SO-CAX-811

"Did he hurt you?"

Gabriel's low voice seemed to vibrate through her arm from where she touched the cloth to his battered face.

"No, he didn't. I told you he wouldn't," she said with some exasperation.

He reached up and caught her hand. "Look at me, Violet," he said in a quiet voice that was underlaid with more steel that she had ever heard from him.

"No lies between us," he said.

Her cloth was going to drip on his shoulder. She tugged her arm away, and he let her. She concentrated fiercely on the cloth as she pressed it gently against Gabriel's cut forehead, avoiding his eyes.

"Violet?"

"I . . . yes, yes, you're right."

"Did he hurt you?" he asked, pressing gently for details. His breath was warm against her hand.

"No. But . . . but I was afraid he might." Gabriel turned his head into her hand, which had stilled again at his temple as they spoke. He nuzzled her hand gently, persuading her fingers to relax until the cloth fell from them. Then he kissed her palm, long and lingeringly . . .

Dear Romance Reader,

In July of 1999, we launched the Ballad line with four new series, and each month we present both new and continuing stories set everywhere from medieval England to the American West—the kind of passionate, romantic stories you love best, written by the most gifted authors. At the back of each book, we tell you when you can find subsequent books in the series that have captured your heart.

Getting this month off to a dazzling start is **Outcast,** the debut story in the passionate new series *The Vikings,* from long-time reader favorite Kathryn Hockett. When a woman proud of her Viking heritage meets the Nordic warrior in search of her father's oldest son, she proves a woman's strength—in battle and love. Next, ever-imaginative Alice Duncan takes us to the 1893 World's Fair in Chicago with her new trilogy, *Meet Me at the Fair.* Everything's **Coming Up Roses** for a trick rider in Buffalo Bill's Wild West Show—until she meets the man who threatens to steal her heart.

Linda Devlin returns this month with **Cash,** the long-awaited sixth installment in the *Rock Creek Six* series, in which a legendary ladies' man—and gunslinger—must face up to his past, and the future he glimpses in the smile of a certain woman. Finally, Corinne Everett ends *Daughters of Liberty* with **Sweet Violet,** as a young Virginia woman determined to find adventure in England discovers danger instead—along with a surprising chance at love.

What a fabulous selection to choose from! Why not read them all? Enjoy!

Kate Duffy
Editorial Director

Daughters of Liberty

SWEET VIOLET

Corinne Everett

ZEBRA BOOKS
Kensington Publishing Corp.
http://www.zebrabooks.com

ZEBRA BOOKS are published by

Kensington Publishing Corp.
850 Third Avenue
New York, NY 10022

Copyright © 2002 by Wendy M. Hilton

All rights reserved. No part of this book may be reproduced
in any form or by any means without the prior written consent of the Publisher, excepting brief quotes used in reviews.

If you purchased this book without a cover you should be
aware that this book is stolen property. It was reported as
"unsold and destroyed" to the Publisher and neither the
Author nor the Publisher has received any payment for this
"stripped book."

All Kensington titles, imprints, and distributed lines are
available at special quantity discounts for bulk purchases for
sales promotion, premiums, fund-raising, educational or in-
stitutional use.

Special book excerpts or customized printings can also be
created to fit specific needs. For details, write or phone the
office of the Kensington Special Sales Manager: Kensington
Publishing Corp., 850 Third Avenue, New York, NY 10022.
Attn. Special Sales Department. Phone: 1-800-221-2647.

Zebra and the Z logo Reg. U.S. Pat. & TM Off.

First Printing: February 2002
10 9 8 7 6 5 4 3 2 1

Printed in the United States of America

For Joan and the Admiral:
I love you, Mom and Dad

ONE

It [marriage] happens as with cages:
the birds without, despair to get in
and those within, despair of getting out.
        —Michel de Montaigne, *Essays*, 1580

London, 1785

Gabriel Isling, Duke of Belmont, pushed his way into the bedroom of his sister Sarah's London home. Servants huddled on the staircase and in the hall, their expressions a mixture of fear and confusion.

The midwife looked up, startled. "You can't be in here, young man," she began.

Sarah, who was as pale as the sheet that covered her, put out a hand weakly. "No, it's all right. That's my brother, the Duke."

"My lady, men do not attend a lying-in," the midwife said to Sarah. "Your lord husband isn't here, and neither should your brother be."

"I don't know who you are, but you will not tell me . . ." Gabriel began hotly.

"Hush, both of you . . . please. . . ." Sarah said

in a thready voice. "Mistress Tanner, there is no one I want to see more than my brother."

"But your labor is not progressing, my lady. This could take hours yet," she said.

"Sarah, are you all right?" Gabriel asked.

"I'm fine, darling boy." Sarah tried to smile, but it looked more like a pained grimace to him.

"Is there a problem?" he demanded, turning to the midwife. He looked at his beloved older sister, whose face was far too wan for Gabriel's liking. Eight years his senior, Sarah had been the only mother he'd ever known. Their own mother had died of a childbirth fever three days after Gabriel's birth.

The midwife looked at Gabriel, then at Sarah. Sarah nodded, and the other woman began to speak reluctantly, only rarely making eye contact with Gabriel. "Your sister's labor is too slow, sir. I've been here since yesterday. She's getting weaker and the baby is no closer to being born. I told her she should have a doctor in, too, Your Grace, but she refuses."

"Where's Wingate?" Gabriel asked.

"His Grace went to his country house two days past, your sister tells me," she answered.

"What difference would it make, having him here?" Sarah asked.

"Because he could order the doctor to be called over your objections," Gabriel answered. "Sarah, you need more than a midwife now."

Sarah pulled herself up on one elbow with effort. "No, Gabriel," she said sharply. "No Wingate. No doctor." Then she fell back against the pillows, reaching for her belly and groaning.

That Wingate wasn't around didn't particularly

surprise Gabriel. He wished for the hundredth time that Sarah had refused to marry the man. He knew she hadn't wanted to, what he didn't know was why.

He cursed the circumstances under his breath. When their father died two years ago, Gabriel had been only fifteen. Three years short of his majority and with only a year of university behind him, the trustees of his father's estate had not allowed him to leave Oxford.

As he watched, feeling helpless, Mistress Tanner helped Sarah through the next contraction. As far as Gabriel could tell, it involved little more than stroking her forehead with a wet cloth and admonishing her not to hold her breath against the pain.

"Sarah, if you are faring poorly, then you must have more skilled medical attention," Gabriel said. To his surprise, the midwife seconded his recommendation, which told him something must indeed be wrong.

But Sarah wasn't listening to either one of them.

"No, I won't have it," she said, but her voice was weaker than before.

Beginning to feel alarmed, Gabriel decided to try a different tack. "Sarah Bel," he said, using the pet name he'd had for Sarah as a child, "if you are going to refuse a doctor, I need you to tell me why, because 'tis not very logical. Will you do that for me?"

"Don't try to charm me, Gabriel, you know I can't deny you anything," Sarah said, a hint of her old spirit showing through.

He said nothing. Sarah was hiding something

and he had to find out what it was and why. She was not just exhausted; her spirit seemed broken.

Their mother had died shortly after childbirth. The reason there had been so much time between his sister's birth and his own was that their mother had suffered several miscarriages in those eight years. It would have been far more logical for Sarah to want the additional medical resources that a doctor could provide.

Gabriel would sooner cut off his arm than see any hurt come to Sarah. She hadn't wanted to get married last year; he was fairly sure he knew why.

As it turned out, he was dreadfully wrong. About everything.

Gabriel had finally managed to get the midwife out of the room, asking her to supervise the preparation of some refreshment for Sarah. The woman conferred with the housekeeper. They decided to ask Cook to concoct a light meat broth that would keep up Sarah's sagging strength. He ushered the women out, watching them descend to the kitchen below with relief.

Then he took the steps three at a time to return to his sister. Seating himself at the edge of the bed, he took her limp hand in his. "We're alone. Tell me, love," he said, summoning every ounce of the considerable charm people said he possessed. "What's wrong? What are you afraid of?"

"Gabriel, you mustn't call for a doctor."

"Why?"

"I . . . I don't need one."

"Sarah Bel, even the midwife says you do."

"Gabriel, you should stay out of this, sweetheart. You're just a boy."

"Sarah, I might be one year short of my majority, but I am no child." He'd had several sexual experiences since going up to Oxford three years ago. Unlike most of the careless young lords who were his friends, he'd been careful not to get any of them with child. And knowing who he was, a duke, and rich to boot, he'd no doubt that if there had been any babes to lay at his doorstep, they most certainly would have lined up at his door.

She smiled sadly at him. "I know you're not a child. Always be the man that Mama wanted you to be, darling. There are many poor examples of men in the world, and I . . ." Her breath caught on a gasp of pain, and under the sheet, Gabriel saw her belly move.

Writhing in pain, Sarah had no breath left to speak. Gabriel flung open the door and, stepping into the hallway, shouted for the midwife.

Dark had long since fallen, and still Sarah labored to bring forth the child. Her breathing was growing erratic; her lips were so pale as to appear bloodless. Gabriel paced back and forth downstairs, ignoring the food that had been set out for him. Finally he could stand it no longer.

He took the steps two at a time and curtly nodded at the midwife to step out. "I'm going to send one of the footmen for a doctor," he said.

To his surprise, she nodded. "I agree. 'Tis time and past time," she said. "I fear that by now, only one of them is going to survive, the babe or your sister. Are you going to send for her husband?"

Gabriel knew that there was no great love between Wingate and Sarah, but it seemed to him that she wanted her husband's presence no more than the doctor's. He rubbed the back of his neck, torn. "If Wingate is in the country, it'll take hours for him to return to London. I'll send one of the servants for him, but I want the doctor summoned immediately."

"Yes, Your Grace."

"Go fetch the footman, please. I'll stay with Sarah."

By the time the doctor arrived, pain wracked Sarah's body with each contraction, but she barely seemed aware of them. Her eyes were sunk deep in her head, her skin clammy and pale.

She tried to protest when Dr. Whitcomb arrived. But the doctor had known them both since childhood, and his quiet air of competence was somewhat cheering as he shut the door on both Gabriel and the midwife in order to examine his patient.

But the door was not closed long. Gabriel heard their voices rise, then fall. Whitcomb came out hastily and beckoned the midwife to enter.

"Your Grace," he said to Gabriel, who stood in the hall. "May I have a word with you?"

"What is it, doctor? Why is she having so much trouble?"

"Your Grace, this is difficult to say, but I fear neither your sister nor the child will survive."

"What? What the devil do you mean?"

"Lord Belmont," Whitcomb said, putting a hand on the younger man's shoulder. "I've known your family since you were both born, and your dear mother passed away. You know that she died soon after birthing you. Forgive me if I speak frankly, but I want you to understand. Your mother had a small womb and a narrow passage for childbirth, which rendered childbirth long and difficult. The longer labor lasts, the more dangerous 'tis for both mother and child. Your sister is built the same way as your mother. Coupled with the injuries she sustained in her recent fall. . . ."

"Fall? What fall? We write every week; she's mentioned no such incident. When I came down from Oxford yesterday, I was told she was already in labor."

"A fall is the explanation she offers for her many bruises, my lord," Whitcomb said. "I fear that the injury may have hastened her labor, and that there may be internal injuries. But, your lordship, one thing concerns me . . ."

"What is it? For God's sake, speak freely. Sarah is my last remaining relative," Gabriel said urgently, seeing the hesitation in the doctor's eyes. "I will take no offense at a man who speaks truth to me."

"Some of the bruises on her back are old, my lord. And the location of the bruises on her arms and shoulders are inconsistent with a fall."

"Meaning she has fallen before?"

"Either your sister is exceptionally clumsy, my lord, or there has been some, ah, infliction of distress."

"Someone has hurt her? Is that what you're saying?" Gabriel was not slow-witted, but he was having trouble believing the doctor, so fantastical did this all sound.

"You told me that she did not want a doctor summoned. That puzzled me. Now I believe it is because she did not want anyone to see the marks on her body. The, ah, individual was careful to keep them hidden from any view that might be observed in public."

Gabriel felt sick. "Wingate did this? Do you mean to say her husband has done this to her?"

"My lord, I cannot be certain, but 'tis likely that he is the one."

Gabriel stared. "Likely? Who the hell else could it be?"

Whitcomb continued in his careful, measured voice. "She might have had this much distress in any labor due to her physical resemblance to her mother, but I see a sharp decline in her general health since her marriage. I have not seen her since then. If the child cannot be born on its own, I will have to cut into her belly to bring it forth."

Gabriel could hardly believe what he was hearing. Sarah had been his world for his whole life. Now she might die because her own husband had beaten her or hurt her? He stared numbly at the doctor.

"Why . . . how . . . could any man do something like this to his wife?" he asked hoarsely.

"Forgive me, my lord. I forget sometimes that you are so young. There are, unfortunately, men whose sexual desires are excessive. Among the upper classes, women of ill repute are usually the unlucky recipients of such attentions. Your sister would not discuss this with me, but I do not believe she has had contact with anyone other than her husband. Therefore, I must conclude that Lord Wingate is the one who inflicted these injuries through his attentions."

Gabriel's rage had grown to murderous proportions. "And I sent for that bastard at the same time I sent for you. I will kill him!"

Whitcomb laid a restraining hand on his sleeve. "Your Grace, please. Your sister needs you now. The law does not forbid a man from ill use of the woman to whom he is married. The law considers the wife's person to be a part of their husband's property."

"That's barbaric."

"That's as may be, my lord, but 'tis the law."

"I'll kill him."

"Your Grace, please think of your sister now. If she cannot push the babe out, I will have to cut it out. Unless you order me to save her life first. In that case, the babe might die a-borning. You need to talk to her, help her decide."

"Decide? There's nothing to decide. Save her life," Gabriel said, suddenly aware that beyond the closed door of Sarah's room, an uneasy quiet had fallen.

"You cannot make that decision for her. You do not have that right," Whitcomb said.

"God damn it, man, I am her family."

"My lord, you are her brother, not her husband."

Gabriel had his hand on the doorknob. "I'm going to talk to her."

"Please try not to upset her further. Do not show her any anger. Lady Sarah needs all the strength and support you are able to give her just now."

"All right," Gabriel said curtly, turning the knob.

Sarah turned her head on the pillow as he entered, a weak smile lighting her eyes, but Gabriel was shocked by the changes in her in just the last hour. Her skin seemed tightly stretched over her bones, and her skin tone had gone from pasty to gray.

It took everything he had to go to her calmly and sit on the edge of the bed. "You need to finish this up, darling," he said lightly. "It's getting tiresome."

"I am trying," she replied. Her efforts to seem normal broke his heart, and neither of them was any damn good at desultory conversation. With every minute, a little more of her strength leached away. She couldn't even talk through the contractions now.

Gabriel couldn't pretend any longer. "Sarah Bel," he said, stroking her lank hair back from her brow. "What did he do to you?"

"I knew Dr. Whitcomb would say something to you. He shouldn't have," she fretted.

"I am glad he did. How dare Wingate lay a hand on you? Why did you marry him? I know you didn't love him, and Lord knows you didn't need his money, but you told me this was a good match for you."

"I lied," she whispered. "But it doesn't matter now. I'm not afraid anymore. I know I'm going to die, Gabriel." She clutched his hand tighter, then her strength failed and her fingers fell away limply.

"You are not going to die, Sarah. I refuse to allow it," he said in his best lord's tone, wrapping her fingers up in his. "What did he do to you? And tell me truly."

She moaned and writhed while another contraction wracked her body. The pain was so intense that when she squeezed his hand this time, his fingers went numb. He didn't care . . . he would have borne her pain himself if he could have. "Just let me go, darling boy. It's all right."

"I'm far too selfish for that. I won't let you go. I'd rather have you than the baby, if one has to choose." He leaned over her, kissing her clammy brow. "Now tell me," he said in a soft but commanding voice.

"I didn't want to bother you, darling," she whispered. "Not when there was nothing you could do about it."

"But I could have, Sarah Bel. I would have killed him for you. How long after you married did this begin?"

"Gabriel," she said, her voice weak. "There's so much you don't know."

Her eyes rolled back in her head. "Stay with me. Damn it, Sarah, don't leave me like this," he said in anguish. "Did you not want this babe? Is that it?"

"I didn't want to marry Wingate."

"Then why did you? Surely with the Belmont fortune, you had no need to?"

"Society doesn't protect women, darling. I had turned down Wingate's suit more than once. But he managed to compromise me and I was forced to marry him."

Truth be told, Gabriel had been more worried about the opposite, women maneuvering him into marriage. That was one reason why he stayed away from the season and its society belles as much as possible. There were many women—or their mothers—who would stoop to maneuvering an eligible man into marriage, but he hadn't considered the reverse.

The more fool he.

"I didn't think a man would do something so heinous either," she said, reading his thoughts correctly. "But I underestimated his desire to get control of my fortune."

"How on earth could he compromise you without your permission or cooperation?" Gabriel asked.

"Gabriel darling, I thought you were a man of the world." She tried to smile but it failed.

"He raped you?" he said, blazing fury erupting within him.

"Gabriel, you're hurting me," she said as his fingers unconsciously tightened on hers.

"I'm sorry. Sarah, bloody hell, why didn't you tell me?"

"There was nothing you could have done. When we married two years ago, you were still a boy. Besides, it wouldn't have mattered. Society doesn't favor women, and in a situation of a man's word against a woman's, who do you think is believed?"

"And after you were married? Once he had you?"

"Send Dr. Whitcomb back in, darling boy," she whispered. "I can't last much longer."

"I want him to save you. The hell with the baby. I hope that doesn't shock you. I would have said to save you anyway because you could always have another baby. But, my God, after what you've just told me, you don't want this baby, do you?"

"It's Wingate I hate, not the child. It might have made things easier between us since he wanted an heir. And I would have had someone to love me."

"I love you. If Whitcomb says to choose, 'tis you. You're my only family, Sarah. Don't leave me."

"I don't think that choice is up to anyone except God."

"The bruises, Sarah? If you're carrying his child, why do you have bruises?"

"I have a deplorable tendency toward independence. I didn't want to submit to him. Wingate has . . . insisted on his marital rights."

"In your condition? He's a monster. And I sent for him just a few hours ago. Sarah, I didn't know. I'm sorry," he said, trying to keep his voice from breaking. "When he gets here, I'll kill him for what he's done to you!"

"No, Gabriel. It's all right, truly. I don't want you ostracized from England, forced to live on the Continent the rest of your life." He couldn't help but notice that her concern was for him, and not her husband. Sarah's nature was so loving and generous that her husband must be even worse than he'd imagined. "Don't waste your life avenging me. I would rather you did something more productive with your life. Be an uncle to my baby."

She coughed, and couldn't seem to get her breath back. Her lips began to turn blue. Alarmed, Gabriel flung the door open and called for both the midwife and Whitcomb. Both Sarah and the babe might be lost, although only Sarah mattered to him now.

He came back to her as the doctor and midwife hurried in with several servants bearing linens, hot water, and other items Gabriel didn't stop to identify. They began to shoo him away from the bedside, but Sarah had a surprisingly strong grip on his hand. He started to disengage so the doctor could step in, but she held on.

Gabriel cupped her damp head with her matted curls against his palm and bent down to kiss her forehead tenderly. "I'll be right here, Sarah Bel," he said softly. "I won't leave you."

"Gabriel, just one thing I ask. Don't kill Wingate." He shook his head in negation.

"I won't let you ruin your life for me. Promise me," Sarah pleaded.

"I can't make you that promise. He's not human."

"I am dying, Gabriel. No, really, it's all right. But that means you have to promise me this." Tears stood in her eyes; as he knew tears stood in his.

"Leave Wingate alone," she whispered. "He isn't worth it. Truly. I want you to keep other women from suffering what happened to me."

"Damn it, Sarah." He dashed tears from his eyes. Her gaze implored him. "All right, I promise."

He would promise her anything, including the moon. And he would make a bargain with the Devil if it would buy her life. But she was slipping away from him as the doctor and midwife worked frantically around them. The light was fading from her eyes even as he tried to keep her with him.

"Don't go, Sarah Bel," he whispered. "Stay with me. Stay with me, please."

"Gabriel, I love you." And with those words her eyes closed, and something resembling peace stole into her pale, pale face.

Gabriel bent his head, his tears dropping freely onto their joined hands. He wanted to gather Sarah close to him and hold her, but the others were still trying to save at least one life, desperation in their hushed voices.

When Whitcomb said that there was no longer a choice, that Sarah had slipped into a coma and the baby had to come out now if they were to save its life, Gabriel let them cut open her belly to get at the babe. But the little boy emerged blue, the cord twisted around his tiny neck.

Gabriel held Sarah's cold hand and kissed her goodbye, although her soul had already fled. At least she had gone to a place where she would no longer be unhappy.

He left the house abruptly. He had to leave before Wingate came, because he knew he could not honor his promise not to kill her husband just then.

TWO

Oh, what a tangled web we weave,
When first we practice to deceive!
  —Sir Walter Scott, *Lochinvar,* 1808

Oak Grove Plantation,
May 1795

Violet Pearson knew she was about to get her way. A few more moments of pleading, and Papa would give in. Her mother already had. She faced her father from the green chair in his plantation office where she sat. He was imposing, seated at his large mahogany desk, but he was her beloved father. Her father Adam Pearson was several years older than her mother Lily, but one would never know it, she mused, admiring his tall frame, which had never run to fat, and the thick dark hair so like her own. The master of Oak Grove plantation still had gray hair only at his temples.

Her papa's extraordinary blue-green eyes were also mirrored in her own, but the arched brows that were so like hers were at this moment raised in skepticism. With difficulty, Violet swallowed the fear that her father would miraculously detect her lie. She had never lied to her parents before, not about anything more serious than how much candy she'd eaten. Nor had she ever plotted anything in secret. This was the most difficult thing she had ever had to do.

"I shall be fine here alone, Papa," she said with her most winning smile. "And I shan't be truly alone, you know that. Will and Betsy are here, and Mistress Steele, and all the servants."

Adam Pearson steepled his fingers and regarded his only daughter over his fingertips. "You have always shown good sense, little one, but you seem almost too eager for this 'adventure,' as you describe it. You are also only seventeen. Why you prefer to remain here, instead of going to Boston with your mother and me and Uncle Peter for the twins' graduation from Harvard College is something I do not understand."

Violet opened her mouth, but nothing came out. She shut it again hastily. Papa didn't appear to notice, so he went on. "Especially since you've been complaining ever since your brothers went to college that life is too slow along the James River and you long to see a big city. Weren't those your very words?"

She nodded; that much was true. "And Boston is far larger than either Williamsburg or Richmond," her father continued. "I still have property there, in Boston Town."

"I know, Papa," Violet spoke up. "I don't mean to be difficult, truly I don't, but I need to be my own person now. The boys have always been considered the heirs to Tidewater Nurseries."

Papa looked startled. "I am far from my grave, Violet, and hardly ready to speak of heirs! Nor is your mother close to relinquishing her flower-arranging business, but you said you weren't interested in the artistic aspect of things."

Violet hastened to reassure her father, jumping up to hug him. "I didn't mean it that way, Papa. Not at all. It's just that Mama and Aunt Rose have always been so independent, and I've had no opportunity to show what I can do on my own."

"So you want to stay home and practice running the business," Papa said, setting her away from him to look up at her from his chair.

"I love the boys, you know that, but once they come back with their fancy Harvard College degrees, I'll never get a chance to do anything."

"Sit down, minx, and let me think." He pretended to glower, but Violet smiled impishly at him as she returned to her chair, and he knew he didn't have her fooled in the least. His only daughter had him wrapped around her little finger, much as did her mother. Twenty years with Lily, and the wonder of the love they shared never faded. Considering what he'd gone through in order to keep it, he never took it for granted.

Still, even though his much-loved wife was in favor of this, he knew she'd also told Violet that the final decision rested with him. Violet's Aunt Rose, married to Lily's brother Peter, would be staying home with her young girls at nearby Willow Oaks. His and Lily's youngest son Peter, named for his uncle, would be going there as well. Violet would be here alone at Oak Grove, but surrounded by longtime servants and family, and Willow Oaks was only a short boat ride or horseback ride away.

Adam supposed he couldn't blame his daugh-

ter for her desire to have the place to herself
for a bit. With three siblings, all boys, she'd always had to be lively to get her views heard. As
a father, his instinct was to protect her, but he
knew her mother had no concerns about Violet
staying here alone. If he maintained his opposi-
tion, he would have both Lily and his daughter
to contend with.

There was no reason to think anything untoward could possibly happen to Violet, but he reminded himself of the unusual legacy of Violet's
female kin. He had been forced to kidnap Lily
for her own protection—twenty years ago now—
while his sister-in-law Rose had been kidnapped
by her own brother and spirited back to England
to be married off. Lily's brother Peter, in love with
Rose, had sailed to England to rescue her.

But Violet didn't know that. She'd been just a
child of seven when Rose's brother had abducted
her future aunt. He and Lily had been neighbors
to Rose Fairchild, Lady Lansdale, and little Violet
had already come to care for Rose. She'd been
told only that Rose had gone to visit her family.
Peter had gone after her to prevent the forced
marriage, but Violet hadn't known that either.
She'd only known love and tenderness from her
family, and seen it in the two families.

History couldn't possibly repeat itself. How
could it? Violet's request was a simple one. Lily
had urged him to let Violet stay. Rose would be
at home; plenty of servants would remain at both
plantations. So, although his heart was somewhat
uneasy, he nodded.

"You may stay, Violet."

"Thank you, Papa, thank you!" she exclaimed.

She did a little pirouette around the room, her long dark hair dancing behind her in waves scented with whatever flower water she used to rinse her hair. Not violet, he knew; she hated being predictable.

She was a beauty, this daughter of his. Although people usually told her she looked like her father, it was the unusual color of her eyes and the dark hair so like his own that strangers saw first. But he saw in Violet her mother's piquant features and the same creamy complexion, as well as the determined chin and the sparkling eyes.

"But behave," he said in a warning tone.

Had she blushed? "Papa, I wouldn't do anything Mama wouldn't do," she declared, just as her mother came in.

Lily put a hand on Rose's shoulder. The two of them looked so alike standing there, down to the mischievous gleam in their eyes.

"That's exactly what I'm afraid of," he said. Lily shot him a warning glance. He shook his head, smiling. He wouldn't reveal the secrets they had decided to keep, unless she wanted him to.

He rose, taking his wife's hand and turning it over to kiss the palm. "Don't make me regret this decision, either of you. But I agree with your mother, Violet, that you should have the opportunity to show that you can responsibly stand on your own with respect to the business. We'll be gone two months at least. Be sure you check your decisions with Will Evans. And if you have doubts about anything, go over and see Aunt Rose. All right, minx?"

"As your father says, Violet," Lily added.

"Yes, Papa. Yes, mama. Thank you. Oh, thank

you." Violet kissed both of them, then left the room with a flurry, her skirts in her favorite periwinkle blue whirling around her slender form.

Violet's plan was daring, bordering on lunatic. She knew it, and felt badly about lying to her parents, but she also knew their extended absence was her only chance to get to London. She adored her parents and loved her brothers—most of the time—but something in her wanted more, craved an excitement she couldn't find here in Virginia. Given how her father and her Aunt Rose felt about the land of their birth, she knew she would find few advocates willing to send her to London for a visit.

Her grandmother would help her once she got there, she was certain. Her father's mother did not visit, but she wrote twice a year. Her father and his mother were not close, but she did send gifts and had written that Violet was welcome to come to London to acquire some "seasoning."

Her father had said Violet wasn't a goose to be seasoned for dinner at a fat aristocrat's table, but her mother had shushed him. Violet had also never learned what bitterness lay between her father and the Dowager Countess of Dalby.

Her grandmother's vague offer and the correspondence Violet had been conducting with a wealthy aristocratic buyer had given her the confidence to concoct this plan. She had a customer with whom to transact business on behalf of the family company, and a place where she was certain she could stay, with the grandmother she had never met.

So while the others prepared for the trip to Boston, Violet hugged her secret to herself and prepared for her own trip. A girl with three brothers could do anything, as she had declared a thousand times since she was a little girl and realized the rules were different for girls than for boys. Her mother and aunt were hardly conventional—both had struggled with the limitations their world put on women—but both had overcome them. Her mother had been Williamsburg's first florist, and Aunt Rose had come here from England to run her family's plantation against their desires.

She was absolutely not running away. This was but the start of a great adventure. Wasn't it?

Violet was certain her ruse would work. After all, she and her brothers had pulled this off a dozen times before. The boys no longer fit into these breeches, though, she thought smugly, pulling them up over her legs and buttoning the flap.

Neither Will nor Betsy Evans, who managed the plantation and were nearly as much her uncle and aunt as her real ones, had seen her leave Oak Grove. Nor had their housekeeper, Mistress Steele, so she no longer had any fear of discovery. And while Aunt Rose had come to America against her family's wishes, she hadn't done so in disguise. Violet was convinced no one would think of her plan.

She needed her brothers' old clothes only long enough to stow away on Uncle Peter's ship at Tidewater Landing. Once they were far enough out to sea that the captain would not risk ruining his precious live cargo of plants and flowers with the time consumed in taking her back to Virginia, she could reveal her identity.

But first, she would have to go to Williamsburg, then ride back to her house with a group of lads looking for work. There were always men seeking to hire on for each trip her uncle's ships took. She couldn't just show up at the landing on her uncle's property with no explanation. Even though she hadn't dressed as a boy for years, she didn't want a family resemblance to give her away. She'd undergo far less scrutiny in a group.

For now though, her chief task was getting a draught of ale in this Williamsburg tavern. Surely a boy—or a youth, that's really what she was— would get a mug of hops. Surely a woman owner would be more softhearted?

"Nay, lad, without your father or employer here to vouch for you, I daren't serve you," the tavern wench said.

Violet tried to deepen her voice still more. "I'm a day laborer, apprenticed right and true," she insisted. "I'm seventeen."

"Yer twelve," the woman said. Violet glowered. The serving maid held her stare, but dropped it when Violet maintained her ferocious expression. "All right, maybe fourteen," she conceded at last. "But no ale during the workday, ye must know the rules as well as anyone. Have a lemonade, there's a lad."

"Lemonade," Violet growled. "That's a woman's tisane."

"D'ye prefer water?" the serving girl asked, empty tray in one hand, and the other fisted on her hips.

"I'll take the lemonade," Violet said with a distinct lack of grace.

"Wise lad." The serving girl winked.

Violet took her despised lemonade, ordered a hot lunch, and went to sit down. She didn't dare draw too much attention to herself. If someone thought her as young as twelve—twelve! she seethed silently—with no one to vouch for her, she could be thrown out.

So here she sat, nursing her lemonade and her grudge against fate. Tavern talk swirled around her, spiced with words her mama and papa would be appalled to hear. She fought to keep a smile from her face, remembering that it was both immature and . . . unmanly.

When the brawl started, Violet was not alarmed. Apparently some other apprentices, new to Williamsburg, had been told their employers had ordered that no spirits be served to them during the workday. They took the news far less calmly than Violet.

When a youth became belligerent, the serving maid disappeared. That seemed to be a signal for mayhem, and suddenly fights broke out all over the tavern. Violet scrunched herself back against the wall and watched the flying crockery.

It was all mildly amusing until the fight came too close to her. A youth was knocked against her table who must have heard her earlier request. He pulled her up to her feet by her waistcoat, and said, "You wanted a man's drink, didn't you? Then fight for it!" And with one pass of his muscled arm, he flung her out into the fray.

As exhilarating as the prospect of a fight was, Violet knew she didn't have the strength to pull it off convincingly, so she looked for a safe harbor. At that moment, a chair came hurtling through the air. She ducked, but not quickly enough.

It caught her shoulder and knocked her backwards. She was tossed up and back, and as she came swiftly down and was about to hit the sawdust-covered floor, another strong arm plucked her out of the air. He set her rather abruptly on her feet so that she lurched against him.

His arm snaked behind her back to brace her as she went over backward, and she found herself arched back against a strong arm, looking up into a face that took what breath she had left away. A handsome man with dark hair and gray eyes held her.

Panic assailed her. Her disguise wouldn't survive a lot of handling, she suddenly realized. "Don't touch me," she ordered in her deepest voice. She cocked her fists at him as she'd done with her brothers.

He looked incredulous, then laughed. He pulled her up to stand with his free arm, then brought his supporting hand from behind her back to cover her fists. Her fists looked tiny next to his hand, which completely covered both of hers.

He squeezed. It seemed a warning. "Easy, lad," he said. "I was only helping." Before she could form a coherent reply, a large yellow jug came sailing at them, and he pulled her down to squat with him below its arc.

"That's it," he said. "We're getting out of here."

He stood briefly, surveyed the crowd and shouted, "Max! To me!"

Then he turned without further ado and dragged Violet along with him, his grip on her hand inexorable.

They were at the far side of the room when two brawny men in blue-checked shirts came out from the taproom. It wouldn't do to be caught and hauled before the magistrate.

Violet let herself be dragged.

THREE

Dissemble nothing, not a boy, nor change
Thy body's habit . . . All will spy in thy face
A blushing womanly discovering grace;
　　　—John Donne, "On His Mistress,"
　　　　　　　Elegies, 1635

Gabriel had known from the moment he touched her that she was no boy. Her slim body was too lithe, too soft. Her startled glance when he'd kept her from falling showed him quickly that her winsome face was far too fair. Yet everywhere around him, men treated her as a boy, or at least took no notice of anything unusual about her.

He found that damned peculiar. Still, they were in the midst of a fight, and he'd been the only one to touch her.

But that body, that face. Women had ceased to surprise him, though he couldn't have said when. Yet this woman-child seemed almost to sparkle. As he'd steadied her, he'd looked down into eyes of an aquamarine intensity he'd never before seen. She had stared up at him, startled, before telling him to get away from her.

Something he was not about to do. He was intrigued, but more urgently, her disguise was in danger of exposure. In his experience, women didn't disguise themselves as men unless they were desperate. But she didn't look desperate.

"Don't squeal," he advised in a quiet undertone as she lay against his arm. She looked fourteen as a boy, but he would lay odds she was older. He'd surprised her when he kept her from falling, but had not made her frightened or apprehensive. Nor did she look ill-treated.

He recognized the secret amusement in her eyes that she had pulled the wool over men's eyes, getting by for this small instant of time in a man's world despite the chaos around them.

Well bred, well fed, he thought as he pulled her down again to avoid a flying bit of pottery. Was she a lady of quality just out for a lark? Despite all the years that stood between him and the tragedy in his past, anger surged anew. This chit didn't know what risks she took.

He called for Maximilian, then started tugging her toward the door. They had to get out of here.

"Belmont, over here," his servant replied, looking exceedingly uncomfortable using Gabriel's name without his title. He was fond of Maximilian Shandling for the years he had put up with Gabriel and his unorthodox household, but the urge to be a proper valet to a proper master had never left the man.

Maximilian signaled to him that he'd found a back exit, which opened onto a kitchen garden. Gabriel pulled the girl through, leaving the door

open for Max. The fight did not follow them outside, but Max closed the door and stood a few
feet away while Gabriel examined his sudden
prize.

He set the girl away from him, strangely reluctant to let his fingers leave her slender shoulders.
Deciding whether to shake her or kiss her was a
puzzle that would have to wait for another time.
She must learn that a ruse such as hers was sur-
passingly dangerous, and it looked like he would
have to be the one to teach her. The men inside
weren't vicious criminals or hardened soldiers.
Nevertheless, men, drinking, taverns, and women
did not mix.

She shook off his hand, but when he reached
for her, he realized she wasn't running away. She
straightened, pulled herself up to her full
height—she came barely to his shoulder—and addressed him.

"I heard him call you Belmont. Are you Gabriel
Isling, Duke of Belmont?" she said, in a deeper
voice than he had expected. She had managed to
make her voice surprisingly low for one so young
and fair.

"Aye," he affirmed, looking at her askance.
Twenty years after the war, Americans were civil
to the British when they had to be—often, for
their trade—but he had yet to hear such reverent
tones outside of London. And how could the chit
know who he was, much less his title? Maximilian
had only said "Belmont" once, inside. He looked
over her head at Maximilian, who still guarded
the back door. An imperceptible shake of his head
told Gabriel that his man had not conversed with
her.

He folded his arms, looking down at her. "I am he. What of it?"

"I . . . that is, my lord, I was on my way. . . ." she began to say without making much sense.

Gabriel set a finger to her lips. "Hush, boy, and start over."

He took his finger away, further annoyed that he now wanted to stroke her lip. What the hell was the matter with him? He was acting most unlike himself.

"But you're the Duke of Belmont, aren't you?" she asked. "I was on my way to see you."

"To see me?" In his experience, only irate husbands traveled to see him. "How could you possibly know I was coming here?"

"No, no, I was going to London. I intended to stow . . . ah, stay on my uncle's ship," she said. "I wanted to conduct our business in person."

Gabriel raised a dark eyebrow. "Indeed. And you are . . ."

"I represent Tidewater Nurseries," she said.

"You are my correspondent? Adam Pearson?" He'd exchanged letters with Tidewater Nurseries about their remarkable stock of ornamental trees and flowers, intent on major purchases for his conservatory.

"Ah . . . Adam the second," she added quickly. "The first is my father."

"I see," he said neutrally, not challenging her now. He had to get her out of here. If she had no idea how precarious her position was, he certainly did. The tavern was hardly a public house on the London docks, but it simply wasn't safe for a woman to prance about dressed as a man.

"Why don't you accompany me to Oak Grove?"

she said. Convenient, just what he'd been about to suggest to her. Did they know at home about her ridiculous disguise? If so, he had some words for her father, the real Adam Pearson. He knew the man was an Earl and had been a top Patriot spy, but was now a prosperous merchant and owner of the south's best nursery. An aristocrat and former British Army officer—Pearson had certainly had an eventful life.

Gabriel had thought to seek his advice about possibly moving his household here. Surely Pearson would understand something of Gabriel's unorthodox life, considering his background. Why Gabriel had boarded ship instead of sending his latest letter as he'd meant to, he didn't know. Perhaps he'd thought someone else would understand the choices that he'd had to make, someone who had faced similar challenges himself.

Or perhaps it was just the restlessness that rode him like the devil these days. London seemed so confined, so confining. Anything, anywhere was better than London. He might even have enjoyed himself inside the tavern—English aristocrats did not usually brawl—if not for his concern about the girl.

"My lord?" said the lovely girl beside him in her dusty breeches, recalling him suddenly to himself. Unorthodoxy seemed to run in this family. Perhaps the father would understand.

"Don't call me that here," he said, taking her elbow. "Come, let us depart." He wanted her out of here before anyone else spotted her disguise or someone tried to arrest them as part of this brawl.

Maximilian had already engaged a carriage and

horses for a week. Gabriel told him to find different lodgings, and took one of the horses to ride
alongside the girl's. Good horseflesh, he noted,
to be expected of a woman from a prosperous
family but not from a mere apprentice or whoever
she was impersonating.

This was one more discrepancy in her story. He
couldn't decide whether to tell her how to flesh
out all the aspects of a more convincing disguise
or lecture her that she shouldn't be indulging in
such foolishness at all.

It would be the latter, he knew. She had no reason to disguise herself as a boy that he could see.
Unjust pursuit or imminent rape were the only
two reasons a woman should ever risk herself by
going into men's company as poorly disguised as
she was.

And so she took him to her home. Gabriel set
a stiff pace, and was surprised and oddly pleased
that she had no difficulty keeping up with him.
He marveled at how trusting she was. As they rode
along the river road, she talked freely. This Adam
the younger she pretended to be must really exist
and be her brother, he mused, because her esca-
pades could not be wholly invented. They
sounded too genuine.

After a good hour of riding, the road curved
away from the river. They passed fields of tobacco,
some of which belonged to her uncle, some to
her father, she explained. They were fields given
to bond servants to work for a season or two while
they cleared their debt. The family didn't grow
tobacco themselves, she explained, because it exhausted the land quickly. Yet these lands, used
only occasionally, provided a quick profit to get

the former indentured servants on their feet, and then they moved on.

He had no time to wonder at the unusual generosity, because the tobacco fields gave way to wave upon wave of beautiful flowers as they neared Oak Grove. Purple, yellow, and white iris. Tulip blossoms in red, white, even the purplish-black color that was unusual and highly prized.

He saw ranunculus on its odd twisty stems, some in colors he had never seen in England. He saw orchards in the distance, some still in bloom, their cascading branches heavy with blossom. In a few weeks' time they would be heavy with fruit. Bees droned everywhere in the warm afternoon air.

Although he had traveled widely, the sheer beauty of the land struck him. It was a gentle beauty, not violently vivid like the tropics, nor the lush green of England's fields that came from unrelenting rain. Yet the young woman riding beside him seemed oblivious to it.

As they rode, he relaxed, feeling the sun's warmth and the breezes off the river, appreciating the scent of the flower-laden air. He'd rarely felt so relaxed. The Pearson girl was safe with him, whether she knew it or not, but her secret would soon be out. He wouldn't embarrass her in public, but it should be safe enough at home for him to expose her ruse.

Violet was so excited meeting the Duke that she hadn't yet thought to be disappointed about the planned stowaway trip. Her correspondent was here, and heavens, was he handsome! Tall, lean, with shoulders that needed no padding in his perfectly cut coat and snugly-fitted trousers.

He wasn't some pampered, worthless dandy as she'd heard her Aunt Rose declare at times about English men. Nor was he really an older man. She'd just assumed he would be about forty, her uncle's age, but she was sure this man wasn't even thirty.

As they rode, she covertly glanced at him. His dark hair was cut on the short side in what must be the latest style. It was thick and wavy and had a tendency to curl at the ends. His smile was swift and charming, and his quicksilver eyes seemed to be shot with light like reflections dancing off the river.

When they arrived at home, she had a moment's fear that one of the stable lads might give her away. She'd certainly had no intention of turning up back here dressed like this.

They went directly to the stables, where Jack ran out to take the horses. Good, he wasn't one of the more inquisitive lads. He blinked twice at the sight of Violet, but she cut him off before he could speak. She didn't want to give her disguise away to him in front of the Duke, whom she was sure she had fooled.

She swung down from horseback, summoning her deepest voice to address the boy. "It's Adam," Violet said, willing Jack to go along. "I've brought a visitor back from Williamsburg. He's expected."

The lad nodded confusedly. Thank goodness, Violet thought. She set about unsaddling the horses expertly. The Duke started to unsaddle his own beast, but she nodded at Jack and he quickly took the reins from Gabriel.

"My lord," she said, indicating the way to the house past various outbuildings, then through a formal garden filled with roses. Dozens of bushes were ablaze with color and scent. Violet was used to the beauty, and temporarily forgot her role as hostess . . . host. She was more worried about whether Betsy Evans or Mistress Steele would answer the door, and what would be said.

So she marched on and the Duke of Belmont kept pace, his arms behind his back. This must be a leisurely stroll to him, she realized. Look how long his stride was. No wonder the tavern girl had thought she was so young. He dwarfed her by comparison.

Had she been running away, Gabriel wondered? Yet he'd seen no sign of trauma. God knew he had plenty of experience with that; she'd shown no such strain.

Twenty minutes later, they sat in an elegant drawing room in the main house. Servants had brought cakes and tea. A woman came in shortly afterward, but the girl jumped up and drew the woman aside before she could speak. Was that the mother? Gabriel wondered.

But no, soon after that the woman re-entered the room and introduced herself as Betsy Evans, wife of the estate's foreman, Will Evans. She seemed more wary of Gabriel than the Pearson girl had been, an attitude he definitely approved. Her husband was out in the fields, she explained.

Mistress Evans seemed willing to continue the deception, though, as the Pearson girl came back to sit and take tea. Occasionally, Gabriel caught

Mistress Evans giving the girl a bemused look, but there was only affection in the glance, not censure.

"The Duke has been corresponding with us," "Adam" explained. "He has a dedicated conservatory in England, and some of our varieties of ornamentals and fruits are of interest to him."

"I have a conservatory," Gabriel confirmed. "When I was a lad, I read about Captain Cook's voyages with great enthusiasm. I became fascinated by the discoveries around the world. I'd been doing my best to go through the money left to me, but just paying out blunt wasn't enough. I had to start my own collection."

He smiled disarmingly. " 'Twas a good thing I did. Developing an outstanding conservatory became an obsession for me. I am constantly in search of new varieties to refine and augment my collection."

"So why did you come here? Surely you're familiar with most of our stock?" the Pearson girl asked.

"Your family's nursery is famous, young Adam. You've developed more varieties of pear and peach than any American nursery. You've cultivated strains of dogwoods and magnolias that are among the most beautiful in the world. And your mother's cut flower arrangements are said to be known for the time they last at peak beauty, indicating your family has developed exceptionally hardy strains for hothouse flowers. I'd like to have some of what you grow in my conservatory."

Violet noticed that while he'd spoken, his face had become more animated than she'd noticed before. He had a ready smile; she didn't think most people would notice that sometimes it didn't reach his eyes.

"We have many acres of trees and flowers between my father's and my uncle's estates. We should tour them."

"Aye, I'd like that." He'd rather have her accompany him as herself, but she seemed keen on preserving the disguise. He'd wait for the right moment, and then show her how ill advised her game was. And he was still curious about why she was doing it.

They arranged to meet the next day for a tour of the two estates that constituted Tidewater Nurseries.

Installed later that day in a townhouse Max had rented in an excess of caution after the tavern brawl, Gabriel asked what Maximilian had managed to learn during the time Gabriel had been out at Oak Grove.

"What is her true name?" he asked. He should have had it by now, but in his correspondence he'd had no reason to think he was dealing with anyone other than a Pearson male. He almost chuckled. She was cheeky. He'd always encouraged his women to be independent, but didn't think any one of them would have been so bold.

" 'Tis Violet, Your Grace," Maximilian answered. "Her twin brothers—older by a year or two—are Adam and Arthur. There's one more boy, Peter. He is the youngest. She is the only girl."

"Call me Gabriel while we're here," he said absently. He knew Maximilan would never do so in

London, and that calling him "Belmont" in the tavern had tortured his proper English soul. But they were in America now. "I wonder what the girl is up to."

"As no one seemed to have noticed her ruse, Your Grace, 'twas a bit difficult to make inquiries."

"I realize that. You are in no way at fault here, Maximilian. I don't employ you as a spy. Nor would it be good to risk the lady's reputation by asking indiscreet questions. It's all harmless in her mind, but she doesn't know how dangerous it can be, does she?"

Maximilian, knowing his employer expected no reply to a rhetorical question, did not answer.

"All right, Miss Violet, you've some explaining to do," said Betsy Evans, when Violet returned to the house some hours later. Violet hadn't come back after seeing Gabriel on the road back to town. She'd needed the time to think about a story to tell Betsy. Thank goodness Betsy hadn't given her away. But that didn't mean she wouldn't get an interrogation.

"Just what were you doing gallivanting about in your brothers' clothes?" Mistress Steele had opened the door, her eyebrows raised in disapproval at Violet's attire. She'd indicated the sitting room where Betsy Evans waited, then withdrew to the back of the house. "I've not seen you dressed this way since you were quite a bit younger. And in front of some British lord, too. What are you playing at, Violet?"

Violet took Betsy's hands between hers, thinking fast, though her stomach was in a flutter. She had to keep Betsy Evans from focusing on why she'd been dressed as a boy.

Her heart was fluttering as well as her stomach. She'd met Lord Belmont, or the Duke, or whatever it was one called such a personage. Younger and more handsome than any man—especially an Englishman of his rank—had any right to be, he was not at all what she'd expected.

"I went to meet him, Bets," she said, trying for her most reassuring tone. "I thought, with all the men away, it would look odd to go as myself."

"Why? Everyone in Williamsburg knows you."

"I don't know about everyone, dear Bets. The town has grown quite a bit. But you know how the English can be, all titles and formality and whatnot." Violet waved her hand around airily, deliberately being vague.

Betsy was indignant now. "What? Neither your father nor aunt have ever put on airs and both of them nobility or aristocracy in their own right, whatever the term."

"Yes, yes," Violet said, "but you know as well as I do they were . . . are . . . different, or they would not have left England and chosen to stay in America."

"And just what does this have to do with you dressing like your brother? Which one are you anyway—Adam?"

"I have to be the oldest, of course. I just thought the Duke might react better to me as a man."

To her dismay, Betsy laughed. "You look a sight better as yourself than as a stripling boy."

Violet drooped. "Really? Is it that bad?"

Betsy patted her hand. "Probably not to a stranger. You go ahead. He seems nice enough. I can't think what your father would say, but. . . ."

"Then don't think!" Violet said nervously. "The Duke would never take me seriously as a girl."

"But, Violet, your mother and your aunt never dressed as boys. . . ."

"And Papa agreed that I had to make my own way. Don't worry, Bets, I'll find a way out of this with no harm done. Just think, my virtue has to be safer with me dressed like this." Violet made Betsy an elaborate leg, flashed her best impish smile, then turned to go.

"I don't have a good feeling about this, Miss Violet, but I suppose 'tis all right for the nonce. Take one of the stable lads with you tomorrow, though."

Violet sped out the door, not answering. She wanted the fascinating Englishman all to herself, and with her disguise, the worst that could happen is he'd think her a shade too young to really transact business on behalf of her father. Even if he would take her more seriously as herself, she'd lose more face by revealing her disguise now. He was only here on a whim; he would soon move on after arranging to purchase what he was interested in.

The whole visit couldn't last more than a day or two, could it?

FOUR

These impossible women! How they do get
around us!
The poet was right: can't live with them,
or without them!
          —Aristophanes, *Lysistrata,* 411 B.C.

Gabriel was not really surprised to find the girl still in boy's guise the next morning. She was better dressed, more like a young master of the estate than the simple garb she'd had on in Williamsburg the day before. But what really shocked him was that no one was to accompany them, not even a stable hand. Of course, he hadn't expected a lady's maid since she pretended she wasn't a young lady, but there should be at least a groom.

"Oh, 'tisn't necessary," she assured him with those big aquamarine eyes gazing sincerely at him. Why were they permitting this farce? he wondered again. When Mistress Evans came out with food for their saddlebags, he realized that she condoned this behavior. He understood that she might not have wanted to embarrass Violet the day before in front of a stranger, but why continue the deception today?

His anger rose. If no chaperone came, then he had all the evidence he needed to know that he must administer a lesson to this young lady. And he would do so today.

With an effort he forced himself to be the polite charming aristocrat, the face he'd always shown the outside world—and most of the women. No one had seen the real Gabriel Isling since Sarah died. He himself hardly knew what he was like anymore.

He almost forgot his anger as they rode along, which surprised him considerably. She was a charming companion, an artless conversationalist, and yet her head was filled with the most ridiculous notions. Though she was clearly knowledgeable about this land of her birth, she seemed to take its richness and beauty for granted. He had known England's squalor, corruption on high and in its underclass, and seen the mess that man had made of his living quarters in ports the world over. She didn't seem to know that what she had here was valuable and so very rare.

This land was still so untamed, so pure and lush. A long buried part of him wanted to romp like a boy, while the hedonist in him yearned for a swim in these fresh blue waters, a nap in a meadow filled with wildflowers. He even imagined he could indulge such fantasies here, make them real, something he could never do in England, constrained as he was by his rank and position.

In the country, there was purity and beauty still, but not in London. And there was no place in England so uninhabited, at least not for such large stretches. He'd read surveying reports; a man could ride for days here and never come within sight of human habitation. Some denizens of London would cherish such solitude; others would find it intolerable. He counted himself among the former.

He concentrated on the scenery around him, beginning to appreciate the flora and foliage. As always in the presence of so much natural beauty, the ugliness of mankind faded, easing the sorrow around his heart that had never fully retreated since Sarah's death ten years before.

There were numerous specimens he wanted to acquire for his conservatories, but he also began to consider whether he might simply transfer everything here to America. He had the resources to do this, but there were others besides himself and his own wishes to take into account.

By the time they had toured the extensive estates, which partially adjoined, the morning was well advanced.

"Might we look around a bit more?" he asked. "I'm thinking of moving my conservatory here. My estate, actually."

"Move? From London?" she asked, as if she could not credit the thought.

He ignored that. "Is there land along the river that is not settled?"

"I don't know," she answered. "There might be estates still abandoned that belonged to those who fled during the Revolution. I do know there is land along the Virginia–North Carolina border that has been difficult to settle. That area contains much swampland, and it is not as well populated as this peninsula."

"I see. Shall we ride along this way?"

"Of course," she replied with a charming smile,

which she quickly abandoned when she apparently remembered her role as a boy. She coughed self-consciously and came out with the lowered voice again. "I guess we can. Why not?" She shrugged with a boyish gesture, as if she didn't care much.

Gabriel turned his head away to look at a stand of willows near the water and smiled. After another hour or so, they paused. Gabriel unpacked the saddlebags to find a feast of Virginia ham and biscuits, a flask of lemonade, and strawberries that were large and luscious. Violet didn't offer to lay it out for them. Perhaps she was afraid of giving herself away if she laid out a table as a lady would. So he tossed the blanket at her and started pulling out the saddlebag's contents himself.

She tossed him a skittish glance or two, but spread out the blanket quite competently, and he poured the lemonade. Mistress Evans had even remembered to include clay drinking and eating vessels, so they were well supplied.

They both stretched out their boot-encased legs at the meal's conclusion, and Gabriel found himself drifting into sleep. He looked over as his head nodded back and found that Violet was already in the land of nod. He watched her for a moment, noting the long, dark lashes that lay against her gold-tanned cheeks, the latter dusted with natural rose. Her hair, even restrained in a queue, looked soft and lustrous.

He found himself appreciating these signs of her femininity and was bemused. A girl dressed as a boy had the power to make him feel longing? It could only be lust, and as such was improper, for she was surely an innocent.

No one who was not innocent could possibly hope to attempt a disguise such as hers. No down would ever touch those cheeks, no coarse hair sprout from her upper lip. The soft bow of her mouth was pink and full, tinged reddish from the juicy strawberries they had eaten. She looked kissable and only the more adorable for the vest, white shirt, and polished boots she wore to disguise her gender.

Gabriel felt a slow building of desire as he looked at her face, dappled with shadow from branches hanging over the glade in which they sat. It was languid, easy, not the sharp push of physical needs that drove a man to distraction. He drifted with her, imagining the touch of that soft skin, the bloom on her cheeks, what her real curves were like under the wrappings and trappings of the boy she portrayed. He would like to gather her up and slowly place his lips against hers, awakening her and her passion simultaneously by infinitely slow degrees. When had he last seen a woman whose innocence was so completely untouched and undamaged?

Gabriel shook his head, trying to shake off the spell of the lazy, warm afternoon. Bees droning in the bushes, the chirping of birds, and the slow lapping of water against the high bank had charmed him into a state of temporary stupidity.

He rose to his feet, dusting off his breeches, turning to look at the horses who stood patiently cropping the grass in the nearby meadow, their reins looped over tree limbs.

There was only one cure for this sort of languor, for thinking thoughts, imagining moments that could never be, so he wasted no time. Activity fit the bill. "Up, boy," he said, clapping his hands briskly. While Violet struggled to rise to her feet behind him, he went for the horses.

Leading them back, he tossed one set of reins at her, then mounted his own hunter.

"I forgot," he said, laughing at her as she caught the reins, still a bit befuddled with sleep. "You aren't tall enough to mount on your. . . ."

"Oh yes, I am," she said, grabbing the saddle horn and pulling her leg up and over with a fluid grace he'd never imagined in a girl her size. She'd practically leaped in the air like a dancer, her bottom landing firm and snug just where it should, her legs gripping the horse's flanks expertly.

She kicked the horse into motion and rode off with a muttered taunt about his slowness. He was perfectly happy to oblige her competitive instincts, so he followed, giving the well-rested hunter his head, leaving the saddlebags and repast behind them.

They tore through the meadow and into the woods that stood back from the river path. It was obvious she knew the terrain better than he. At any moment he might unhorse himself from an unexpected tree looming in his path or foliage-covered stump.

He headed the animal back out of the woods and onto the low bluffs that lined the river. They passed a square plantation house, a perfect brick cube that commanded a beautiful view of the river.

"That's Shirley," she pointed. "The Carters own half the land hereabouts," she called out. If she said anything else, it was lost in the ride's wild

rush—the water flowing past or the wind stream-
ing through their hair.

He led her now, having passed her but a moment before, and found himself grinning with enjoyment. The horses were starting to lather, and
he knew they would need to slow down soon.

The bluffs above the river, never terribly high,
diminished until they were nearly at river level.
Violet looked around, came to the same conclusion he had about the horses, and slowed. She
flung herself from the saddle before her horse
had fully stopped and he swung down quickly in
case she hurt herself.

Instead, she was clinging to the horse's flanks
and laughing animatedly. He found, to his cha-
grin, that he was smiling the same way himself.

"Oh, that felt good, didn't it?" she said, her
eyes sparkling with pure fun.

"I am too old for such goings on, lad," he
panted, but he didn't mean it.

She knew. "Pshaw," she said. "You are not old.
The only advantage I had is that I know the land
better than you. Take that away and. . . ."

"No mercy, young . . ." he caught himself a
moment before saying "lady," adding instead,
"young one. You'll recall I caught you at the end.
I don't need your pity."

"True." She patted her horse's steaming flanks,
then flopped down on the ground nearby. "I
need to catch my breath," she said.

"No more sleeping," Gabriel said, and he
meant it in earnest as much as in fun. He wasn't
going to make calf-eyes at her again. As he moved
to stand over her where she sat clasping her hands
around her knees and smiling up at him, he fisted

his hands at his sides in a posture of mock domination.

She was still laughing, eyes sparkling at him in a way that in most society women would be the definite start of a flirtation.

But this wasn't London and she wasn't a lady. She was a child who shouldn't be out alone with a man of his reputation, and he remembered that he intended to teach her a lesson.

Gabriel stepped away from her, sat down, and began to pull off his boots. The two of them were hot and sweaty. The river beckoned. He knew what he would do now, and how.

He refused to allow himself time for second thoughts. He was not a tame old man who could be led about by the nose. The control he had learned came from experience and knowledge; most men were not inclined to exert such self-discipline when they wanted a woman. Whatever she knew of men—or thought she knew—it was not enough.

"Come on, lad, into the river," Gabriel called across the space separating them. He tossed his coat aside and stood. Striding over to where she sat, he offered her a hand. When she continued to just look up at him, he extended it, grasped her arm and pulled her up to stand before him.

"Let's go for a swim, lad," Gabriel said in a hearty man-to-man voice. He watched as her eyes went wide for a brief moment, then she recovered herself.

"I can't swim, Your Grace," she said, dropping her gaze and scuffing a toe in the dirt.

"Oh, enough of the title business, now, Adam," he continued in the same hearty tone. "I rather

like your American egalitarianism." He stepped
closer to her, watched her flinch when it looked
like he might lay a hand on her shoulder. Did
she begin to perceive how fragile her disguise
was? he wondered. "How could you possibly live
along this river and not learn how to swim?"

" 'Twas my mother, sir," she answered.

"She made you a coward?" he asked, folding
his arms.

"I caught a terrible chill from a tumble into
the James once, sir," Violet said. "When I was
six."

"And?" he inquired. She was lying, but he'd
point out how badly she lied later.

"And she wouldn't let me go back in."

"Ever?"

"Not ever," she affirmed, her eyes solemn.

What else had this chit lied about, Gabriel wondered. Well, he would prove her boy's tale a flum-
mery. She was so obviously entranced by her
success that she had no worries, no cares—and
had not even brought a chaperone.

He could do anything to her, out here alone.
The thought didn't fire his blood, far from it. It
made him feel ill, as nauseated and disgusted as
when he'd learned what had been done to Sarah.
Men shouldn't have that kind of power over
women. What God had created, man had perverted.

This was not the time for such reflections. Moving briskly to her side, he gave her a playful shove
to indicate she should continue down the bank
with him. He pulled off his coat and shirt along
the way.

At the water's edge he turned, one hand on the

buttons of his breeches. In other circumstances he might have enjoyed seeing how he affected her. But determined to prove his point, he had to goad her into revealing herself, or he would have to do it for her. Still, he had to keep his attraction to her under control, something he'd never had trouble doing before. Women still threw themselves at him, despite or perhaps because of his unorthodox household. Given who they were and what had happened to them, he'd had to both learn restraint and practice it.

Violet turned as if to retreat. "Oh no, you don't," Gabriel said. "You wanted a picnic along the James. What could be more pleasant than to end the afternoon with a swim?"

"I told you, I haven't been in the water since I was six," Violet protested.

He feigned disapproval. "This is how you present the virtues of your native territory to someone interested in it? Perhaps I'd best head to the Carolinas, find someone more enthusiastic about working with ornamental horticulture."

As he'd hoped, the threat of competition fired up her own instincts. "There is no nursery better than ours in the southern United States," she announced proudly. "But swimming with you won't prove that point."

Gabriel smiled. He couldn't help himself. A man would have understood the implicit challenge and raced into the water. "I'll just sit on the riverbank, then," she announced. Gabriel grimaced. He hadn't inspired her; not enough, at any rate.

"That's it lad, just dangle your feet." Gabriel walked into the water abruptly. If she came any

closer than she just had, she couldn't miss his condition. He'd been about to dispense with his
breeches, certain that the shock would force her
to reveal her own subterfuge, but those wide
aquamarine eyes and the thought of her lissome
body had called his bluff.

The water was cool but not cold and the sun
dancing along the blue expanse shot bright reflections everywhere. Violet sat down, removing
her shoes and stockings, then dipped her small
feet into the water up to her ankles.

Gabriel swam idly back and forth, waiting for
her to lower her guard and once more lose her
fear of having her disguise revealed. He flicked
water at her with his fingertips, she did the same,
and in the resulting play she relaxed, her unaf-
fected laughter pealing out merrily.

She was in the midst of laughing at him because
she'd splashed water into his eyes when he
ducked under water, swam at her, and pulled her
down into the water by her dangling ankles.

"No, my lor—" she cried, the last syllable ending in a wet gurgle. It had never occurred to him
that she might have told the truth about not being able to swim, but when he surfaced a moment
later, he was alone.

He started to look around anxiously when she
pushed up through the water's surface fifteen feet
away and spitting mad.

"How dare you?" she sputtered.

"You seem to be floating perfectly well. I see
your early childhood swimming ability has all
come back to you," he said blandly, proffering
her his best charming smile.

She swam for shore immediately. He gave chase,

and clapping a hand on her shoulder, pulled her under again.

When she came up, her hair had fallen. Gabriel realized she'd had it in a double queue, turned up twice so it didn't look too long for a lad's. He didn't think she realized it, though, because she swept her hair out of her eyes with one hand, shot him a fulminating blue-green glance, then resumed swimming toward shore.

Gabriel followed slowly, not trying to catch her again. He couldn't resist saying, "That looks a lot like swimming to me." Violet didn't answer. She found her feet in the shallows and surged up the bank.

Sighing, he grabbed her ankle. He wasn't really enjoying this anymore, knowing what he was about to do. But he told himself this was for her own good.

"Not again," she cried as he unforgivably dragged her under the surface for a third and final time. This time she came up coughing because her mouth had been wide open when she went down. He slapped her on the back. Her hair floated around her in the water as he put an arm under her shoulders and dragged her against him and back to shore.

"I'm sorry," he said in a low voice, but she floated like dead weight, limp and lax in his arms. "Bloody hell," he swore softly. "I think I went too far."

No answer. Alarmed now, Gabriel found his feet and surged up the bank with her until he reached soft, dry grass. He picked up his discarded coat, wrapping her in it and propping her up in his lap so he could use his arms to warm her torso.

"Damn it, why did you have to try my patience, girl?" he muttered as his ministrations bore no obvious fruit. Her skin was pale, almost blue, her lips a pale violet, her dark hair hanging limply.

FIVE

*O'er her warm cheek and rising bosom move
The bloom of young Desire and purple light of
    Love.*
    —Thomas Gray, *The Progress of Poesy*, 1754

Something finally reached her, because after another heart-stopping minute, she stirred. She gasped, spitting out a mouthful of water. "Why . . . did . . . you try to drown me?" she asked from between lips that barely moved.

He kept up his steady, brisk rubbing up and down her back. "I didn't, my dear. Your disguise brought this lesson on yourself."

She struggled to sit up in his lap. "What did I do?"

"This little game you're playing. It's dangerous." As dangerous as the effect her supple, youthful body was having on him. She was slightly built and the coat he'd wrapped around her was voluminous, yet still he felt the feminine curves beneath. She wasn't a child; she was certainly older than she seemed as a boy.

"W-what's dangerous?" Her voice was still little more than a whisper, her lips and skin still bluish.

He hadn't counted on the fact that her lesser body weight meant she would chill far more quickly in deep water than he. Her innocent question reminded him of why he'd done this.

"I never meant to hurt you, child, but your masquerade is far more dangerous than you realize."

She began to protest, realized her hair was draped about her shoulders and kept her mouth shut, though her full lips were mutinous. He wanted to shake her for her obstinacy.

"I'm not a child," she said vehemently.

"You are acting like one, Violet Pearson, playing at a game you know nothing about," he said harshly.

"It harms no one," she shot back defiantly. She didn't even notice that he knew her name.

"Oh no? If someone discovers you are a woman and you have no indulgent servants or relatives around. . . ."

She snorted.

"You could bring harm upon yourself," he said, his anger replaced suddenly by a sadness Violet had never suspected lay beneath his charming exterior.

"How could I?" Clearly she intended to brave this out, did not want to let him intimidate her.

"Go down to the waterfront of any town in the world, Violet, and see what rolls off those ships. Men who haven't had a woman or seen land for months. That breeds a lustfulness no lady should ever see. And no lady ever goes there," he added before she could interject again. His finger traced a soft path over her mutinous lips.

"Who goes to the docks to service these men, sweet Violet? Do you know?" his soft voice and sensuous touch at odds with the ugly truth he'd been telling her.

He bent over her, taking her lips with such gentleness, such sweetness that she forgot he'd pinned her to the riverbank beneath him in their sodden clothes. He pressed light kisses one after another on her mouth, her chin, her cheeks, her eyes. But always he returned to her mouth, deepening the kisses until she began to kiss him back.

Violet was so entranced that she forgot their quarrel and ceased to wonder at his sudden change in mood. Gabriel's lips pressed deeper against her mouth, slowly kissing apart the seam of her lips. "Open for me, sweetling," he breathed.

She did, aware that no one had ever kissed her like this, tasting him in her mouth and wondering at the shuddering, delicious feelings he evoked. After angling his mouth over hers, and widening her parted lips, his tongue stole in to explore her mouth.

Reeling with sensation, Violet was barely aware that his leg had insinuated itself between hers, and one of his hands had slid inside the opening of her shirt. At the same time that she dared to let her tongue touch his, a warm weight descended on her breast, covering it, rubbing. Had her nipple puckered on its own or was it Gabriel's searching, caressing hand that had shaped it, molded it, as he was doing now?

Gabriel's legs were now between hers, and his manhood was rigid against her. She had lived too long on a plantation watching horses and other animals mate not to know what pressed against her now.

What she had never realized was how good it felt, or how his hardness pressing against her seemed to make her softer, warmer . . . wanton. Her legs fell apart wider of their own accord, and into that breach he pressed.

At the same time, his kiss changed. The exploring became deeper, his tongue thrusting in her mouth the way his manhood had begun to thrust against her own secret place.

Gabriel's mouth left off its plundering; he raised to one elbow. One hand remained at her breast, having slipped under the sodden binding wrapped around her breasts. He pulled at her nipple, distending its hard tip, lengthening it. He looked down at it and her gaze was drawn there as well.

The most illicit thrill she had ever experienced shot through her in one heady, indecent rush. She moaned, ashamed and aroused all at once. Violet looked up at Gabriel looming over her, blocking out the sun. She knew she was begging wordlessly for something she couldn't name: an answer, a clarification, relief from these wild emotions.

"Look, Violet," Gabriel said in a darkly compelling voice. "Look at your breast in my hand." She did and the rush of sensation where he pressed against her was instantaneous.

"I could take you now and you would want me to, wouldn't you?" he asked, his strong fingers kneading her breast. His manhood pressed against her once more and she wished suddenly that he would touch her between her legs.

She nodded weakly, her eyes on his face.

Gabriel suddenly removed his hand, levered

himself off her, and sat her up with a hand behind her back. His eyes seemed to bore into her and she watched, fascinated, as his expression went from fierce to stony, the silvered gray of his eyes transmuting to something darker, harsher.

His hand was still at the opening of her shirt, which gaped open. "And that's what women do at the waterfront, Violet," he said in a low, ruthless voice stripped of all emotion. "They service men. They're whores. And don't tell me you are not one of them, because I already know that. You are an innocent. But you would be their sport if you were caught at this game that you're so proud of."

Her state of arousal ended abruptly with his words, as if she'd been doused again in cold water. He disengaged his hand, reaching to smooth a wet lock back from her cheek, his face impassive.

Violet slapped him. She jumped up, sobbing, and ran. Anywhere, anywhere to get away from this debonair man who had such darkness in his soul.

Gabriel stared after her only a moment before rising to go after her. He didn't bother lifting his hand to his stinging cheek. He'd deserved it. Oh, he had deserved it. He had also taught her a harsh lesson in far too harsh a fashion.

She wouldn't have listened any other way, he told himself, and knew he was correct. Still, that didn't make what'd he'd done any more palatable. He'd been no better than one of those sailors in rut himself, so fierce had been his own arousal. She might be innocent enough to believe it was part of the lesson, that he could control his reaction to her, but he knew the truth.

Violet affected him in a way no woman had in years. He pushed the thought away, telling himself he would consider it later.

He found her not far away, hunched over, shoulders shaking with silent heaves. The binding lay in a sodden heap beside her; she had put the shirt back on. She resisted him at first but was too tired to fight him. He gathered her up against him, telling himself she was just a little girl in trouble. She still turned her face away but he pressed her head against his shoulder and began to stroke through her hair with his hand. He talked softly, soothingly, little bits of praise for her beauty, her daring, her cleverness.

She softened against him finally, like a wild creature he had to treat gently to get her to trust him again. Still talking softly, just above her ear where she could barely hear him, he said, "You're a beautiful girl, Violet. But you mustn't trust men. I could have taken you; the kind of man I warned you of would not have stopped. It was damned hard for me to stop." She shook her head violently.

" 'Tis true. There is no lack in you, little one. It's not your fault; I'm not saying that. You must never believe a man who tells you that 'tis your fault he cannot stop. But you must never put yourself in that position, must never give a man a chance to take advantage of you that way. I did it knowingly, trying to teach you a lesson."

Violet lifted her head to look into his eyes. "I didn't do it to hurt you, sweetheart, not ever," he said. "And 'twas a stupid way to teach you a lesson."

His words penetrated, her eyes cleared. "You did that on purpose . . . to teach me a lesson?"

"Yes, I'm sorry, Violet. I meant the swim to show you how flimsy your disguise is, that you shouldn't use it to go out into the world, nor to rely on it."

"All this, you planned?" she asked, the dullness fading from her tear-streaked eyes, and the light of battle entering them suddenly.

"No, sweet, only the swim. I didn't mean . . . the rest. I meant it, that is, but I didn't plan it." He stopped, aware he was digging a chasm for himself he could only fall into. He was ten years older than she, and she had him babbling like a schoolboy.

He eased her off his lap, and then drew her up to stand with him. The horses were not far off. "I apologize for what transpired between us, my dear, but it was a mistake for you to wear boy's garb. Your guardians should have seen that you did not leave the house that way, and you should know now the dangers that could transpire." He sounded pompous. He'd been called many things but pompous was not one of them.

He should be advising her with disinterest, with concern only for her welfare. Instead he'd half seduced the girl, lost his own control, made up for it by saying blasted stupid things, and he suspected he'd insulted her but she was too dazed to realize it.

Either he had meant to kiss her senseless or he hadn't. He had not meant to lose his head and go farther, and yet he had. He had not told her how appealing she was, and she was, oh, how she was.

Blast. He'd taken her hand as they walked over to the horses but now she pulled away from him.

Without a word she mounted and turned in the direction of home, back to where they had left the picnic.

The ride home seemed long when little was said between them. She urged her horse forward when they came within sight of Oak Grove, and he let her go. By the time he arrived at the stables, her steaming horse was being wiped down by the stable boy and Violet was nowhere in sight.

Gabriel knew there was no point in going after her, not now. He would need to find out when her father would return. He wanted the nursery stock but he also had a few things to say to the father about how he let his daughter conduct herself.

Violet was furious. Furious, hurt, and betrayed. The Duke had seemed such a gentleman. Everything had gone so well. She didn't think he'd suspected a thing. And then—what he'd done. He had guessed that she wasn't what she'd said, and decided to make a fool of her.

How was she going to look him in the eye after this? Violet wondered. Even though she'd slapped him, it was more her own shame and humiliation at the root of it, not his caddish behavior. After all, he'd only been making his point.

Her recent deception notwithstanding, Violet had always been fundamentally, unflinchingly honest. When she set aside her own hurt feelings and the wish that he'd chosen some other way to deliver his message, she knew she wouldn't have listened to mere words. His demonstration had been effective beyond words.

And the opportunity for that was something she would never, ever allow to happen again.

"Someone was following me, Lady Pen," Tessa said, entering the Duke of Belmont's dining room in London with her market basket still over her arm. "I'm just back from the market and there were footpads, I know it." She was barely out of breath, but Penelope suspected she'd run most of the way here.

Lady Penelope Henley put down the morning newssheet and regarded Tessa Lindon thoughtfully. Tessa was a young woman given to strong emotions but she had never lied. Nor had she any reason to invent enemies. In her short life, her family had taken care of that for her.

"What did they look like? Were they in livery?" she asked. Gesturing to Tessa to sit at the long table, she pushed the silver chafing dish of eggs toward her. They were the only two in the dining room so far, since it was early. Tessa, who was London-born and had lived on the streets, liked to go to market at dawn. Penelope rose earlier since Gabriel had left: there were so many responsibilities to handle, and she never slept well anyway. Though she had been with Gabriel for nearly four years, she still had nightmares sometimes when he was away.

"Naw, they weren't in livery. A lord would be a

fool to send men in his own colors, wouldn't he?"
Tessa scoffed.

"Sometimes the higher the lord, the less common sense he has," Penelope observed.

"I know a man'll do almost anything if he's provoked enough," Tessa said, "but these two were careful."

"Did they look like Runners?" The Bow Street Runners had a formidable reputation for finding what they sought, and their investigators were well trained and highly competent.

"Naw, they were private, I think," Tessa said. "I don't know if they were trained. Don't think so, though, because I lost 'em quick enough."

"So you did lose them. Good. Do you think it was you they were after?" Tessa's father had tried to find her before. Because she went out so often, her whereabouts were likely to be discovered more quickly than some of the other women who only went out when they were at the Duke's country seat.

"My dad, put up blunt to find me? Even if he was desperate for help in the tavern, he'd never spend his ready on me. He'd just do it himself."

The truth was sad, but Penelope also believed firmly that as the Bible said, the truth would make one free. Tessa had faced the truth about her father and would never again be taken in by his lies. Some of the other women had not yet—and might never—reach the painful clarity that Tessa had learned. Some left "Belmont's," as they referred to the Duke's home, to return to their abusers who were their husbands, fathers, lovers.

Penelope understood how hard it was to leave.

It had taken the death of her unborn child for her to realize that reforming her husband was not possible, and that if she stayed, sooner or later, he would kill her and any children she might eventually have. Or perhaps his last beating had removed that possibility forever.

She took a last bit of toast. Then she waited until Tessa had finished eating her poached eggs—a matter of seconds, because Tessa had learned early that food came her way infrequently. Breaking the habits of a lifetime took years.

"Do you have any idea who they might have been after, Tess?" she asked.

"Who's the newest? Lady Margery? Lord Albie has plenty of the ready to chase about London looking for her."

"Good thought. She's still so new. . . ."

"And rabbity, yes, I know," Tessa interrupted. "She might run out into the street like a chicken with 'er head cut off if she thought it wasn't safe here. She'd just panic, like. Don't you think it's best not to tell her?"

"As long as she doesn't go outside, I think 'tis all right not to tell her. She's not shown any inclination to go out anyway. I will tell the guards Gabriel hired to keep their lookout sharp. And no one is to go out alone for the time being. That includes you, Tessa."

Tessa, whose small features could show an amazing variety of expressions, wrinkled her nose. "I know. Don't mean I have to like it, though."

"It's for your safety," Penelope began.

"Save the speech, Lady Pen. I know it by heart." Tessa smiled to take the sting from her words, and Penelope marveled again at the change in her that a smile brought. Her features were unremarkable—Tessa preferred to look like an ordinary brown sparrow with her brown hair, hazel eyes, and drab clothing—but when she smiled, Penelope could see how her wide, generous mouth and radiant smile might make a man look twice and think of sin.

"I know you do." Penelope smiled in return, although with her pale coloring, she would never look half as intense as Tessa could when she was wrought up about something.

"Be sure to tell me if there are any more incidents," she continued. "Make sure the less observant among us have someone with them like you who is good at spotting when they leave the house."

"You can count on me, Lady Pen." As if sharing the news had relieved her of her burden of fear, Tessa gave her a wink and left the dining room.

Penelope gave in to a moment of quiet panic after Tessa left. This time Gabriel wasn't in the country or elsewhere in Great Britain, where a courier could reach him within a day or two. He was in America, separated from them by an entire ocean. She bowed her head in a quick, silent prayer, then composed herself and rose to go about the day's business, tamping down her terror.

They all had their devils. It was why they were here. Penelope's veneer of control went about as deep as Tessa's forced air of cheerfulness. They had all experienced the terror of realizing that they were never safe. Even here, sheltered within

Gabriel's embrace, none of them could fully give up the fear and watchfulness that had enabled them to stay alive, when other women just like them had lost their lives.

SIX

What is your sex's earliest, latest care,
Your heart's supreme ambition?
——George, Lord Lyttelton
Advice to a Lady, 1770

Violet decided to ride over to Willow Oaks to see Aunt Rose, her cousins, and her little brother Peter. She'd always been able to tell Aunt Rose anything. This particular tale would take some careful censoring, however.

"Violet, how are you?" Her tall, red-haired aunt bent to kiss her at the front door that faced the river. Shrieking sounds emanating from the opened rear door of Willow Oaks revealed the location of her little brother Peter and his partners in crime.

"I see that I don't need to ask if little Peter is having a good time," Violet said, smiling. Aunt Rose's girls, Martha, nine, and Catherine, five, adored their cousin, and she suspected from the noises she heard that they were using him as their "pony."

"Come in, darling," Rose said. "You can romp

with the children after we sit and talk a while. What have you been up to?"

Violet's face must have shown something, because Aunt Rose dropped her light tone. After ringing for tea, she had Violet sit in one of the elegant wing chairs that sat beside the long front windows, and said simply, "What is troubling you, Violet?"

"Troubling me? Nothing," Violet said, mustering her best smile. "I've just had the most amazing experience." And she found that once she started talking about her correspondence with the Duke, the initial excitement and sense of adventure came back. She was able to push her second encounter with Gabriel Isling to the back of her mind.

Aunt Rose knew the family name but little about Belmont's reputation, just that the family was immensely wealthy. Violet wasn't about to tell her aunt either her daring plan to stow away or how her disguise had been so recently foiled by the Duke of Belmont, but she did reveal that she'd been corresponding with him.

"Under false pretenses?" Aunt Rose asked with an amused look.

"Not to put too fine a point on it, yes," Violet confessed.

Much to her surprise, Aunt Rose laughed. "Darling Violet, it seems you don't know how I came to America. Did your mother never tell you?"

"No."

"I think I know why she didn't. Your mother and I had some . . . ah, rather unusual adventures with your father and Uncle Peter. I believe your mother wanted to protect you so she hasn't told you a number of the stories."

"What on earth did you do?" Violet asked, feeling a sudden spurt of jealousy about this secret history of which she had known nothing.

"When I came to America, I had been corresponding with your Uncle Peter, posing as my father's heir."

Just like she had, Violet thought excitedly, but bit her lip before she could say so. She wouldn't tell about the disguise. Aunt Rose had an extremely sharp mind and now that Violet knew she had once fled her home, it surely wouldn't take much for Rose to guess that Violet might have planned the same.

"Is that how you came to inherit Willow Oaks?"

"Mmm, not exactly. My brother Bertram became the heir after the death of my brother Ralph, but Bertram was away in India. I knew he would only sell the land at my mother's bidding. I loved Willow Oaks and couldn't bear that to happen. So I came here to take over the plantation and run it myself, thinking I could make enough money for my family so that I wouldn't have to live in England or marry a horrid man who wanted to buy my family's title."

"Did you stow away on a ship?" Violet asked, and then bit her tongue, hoping she hadn't revealed anything.

Aunt Rose gave her a sharp glance, but said only, "No. I did sneak out of my house at night with my maid Eunice, but not in disguise. We bought passage as a lady and her traveling companion, which we were."

"Did you and mother ever dress up as boys like

I do . . . did?" Violet asked, eager to learn more of this side of her mother and aunt.

"Mmm, not that particular bit of rebellion, no. Yours is actually quite harmless, I think, dressing as a boy to go to town." If she knew what trouble that had gotten Violet into last week, she didn't say, bless her.

"I ran away and crossed an ocean, a feat I wouldn't wish either of the girls to undertake without my knowledge," her aunt continued. "I know, though, that it all looks different when you're young and impetuous, something that also seems to run in the family," Rose said with an affectionate frown.

Her aunt's confession gave Violet a secret, guilty thrill. No wonder her mother hadn't wanted her to know about the past. And yet it seemed that history had a way of repeating itself.

"And mother? What was her rebellion?"

"Apart from being Williamsburg's first florist and passing messages to the Patriots, do you mean?" Violet nodded; these stories she knew.

"She defied your father and he kidnapped her."

"What?" Violet was flabbergasted. "Why?"

"There were fairly personal reasons mixed with the imminent war, from what I understand," Rose said. "I think I'd best leave that one to your mother to relate. 'Twould not be my place to speak of it."

Violet nodded, though she was disappointed.

"So why did you decide to correspond with the Duke of Belmont?" Aunt Rose asked briskly, bringing the subject back around to Gabriel.

Violet fidgeted on the elegant chair, feeling like

a child again. After what she'd said, would Aunt
Rose understand that Violet's motives were in
many ways the same? "I wanted to do something
on my own. All my life I've spent running after
the boys. Perhaps 'tis also due to their being twins.
Adam and Arthur were a closed society of their
own. They never needed anyone else, and being
boys, knew they would be running the plantation
and the businesses one day. Even Peter being
born didn't change that, because he was also a
boy. Then 'twas three to one."

Aunt Rose looked at her seriously. "Perhaps we
did you a disservice without realizing it, love. You
seem to want to tread the same path your mother
and I did, even though you know so little of what
transpired when we were younger. How odd."

"It must run in the family," Violet said brightly.
The last thing she needed was to have to explain
her own plan to her aunt. But now that the Duke
of Belmont was here, surely she could go legiti-
mately to London with him, while representing
Tidewater Nurseries.

Her desire for adventure had not altered one
whit. She didn't care what the Duke thought of
her disguise. And she could always smuggle herself aboard his ship, surely, should continued subterfuge be necessary. Having Gabriel Belmont
find out she was a woman didn't mean she had
to start acting like one.

Gabriel waited a bit longer, but Maximilian's
discreet inquiries had turned up very little. No
one remembered seeing Miss Violet Pearson of
Oak Grove in town lately, dressed as a boy. Nor

could he conceive of any reason why she would have come to town like that, and for what purpose.

In the end, he concluded that it must have been her idea of a lark. And now that he'd discovered Violet at her ruse, surely she would start acting like a woman. After all he'd caught her—and humiliated her—and then nearly made love to her. It had been the closest he'd come to losing his control that he could remember.

So it was with considerable surprise that Gabriel reined up at Oak Grove and found the servants still going along with the fiction that Violet was Adam Pearson the younger.

There was no point in berating servants, Gabriel knew. It wasn't their fault. But if the plantation's factor tried to pull the sophistry of Violet's identity on him, Gabriel intended to pin his ears back.

The housekeeper, Mistress Steele, told him that Will Evans was in the fields, but that Will's wife was in the estate office.

Gabriel waited, and presently a handsome, sturdy woman came toward him from the back of the house. Her features were open and honest, and she showed no reserve at shaking hands. She did not mention Violet, and Gabriel did not ask for her, not at first.

He discussed what he was looking for, and she proved knowledgeable about the estate's inventory. She knew a fair amount about Willow Oaks, too, but told him to go see Rose Walters for more details. She offered him tea and biscuits, which he accepted, and he began to ask her more general questions about the Tidewater area, the plantations, and the way of life along the James River.

He liked what he heard, but he wasn't going to tell her his own thoughts. Any decision to move his household to America had to be carefully considered. There was nothing usual about the way he lived, and he would not move everyone here without at least some sense first that they would be accepted. And if not accepted, at least left alone.

When he rose to go, she offered him her hand, and without thinking, he took it to kiss it. She pulled back and he looked up.

"Have I offended, mistress?" he asked.

"I . . . no, that is," she said, flustered. " 'Tis just that I've never met an Englishman before, and . . ."

"Your employer? Your employer's sister-in-law?" he inquired in a level voice.

"Well, they're different. They left England, good riddance to bad . . ." She stopped, put a hand to her mouth. "I'm sorry. I don't mean to be rude, sir."

Gabriel smiled. " 'Tis perfectly all right, madam. You've only had your independence but a few years, and I understand that affection for the former home country is not unalloyed."

At her bewildered look he said more simply, "There are many Americans who have no use for Britain."

Put that bluntly, she couldn't mistake his meaning. She nodded, then lifted her hand again to cover her mouth, looking abashed. Gabriel held up a hand. "You needn't clarify, madam. Nor do you need to apologize. But I do hope bygones can be bygones in at least some part of this pleasant land.''

"Of course, sir. 'Tis just that this particular family hasn't had the best of luck with the English families they came from, and I'd not have Miss Violet hurt by truck with you."

Ah, the heart of the matter. Gabriel took a step toward her for emphasis, looking into her clear brown eyes. "Your young mistress Violet is only going to hurt herself by pretending to be a boy," he said. "There are men who would take advantage of that fact if they knew. Her disguise is neither clever nor prudent. I strongly suggest you advise her against it."

Her brown gaze flew to his, stricken. "You knew? When? She said she had not told you."

"Nor did she. My dear lady, I knew from the first. It may be that I am unusual in that regard for reasons that I do not choose to name. But if I guessed, others might. With her family away and her penchant for traveling about, she should ride with a companion, or dress as herself and take advantage of every privilege of courtesy and respect afforded to a lady."

"I . . . yes, yes, your lordship, you are right. I shall have to speak to Violet. But she's. . . ."

"Headstrong?" He smiled ruefully. "Ah yes, I've learned that already. I do not think your task is easy. But if her parents are away, you are standing in their stead, are you not?"

"My husband and I are in charge of Oak Grove while the Pearsons are away. Her aunt is nearby at Willow Oaks," Mistress Evans said.

"I do not wish to pry, do you understand, Mistress Evans?" He held her gaze while the indignant expression softened as she realized that he meant what he said, and probably had some basis for understanding that ill could come of such a charade. To the open question in her eyes, however, he did not respond. He had his own demons, which no one here needed to know anything about.

"I wish only the best for the young lady. Only the best," he repeated. "I give you good day." And so saying, he donned his hat and began to take his leave.

"Surely, sir, you are not so old yourself," said Mistress Evans rather daringly.

He turned as he reached the door. The smile he offered her was tight, he could feel it. "I have more experience than you could know or possibly guess."

Betsy's thought as the handsome Duke went out the door was that the set of his shoulders was proud and unbowed, but something in his eyes told of a world of experience that was very hard won indeed.

Her half-formed thoughts of matchmaking fled. This man had some darkness in his past that was still with him. He was not for sweet young Violet. He knew it too.

But Violet's face had been so alive and excited when she'd talked of meeting the Duke. Betsy sighed, heading back toward the plantation office where she had left the household accounts ledger open on the small desk her husband used.

What to do? If she warned Violet away, the stubborn girl might be like a moth to flame. How easy the temptation, how painful it would be to fall into the fire. But Violet had great good sense; surely Betsy could rely on that.

Violet had seen Gabriel from the paddock where she was exercising one of the horses but she had not looked in his direction or ridden closer. Yes, she was still in breeches, but she had a very good reason for them today, working around the stables. She didn't know if he would find that an acceptable reason.

Suddenly she felt resentful. How dare he, a stranger, come here and tell her what she could and couldn't do! She turned her back deliberately as she saw him leave; he did not approach her.

Good! That was exactly how she wanted it. Except that if she wanted to sell him Tidewater Nurseries stock, she was going to have to negotiate with him. She didn't want to lose his business and with it, her chance to persuade him to take her to England when he left, just because they had argued over her style of dress.

But not today. She was still far too angry—and heart sore—to want to see him or talk to him. And she refused to hear another lecture about the impropriety of breeches.

SEVEN

Some man unworthy to be possessor
Of old or new love, himself being false or weak,
Thought his pain and shame would be lesser,
If on womankind he might his anger wreak.
      —John Donne, "Confined Love,"
      Songs and Sonnets, 1633

When next they met, he saw awareness of what had happened near the river leap into her eyes and color her delicate face and neck in what seemed a heartbeat. She was dressed as a woman, he saw. Thank God. To his inflamed senses, however, only a burlap sack could have hidden her charms.

The resulting disappointment in himself and his unruly urges made him more curt than he had intended to be.

"I see you have resumed acquaintance with your gender, Miss Pearson," he said.

Her face flamed but she bit off any retort she might have made.

"I regret what happened, Violet," he began.

"Don't," she said. "Oh, please don't."

Don't what? Rub it in? Make it worse? Remind

her of her humiliation? Or of those brief, intense moments of pleasure they had shared?

It didn't matter. He sighed, his eyes searching her face, taking pleasure in the sight of her fine, sweet form, and the spirit in those rich blue-green eyes. What had happened, had happened, and nothing could change that.

"I am Violet. Just Violet," she said at last, holding out her hand. He didn't shake it as he had when she'd been "Adam." Instead he lifted her hand to his lips and smiled as if they had indeed just met.

And that became the pattern of their days. The stern admonisher had disappeared along with the intense lover. Mornings they spent going over twenty years' worth of records of her family's business, going back to her parents' marriage and move to Oak Grove. That was when her mother started seriously cultivating florists' flowers and her father, after the war, became involved in breeding and crossbreeding. Cultivation of fruit trees began then, an effort considerably strengthened when her uncle Peter had joined the project.

Afternoons Gabriel visited the fields with Will or once, visited the greenhouses at Willow Oaks. Uncle Peter had added a second greenhouse at Willow Oaks to the one he'd built years ago by the Tidewater Nurseries dock. Gabriel was fascinated by the various techniques used in the orchards and greenhouses, which trees had been espaliered to grow against trellises or walls, which had been grafted onto root stock, and so on. He also found interesting the records of attempts to breed for flavor, or color, or other desirable qualities. Not everything they had tried had worked, of course. The records were liberally scattered with failures: pears were notoriously difficult to grow, for instance; peaches were also delicate breeders.

Producing wine from grapes the family grew, well, they had given up on that altogether. The Tidewater was too hot, too humid. Rot infected the grapes, and they would not hold their flavor when fermented and mixed with sugar. Although Thomas Jefferson had renewed his efforts at Monticello since returning from France the previous year, Violet had heard her father say that the countryside near Monticello, in the central mountainous region of Virginia, was more like Tuscany. Perhaps Jefferson would have more success, but the grapes grown at Willow Oaks were used as fruit only.

Gabriel had befriended Will Evans, impressing the Oak Grove foreman that he was no idle English lord. With Will's conversion had come Betsy's. Soon Gabriel and his right hand man Maximilian were invited to share the hospitality of Oak Grove. Because the trip back to town was so long, they often spent the night.

If only they hadn't been in Virginia, everything would have been perfect, Violet thought more than once. Among the sparkling society that London boasted, everything that was wonderful now would have been even more so. Gabriel was the very image of all she had imagined a British lord would be: bright, witty, charming.

Thank goodness, he acted as if that day at the riverbank had never been. There was no censure in his face or voice, and he was nothing but the

picture of a gentleman. For Violet, it was
enough—mostly. Every now and then, she longed
for the passion he had shown her, the depths in
his personality she'd glimpsed, but such thoughts
were as frightening as they were intriguing.

Occasionally she slept poorly, fidgeting in her
sleep as dreams plagued her of that afternoon.
Sometimes her body felt heavy, vaguely unsatis-
fied, and she dreamed of his mouth on hers and
of his caressing hands. Her lips longed for those
deep kisses she'd never received from any man
before, never known she could want so much. But
mostly, she found it better not to think about that
strange interlude with Gabriel. This light, carefree
lord was the one she preferred, and he obligingly
acted the part.

One morning Violet came down to breakfast to
find Gabriel still at table. When he spent nights
at Oak Grove, he was usually up and about early
the next morning with Will Evans, or rode back
to Williamsburg if Maximilian wasn't with him. At
the moment, Maximilian was away from Williamsburg on some errand Gabriel hadn't explained, so Gabriel had accepted Betsy's invitation
to stay with them an extra day.

Violet had enjoyed Gabriel's company at the
dinner table the night before, since usually it was
just Will and Betsy eating with her. Their conversation was always predictably—and boringly, she
thought (in private only)—about the plantation.

She'd hoped Gabriel would be more entertain-
ing, and he was. He'd talked of fêtes he'd attended in London, of the occasional ball to which

he'd been obligated to go. One thing only surprised her, and that was that he didn't show much
enjoyment in the social whirl. He seemed to speak
more for her pleasure than his own.

"My life in London is a rather unusual one,
sweet pea. I don't go to balls unless I have business to transact that cannot be done anywhere
else," he'd said, then had changed the subject.

Gabriel frequently called her by flower names
not her own. It sounded like flirtation to a casual
observer, but after the first few times, Violet realized he employed the pet names as a way of dis-
tancing himself from her. She might be young,
but as her mother had long ago observed, Violet
had good acumen when it came to judging
other's emotions.

She thought this whimsical practice was
Gabriel's way of keeping things between them
light and uninvolved. Since her physical desire for
him was one that usually came at night, and she
worked hard at forgetting it, she refused to be
annoyed by his tactic or to show him that she
understood what he was doing.

Yet this morning she was excited because she
had news to share. The annual Independence Day
celebration would be held along the river with
picnics, bonfires, and fireworks. Usually her family were among the key organizers of the event,
but with Aunt Rose alone at Willow Oaks and her
parents absent, she wasn't expected to fill in for
them. But the uniquely American festival would
take place regardless.

People would ride or boat along the river all
day, from plantation to plantation. The Harrisons
at Berkeley would offer fried chicken; the Carters

at Shirley, their best Virginia ham. The Byrds at Westover would carve ice from their blockhouse and cool down beverages for everyone with it. Oak Grove and Willow Oaks would supply dozens of tarts and fruit pies.

At dark there would be bonfires, singing, and dancing. The evening would climax with the fireworks of which John Adams had written predicting that July 2nd—the day the Continental Congress had actually voted for independence—would be commemorated. The young nation had instead fixed on the day Thomas Jefferson's Declaration of Independence had been signed, but the activities were all that John Adams had foreseen.

Gabriel watched her bustle into the room, her narrow-skirted dress in the new fashion draped gracefully about her lithe figure. She was the picture of youthful excitement. Sarah had been like this when he was a little boy, he remembered, before he'd been sent away to school. The excitement of attending a grown-up ball had lit her sparkling hazel eyes and the full, generous mouth that had used to smile so much.

He smiled now at Violet, her image overlaid with the fading one of Sarah. But Sarah still smiled, and he felt not haunted but blessed. Sarah would have liked Violet very much, he mused. And what he felt for Violet was not at all sisterly, but he tamped that thought down. He should think of her as a sister, the little sister he'd never had.

"Of course I'll attend, my little rose," he said, her smile sparking his own.

"You can't call me that, Your Grace," she said.

"Gabriel," he said, frowning slightly at her use of his title. "And why not?" he asked lightly.

"My Aunt Rose, that's why. You've not met her, I think."

"No, I haven't. I have been near the big house at Willow Oaks only once with Will to see the greenhouses. I didn't want to intrude."

"Well, it's time you met her. If you don't mind children."

He shook his head, still the charming guest. "Of course not." Inwardly, the pain of never having had Sarah's child to raise stabbed at him as it always did.

"Good. My baby brother is staying there, along with Aunt Rose and Uncle Peter's daughters." Gabriel had learned by now that Violet's parents were in Massachusetts for the twins' graduation. Privately, he wondered again why they had let her stay virtually alone, because the Evans woman and, he assumed, the aunt had known about the escapade and not stopped her.

But he said nothing, and smilingly acquiesced to her plans. "Are you sure I won't be attacked by your patriots?" he asked jokingly, but she took him seriously.

"If you don't dress in silks and satins—not that I've seen you ever dressed like that, come to think of it—I'm certain you'll be fine. Hospitality is paramount here, my lord."

"Gabriel," he said automatically, as he did every time she used his title. Technically it should be "Your Grace" but he hated that even at home. Did she use the formal address in the same way he used pet names for her? If she did, good for her, he thought. He needed no complications of the emotional sort. His life was too complicated as it was.

Penelope was in the conservatory with the gardeners when Athena came in at a run. Athena, whose ravishing looks belied her scholarly nature, was always in a hurry. For a scholar interested in such long-dead antiquities as the Hanging Gardens of Babylon, she was always in a remarkable hurry. And yet, she would sit for hours with her books and manuscripts. She had helped draw plans for Gabriel's country garden that imitated part of those gardens, as well as those in the Vale of Kashmir, but the actual plants and flowers interested her not in the least.

Penelope felt the first faint stirrings of fear. She handed the watering pot to one of the other gardeners and gripped Athena's hands between her own when the young woman came up to her. She could see they were shaking. Now she was fully alert; Athena had traveled to so many strange places that travel throughout London never fazed her.

"What is it, Athena?" she asked.

"A-t-t-tacked," she said. The stuttering that was the legacy of her father's and later, her husband's, emotional abuse returned when she was under stress.

"Who was attacked? You? Are you all right, dear? You weren't alone, were you?"

"N-n-n-no. T-t-Tessa made that quite clear. No, Cleo and Diana and I had gone to the lecture at the Historical Society. With Gabriel's open invitation in hand, they let us in. We all wore veils."

There was no place more likely than the Historical Society for Athena to run into her father, the man who had made her marry under his browbeating, Penelope thought grimly.

Athena's unearthly amber eyes glowed at her. "It's not what you think, Penelope, really. No one bothered us while we were there. We didn't stay for refreshments, of course. We were going to go to the tea rooms near here, where they know us."

Athena was holding onto her hands so tightly that Penelope thought she might sustain bruises, but she said nothing about that. If Athena thought she was being judged for slowness of speech or thought, she would retreat into herself again. Sometimes she didn't speak for days.

"What happened?" Penelope asked, trying to mask her apprehension. " 'Tis all right, you're safe here. You know that, don't you? Take a deep breath. That's it. Good girl," Penelope said in her most reassuring tones. "Are the others here with you? Are they safe?"

"Yes. Diana took C-C-Cleo up to her room. Diana said she'd be d-d-down in a moment." At that moment, the thundercloud that had been threatening all day opened up and Athena had to shout above the noise of the rain pouring down upon the greenhouse roof.

"Come back inside," Penelope said, drawing Athena after her into the sitting room. She asked Liza, one of the inside maids, to get them some tea and cakes from the kitchen.

"All right. One more deep breath. That's it. You can do it," Penelope said as Athena folded her long legs into a chair by the hearth.

Athena took a deep breath, then a sip of the

tea that had just been brought in. Pulling her composure around her like a cloak, she resumed. "Before we turned into Half Moon Street, we saw two men walking toward us. We didn't think anything of it at first but then Diana said, 'Those gentlemen aren't out for a walk.' We'd crossed Hyde P-P-Park and it was behind us, but we weren't sure 'twould be any safer there. Most of the carriages and phaetons had already left the Walk. So we just k-k-kept going."

The park should have been safe, Penelope thought. The Season was in full swing, although the afternoon had been well advanced. "As we drew closer, they split apart, and before we knew what to do, there was one of either side of us. One had a p-p-pistol." She stopped for a moment, her hands clenching on the wrapper Penelope had given her, which was still in her lap.

"He took a pistol from his pocket and pressed it into Cleo's side—that's why she nearly fainted—while the other had a dagger tip imbedded in his walking stick. He brought it up near my face, and said 'We're not to carve up your p-p-pretty faces, not today anyway. But if she knows what's good for her, and the rest of you, she'd best leave. His Lordship says she has three days.' "

"Do you know whom he meant, Athena?"

"None of the three of us," she replied, shuddering. "Or we wouldn't have gotten home. We weren't the ones he was looking for. He pulled a signet ring out of his pocket and held it up to my face, keeping the dagger close at me."

"Can you draw the ring?"

"Of course." Athena had sketched hundreds of tombs, vases, pottery, and other ancient artifacts.

It was probably the one skill her husband hadn't been able to rob her of by shattering her will and spirit.

By the time she'd finished relating the story, and paper and charcoal had been found for her to draw, Diana had come down from Cleo's room.

Diana confirmed Athena's story, and added that she thought the men were in some lord's regular employ. They were respectably dressed and hadn't smelled of liquor or the gutter.

Penelope, Athena, and Diana stared at the sketch of the signet ring Athena had drawn. None of them recognized it.

"Athena, can you do one thing more?" Penelope asked. "Could you draw the faces of the men who assaulted you?"

"Penelope, you know I'm not good at people."

Penelope patted her shoulder. "I know, dear. But you're better than any of us. Diana can help you with the description. I'm sure you can do it. I'll go gather everyone together once you're done. Then we can try to figure out who among us is being threatened. Did any of Gabriel's security men see them?"

"No, since there were three of us, we told them we didn't need to be accompanied to the Society lecture. They saw us into the hackney. And the men stopped us near the teashop, not the house. The security men that Lord Belmont put at the end of our block were too far away."

"Did you tell the men you intended to walk back? They should have accompanied you to the lecture."

"No, we told them we'd be taking a hackney,"

Diana said. "We only decided to walk to the tea rooms at the last minute. That was our fault."

"But how did they know you would be at Half Moon Street?" Penelope wondered.

Diana, who had been once been London's most celebrated courtesan, was less sheltered than Penelope, an Earl's daughter. She pushed a lock of red hair off her shoulders before replying. "They didn't. I imagine they were either lurking about just past where the guards stand, or they figured one of us would be in Hyde Park eventually. After all, we're so close to it and we do go into the park frequently. Dressed as they were, it wouldn't have been that strange to a passerby for them to have pretended to greet us."

When Athena was done, Diana and Penelope looked carefully at the sketch, but recognized neither man. Penelope called in Tessa to see if one had been the man following her back from market the other day.

But Tessa hadn't seen her pursuer; it was more her street sense coming into play. She could read shadows better than any of them, but a shadow was all she had seen.

The four women looked at each other somberly. This was the second time in as many weeks that their security had been breached. If Gabriel's hired guards could not be counted on, if someone was determined to threaten them all to get one among their number to come back to him, they were all in serious jeopardy.

EIGHT

One crowded hour of glorious life
Is worth an age . . .
> —Thomas Mordaunt, *Verses Written*
> *During the War, 1756–1763*

Independence Day dawned with the sultry heat so typical of July in southern Virginia. The humidity was close and oppressive. Violet told Gabriel that an open-necked shirt and rolled up sleeves were perfectly appropriate attire. She watched as he discarded his coat and stock and rolled up his sleeves with apparent relief.

He had already been out in the fields informally, she saw, since the forearms and throat revealed by his actions were strong and brown. The evidence of the powerful frame beneath the tailored clothes made her throat go dry, so she resolutely looked away, but the image lingered.

She herself had chosen the lightest muslin dress she owned and discarded all petticoats but one. She wore an old fashioned hat of chip straw because its wide brim shaded her face and was more practical than the bonnets currently in fashion.

Gabriel wanted to look at the land from the

water, so they would go from plantation to plantation in a skiff. He'd agreed to stop by Willow Oaks and pick up Peter. Later they would reunite him with his cousins.

By mid-afternoon, little Peter was nearly asleep in the boat, worn out with stops to play with friends and frequent food forays. Gabriel took them to Willow Oaks and helped the sleepy boy onto the dock. Violet led them toward the house. Midway there, Peter stumbled, and Gabriel simply scooped him up and kept going.

Peter was actually asleep when Gabriel followed Violet into the house. A servant stepped forward, but recognized Violet and smiled when she pointed to the sleeping boy.

Aunt Rose came down the stairs, and Violet introduced her tall, flame-haired aunt to Gabriel. Rose greeted him politely, but there were a dozen or more visitors in the house and they did not talk at length.

"Violet, your friend Edgar is around somewhere. He was here a little while ago, but may be preparing to go across the river to help with the fireworks."

Violet jumped up. "Edgar is here? Did he come with his family from Richmond?"

"I believe so," Aunt Rose said. "Why don't you go find him?" She turned inquiringly to Gabriel. "May I play hostess in Violet's absence, sir?"

"Of course." Gabriel waved her on. "Go, little Violet, I can fend for myself, at your aunt's kind sufferance."

"The Duke can catch me up on news of London. We'll be fine, my dear," Aunt Rose said. "The girls are having naps under protest, so that they might see the fireworks tonight. They want you to see their frocks, and they remember that you said you would braid their hair, so please do remember to come back. Now run along and find your beau."

Violet noticed that at the word "beau," something in Gabriel seemed to come to sharper attention, although the pleasant expression on his handsome features did not alter. His hammered silver eyes were as hard to read as ever, although she thought she heard him murmur Edgar's name in polite inquiry of her aunt as she sped from the room.

Violet had not seen Edgar all summer. As childhood friends, they had played together every summer when Edgar came to visit his cousins' plantation just upriver. Her family always visited his when they traveled to Richmond. Edgar's sense of adventure had helped her keep up with her brothers when they hadn't wanted a sister around, because Edgar was always prepared to range himself on Violet's side.

She saw him preparing to get into a skiff with several of his friends and cousins at the dock. "Stop, you blackguards," she called out in her deepest voice.

They all looked up. "Vi!" Edgar called, rocking the boat as he leaped back onto the dock. The others shouted and complained good-naturedly, but they managed to right the boat before it tipped over. Edgar hadn't even noticed because he was racing towards her.

Edgar, fair-haired and sturdily built, grabbed her in a typically exuberant hug. "How are you, you minx?" he asked, lifting her off her feet with a sound buss to each cheek, then one on her lips. He waved their companions on. "We'll take another skiff across the river," he called to them.

"How is my darling girl?" he asked, looping an easy arm about her shoulders. "You're looking particularly fetching today," he went on. "Almost too pretty to row across the river and muck about with the gunpowder. Have you decided to stop being a tomboy at last, Vi?"

"I thought you liked me the way I am, Edgar. And don't call me Vi," she said, tossing her head in the flirtatious gesture she'd seen other girls use but had always disdained herself. Her dark curls touched Edgar's open shirtfront. He looked down at the locks that had caught in the vee of his shirt and his expression changed. It took on an intensity she'd never associated with her friend. She'd seen that look in Gabriel's eyes, and her thoughts involuntarily flew to him.

"You are ready to grow up, I see," Edgar said in a teasing tone, although his arm had lowered to her waist. "In that case, it's time for a proper kiss." And instead of the smacking kiss he'd given her before, his lips descended to hers in a gentle sweethearts' kiss.

She was stunned and remained without moving. Edgar's lips were firm and warm, but all she could remember was the taste of Gabriel's lips against hers.

Fortunately their companions had pushed off or Violet had no doubt there'd have been any number of catcalls and cheers. She pulled away slightly from Edgar, confused. He'd always said he intended to marry her but she'd treated him as just another of the boys—much as he'd always treated her.

But now the look on his face was entirely too serious and intense. "Well, enough of that," she said, "or I'll be afraid to get in a boat with you alone."

His smile was broad and confident. "I'll behave myself, Violet. But make no mistake: the time has come to court you, and I've already staked my claim."

Violet pushed at him, a little annoyed. "I'm not some piece of property to 'claim,'" she said, but she didn't feel particularly playful as she said it. "You'll have to get in line like all the rest."

Edgar gestured around the riverbank. "I don't see any line, dear girl. It must just be me."

"We'll see about that," she said, tossing her head again. "Come on, let's go find the others."

She dared him to race down the bank, and they did, jumping into the boat as they had when they'd been children.

Later Edgar and Violet rowed back with their friends after all the preparations were in place. The fireworks would be shot off at full dark from the opposite side of the river. It was dusk now, and they'd run out of all the food supplies they had taken across the river with them.

Violet wanted to be sure Gabriel saw the fireworks, and she'd promised Peter that he could watch with them. He'd formed a strong attachment to Gabriel, and had abandoned even his cousins Martha and Catherine in order to follow Gabriel around today.

Edgar, Violet, and their companions trooped up to the house to fetch Peter. The young men also wanted more pie, if they hadn't all been eaten.

"Aunt Rose, where is the Duke?" Violet said as she went upstairs to help braid her small cousins' hair.

"Gabriel went to look at my knot garden and the gazebo, dear." So he'd convinced her aunt to use his first name already, she noticed.

"I'll just go fetch him," Violet said a few minutes later, when the girls' hair was done. They would be watching from the upstairs gallery Uncle Peter had added to the house a few years ago.

"The gazebo is as good a vantage point as any to watch the fireworks," Aunt Rose called as Violet went down the stairs.

"I know, but we already promised Peter that Gabriel would take him up on his shoulders to watch, and they won't fit in the gazebo that way."

"Violet, wait for me," Edgar said, coming in from the pantry where the servants had brought the pies from the bake house out back.

"No, no, it's all right," she said laughing. This was the Edgar she remembered—a broad smile on his face and cherry juice on his fingertips. "I'm just going to get our English guest."

Violet flew across the path leading to Aunt Rose's garden, the one she'd first planted to express her feelings for Uncle Peter. Ten years later the yellow tulips for hopeless love were gone, the ivy for fidelity was abundant, and the lavender for success also flourished. Aunt Rose made sachets from the fragrant herb that her mother sold in her store.

In the dusk, Violet almost ran into Gabriel leaving as she stepped up to the gazebo's floor to enter.

"Steady there," Gabriel said, reaching for her arm. The connection she'd felt the last time she and Gabriel touched instantly renewed itself. Gabriel's arm encircled her waist, and the touch between them prolonged as if they were both reluctant to let go. Violet had put her hand out when she bumped into Gabriel, and it now rested on his bare forearm. The warmth from his sun-browned skin and his own innate vitality made her feel warm all over.

Violet felt a touch from behind and whirled to find Edgar there. "Are you all right?" he said. Gabriel tightened his hold slightly, although Violet made no move to pull away.

"Of course I'm fine. This is my . . . our guest, our guest at Tidewater Nurseries, Gabriel, Duke of Belmont."

"Gabriel Isling," Gabriel said, reaching out with his other hand to shake hands with Edgar.

"Edgar Randolph," Edgar said as they shook hands. Violet suddenly became aware that the air seemed charged, much as before a storm, when senses felt heightened and a freshening breeze pregnant with anticipation of rain stirred damp hair at the temples.

Except that she felt the electricity in her body and there was no storm imminent.

The men studied each other with Violet between them, as if they were two predators circling their prey. What a ridiculous notion, she thought, trying to clear her head. She took a deliberate step away from Gabriel and he released her.

"Gabriel and I are going to fetch Peter to see

the fireworks. Do you want to come?" Violet asked.

"You're not coming with me to the bonfire?" There was usually dancing around a bonfire before the fireworks began, a brief period of silent wonder while the pyrotechnics took place, and then more dancing, while some couples would sneak away into the dark in quiet pairs.

"I'll bring Gabriel down to the bonfire later," Violet said.

"Sure," Edgar said curtly. "See you then." He turned away into the gathering dusk and he was lost to sight.

"Is that your beau?" Gabriel asked lightly.

"We have to fetch Peter," Violet said, not answering his question, not knowing what to say. "He's ready but insists that you must carry him on your shoulders from the house to the riverbank."

"Cheeky lad, isn't he?" Gabriel asked. "Does he get that from you?"

"The cheeky part or being a lad?" Violet returned, grateful that the easy banter between the two of them had resumed. Before they reached the house, however, a small form came hurtling out of Willow Oaks and launched itself at Gabriel.

Gabriel plucked Peter out of mid-air, it seemed, and swung the laughing boy up to sit on his shoulders.

"He really misses his father," Violet observed.

"How do you know?" Gabriel asked.

"Because that's exactly what he does when Papa comes home from Williamsburg or Richmond."

"I see. And here I thought I was his new friend." Although it was said lightly, Violet had the oddest sense that it rendered Gabriel sad in some ineffable way. Had he left a child at home? Did he have a wife and family after all, even though he never mentioned them?

She remained quiet as they went back down to the river. This didn't seem to be that kind of sadness, of missing loved ones with whom he'd soon be reunited. No, this was more like a longing for something he'd never had. And he had spoken of moving his household here, not his family. Surely a man with a family would not speak of them in such a detached way.

"Mistress and Master Pearson," Gabriel said formally, with a smile in his voice, "What is your pleasure? Do you want to stand, sit, or lie down?"

"You promised to carry me," little Peter said. He looked so like his namesake, Violet thought. The twins were tawny like their mother with her father's strong jaw and aquiline nose, but little Peter took after his uncle, although his eyes were hazel, a mixture of Papa's blue-green and Mama's golden hue.

"Yes, I did promise to carry you, little man, but you can sit upon my shoulders even if I am sitting down. I will keep my promise, never fear," he added.

"Peter, you mustn't say such things to the Duke," Violet said.

Gabriel took his hand off Peter's leg where it dangled from his shoulder and squeezed Violet's hand. "I'm just Gabriel here, Violet. Master Pearson is quite right to remind me of my pledge." He disengaged his hand from hers.

Gabriel gripped Peter's sturdy little legs in his hands, tickling him. While the little boy giggled,

he added, "But there is more than one way to
carry a boy."

He grabbed the wiggling child, then dangled
him upside down to Peter's shrieking delight.

"I can see the fireworks upside down," Peter
crowed, and Gabriel and Violet laughed.

"I can't hold you that way forever, my boy,"
Gabriel said. "The blood will all run into your
head and make you dizzy."

"I like being dizzy," Peter declared, but when
Gabriel tumbled him into the grass from his up-
side-down position and followed him down to
tickle him, Peter forgot his insistence on the fun
but difficult position.

"Didja know my sister's ticklish too?" Peter con-
fided when Gabriel had eased off so Peter could
catch his breath. Violet had remained standing,
not wanting to get her pale blue gown dirty, although she enjoyed watching the elegant British
lord and the little boy tumble and tussle together.
When Gabriel reached a hand up toward her foot,
she thought the sparkling look in his silver eyes
made him seem years younger.

Not that he was old, she thought, instinct making her jump back just in time to avoid his seeking
hand. From the book on British peerage her aunt
had, she'd worked out that he was seven and
twenty, ten years older than she was. But his experience seemed so vast . . .

"Oh no, not another drowning, my lord," she
said as she evaded him.

Gabriel rolled onto his stomach to better extend his reach. But as he looked up at her from
beneath the fall of dark hair over his brow, his
playful expression turned intense and she knew

that he was remembering, as she was, what had passed between them the last time they had sat by the riverbank.

Even though the look on his face promised a passion with no lessons attached, her sense of shame returned. She couldn't linger here. "I'm going to the bonfire," she said. Gabriel had no chance to come after her because Peter pounced on his back like a cat on a mouse, although their sizes were reversed. Amid her brother's renewed shrieks of delight, Violet made her escape.

Gabriel watched Violet go, regretting her sudden retreat. Obviously she had remembered being pulled down into the water and feared he might do something similar. Or had she reacted to the burning look he'd given her, one he couldn't suppress, as he'd remembered the feel of her in his arms that day.

With Peter Pearson on his back like a lion's cub, he knew he wasn't going anywhere right now. He'd find her later, but his blood was up, and he didn't want to find that pup Edgar with his hands all over Violet.

Gabriel made growling noises while trying to shake the clinging Peter from his back, who was enjoying the ride tremendously. Was he jealous? Gabriel wondered.

Jealous? That wasn't possible. Violet was a child and belonged with a child herself.

A man-child who at his age—he couldn't be older than Violet by more than a year—would want only to press his face between her breasts and put his tongue in her mouth. Gabriel sur-

prised himself at the vivid pictures that flashed
through his head, but he knew what randy young
men were like. He'd been a fairly normal speci-
men himself, until Sarah's death. Certainly he
knew what the urges were like, and that most
young men didn't have a great deal of control.

Violet was a lady, not a trollop to lead a man
on, but she and the boy were obviously friends of
long-standing. And Rose Walters had indicated
the boy was fond of her niece. Considering how
quickly Gabriel had lost his own discipline with
Violet, he didn't think the boy's willpower would
last more than a minute if he got her in his arms.

But Gabriel was stuck playing the role of hon-
orary uncle, and with so many people about, he
doubted that there would be trouble. Not now,
with everyone milling about to see the fireworks.
There were too many people, too much excitement. Afterwards, perhaps, when the fires burned
low, then there would be trysting. American men
and women had the same passions as their English counterparts, after all. They were all human.

So he entertained the laughing boy, putting
him up on his shoulders again when the tussling
match settled down, and Peter directed him to
the spot he thought best for viewing. Last year he
had been at Oak Grove with his family, he in-
formed Gabriel. Then he suddenly remembered
that his girl cousins were extending their "hop-
si-tal-ity," and asked if they could go find them.

"Do you mind, Gabr'el?" he asked. "They're
littler than me, and they might get upset that I
got to go with you and they didn't."

"Your aunt knows you are with me, does she
not?"

"Yes, but she also thought my sister was gonna be with us, and now she's not."

"Are you upset, little man? Shall we go look for your sister?"

"Naw. She'll be with all the boys, Edgar an' his friends. Let's go find Marth and Cathie." Out of the mouths of babes, Gabriel thought, renewing his inward pledge to find Violet. It was only for her own safety, he told himself. It had nothing to do with jealousy. He just needed to make sure she was safe.

Was he worried about her safety with boys she had known her whole life, when he had known her but scant weeks? Who was he fooling? Gabriel asked himself. No one, he admitted as he swung the child up to his shoulders once again. No one, so it was just as well there was no one to talk to. Maximilian would just have lifted that eyebrow of his, but it would have had the same effect.

NINE

. . . solemnized with pomp and parade, with shows, games, sports, guns, bells, bonfires, and illuminations . . .
—John Adams, *Letter to Abigail Adams,* 1776

Little Peter yelled for his cousins as he ran into the house. Gabriel followed more slowly. They found Aunt Rose and her girls, two adorable redheads who regarded him with big appraising eyes. They had been just about to ascend to the second floor gallery. Violet and her cohorts were nowhere to be found, although there were still plenty of folk wolfing down pies under the watchful eyes of Eunice, the housekeeper.

Gabriel watched as the little girls challenged their older cousin to a race up the stairs. Martha had red-blonde hair and cornflower blue eyes, while Catherine had green eyes and her mother's flawless cream-colored skin. After Peter's whispered tales of his adventures to them, each of the girls had demanded a ride on Gabriel's shoulders. Gabriel was happy to oblige.

Unlike the fearless Peter, however, they had a tendency to clutch at his hair whenever they felt their perch threatened. It was giving him a headache but he didn't want to complain. Rose took a look at his pained expression when Cathie had gotten a particularly large hank of hair in her little hand, and said, "This is the last ride."

Cathie began to complain but the sound of explosions outside captured both girls' interest. Now she was happy to get down from Gabriel's shoulders. All three cousins raced up the stairs and out onto the gallery in record time.

"Poor Gabriel," Rose said. She and Gabriel stood just inside the door leading out onto the gallery, where the noise was less. "Do you want a compress for your head?"

"No, madam, I shall be fine," he said, rubbing the top of his head gingerly. "The removal of the cause is its own cure," he said.

"You are too kind. Do you have children of your own?" Rose Walters asked.

"No. I am unmarried."

"How unusual for a peer," she said candidly. "My mother was desperate that I should marry. Do you not have a mother who presses you for a grandchild and a father who wants to preserve your line?"

"I had heard you were unusually direct, Lady Rose," he parried gently.

"Rose, please. I am but the wife of a Virginia planter now, Your Grace," she replied. "And yes, I will acknowledge my question was rude by London standards. Perhaps even American standards," she said, charmingly admitting her tactlessness.

"Just call me Gabriel, please. Let's not go back on what was a promising beginning."

"Agreed. How fares my mother?" Theirs was a small world, that of London society. Rose Fairchild had been here ten years, though, so she could not have known what he himself had become. But he did know the status of her family, and was prepared to share it with her.

"Your brother Bertram married, a respectable match that allows him to keep up the house in town, where your mother lives. He and his wife are said to prefer the country."

"I don't wonder that he prefers anywhere but where my mother is. Forgive me, does that shock you?"

"No, madam. The Earl of Lansdale is also said to manage his estate wisely, with the help of his father-in-law, and he owns a sugar plantation in Antigua."

"That is good to hear. I thank you," Rose said formally. "I don't hear about my family often, since my mother no longer communicates with me."

"Mama, come look! It's a giant flag in the sky!" cried one of the girls. And sure enough, there was a pattern to the final bursts of color coming from across the river.

Gabriel stood to one side while the girls and Peter chattered at Rose. His gaze scanned down the crowd at the riverfront. It was hard to make out figures in the darkness and individual features were nearly impossible.

Then the sky lit up in a final explosion of color, searing whites and yellows that whizzed and popped to the crowd's awed exclamations. Gabriel had seen fireworks at Vauxhall, the pleasure gardens in London, so he was not that attentive.

Truth be told, he was really only looking for Violet. The finale of the fireworks gave the scene below him a brief, unreal glimpse of artificial day, and in it, he found what he'd been searching for.

Violet. She was with Edgar and he was pulling her by the hand toward a copse of willow oaks whose branches provided a snug haven for the seduction he was sure the young man intended.

Gabriel left the gallery after the briefest of goodbyes to Rose Walters. He ruffled Peter's hair and told him to be a good boy; that he would see him soon. Then he took the stairs two at a time, moving as quietly as haste permitted.

They were gone from sight by the time he'd filtered through the crowd, as people around him gathered up their belongings and got back into their boats to return to their own homes. But he'd seen the copse and headed straight for it.

Gabriel heard Violet's protest as soon as he breached the curtain of leaves.

"Edgar, this isn't a good idea."

"Why not? I've told you we're going to marry, Vi, don't be so coy. Here, have some more mobby," Edgar urged, his voice a little thickened by drink. "It's from your house, after all."

"I think you've had enough of it. And I never said I would marry you." Gabriel halted to listen to their exchange, his heart beating with an oddly erratic rhythm in his chest. What kind of drink was mobby anyway?

"You don't have a *tendre* for that boring English Duke, do you? Ah, your cheek's heating up. You do like him," Edgar said accusingly. "Silly girl, he won't marry you. You're a provincial, just one step removed from being a colonial."

Gabriel heard a smack followed by an "Ow!" from Edgar.

"Don't take on, Vi, I wasn't trying to insult you. You know I think you're beautiful and I will marry you, you can count on that. I just meant that a Duke is too far removed for the likes of us."

"My father is an Earl," Violet said in a proud voice.

"Oh, come now, don't give yourself airs. You can kiss as well as any other girl, I reckon. Come on, give us a kiss."

"You've been drinking," Violet declared. "Have you been at the brandy?"

"Just like every year," Edgar replied. "What made you the minder of morals all of a sudden?"

"We all snuck a taste of mobby or perry when we were younger, Edgar. But you were never drunk like this before, and you've never tried to take me off somewhere to kiss me."

"You were a baby before, Vi. But not this year. I told you I'd stake my claim."

"Stake your claim? I'm not a piece of property! You're just talking this way because you're jealous of the Duke."

"Jealous? Of what? Is there something going on between you?"

"And if there were, 'twould be none of *your* affair, Edgar Randolph."

"The hell it wouldn't. You're mine, Violet Amanda, and you have been since you fell in love with me when you were six." Gabriel imagined that the arrogant statement would set Violet's teeth on edge.

"But I'm not six now, am I?" she retorted. "And

I've always had a choice. It doesn't have anything to do with Gabriel. I just don't choose you."

"Gabriel, is it now? Has he been dallying with you, a great fop like him? I'll show him how Americans act towards their ladies."

"What, the way you act? A fine example you are, Edgar Randolph."

"I've done nothing but give you a little peck on the lips. He's done more? Damn it, Violet."

And from the muffled sounds he next heard, he knew Edgar was proving his ardor to Violet. This was exactly what he had most feared. The next moment, as he pushed through the over-hanging branches, he heard a louder smack.

"Ow! Damn it, Vi, what's the matter with you?"

"Maybe she doesn't like her virtue being assaulted when she's told you she's not interested in your attentions," Gabriel said in a deadly cold voice as he found them.

"As if *you're* not snooping around to get beneath her skirts," Edgar said. He released Violet's arm and turned toward Gabriel with his fists raised.

That much was most assuredly true and Gabriel would not be a hypocrite by denying it. Instead, he stopped where he was and let the younger man get in the first blow.

It was a solid cut to his jaw. The lad was strapping and had a good right, he'd give him that.

"Stop this now," Violet said, her voice like an angry swarm of hornets to Gabriel's ringing senses.

"Leave the lady alone," Gabriel said to Edgar.

"She's mine," Edgar retorted.

"I am no one's!" Violet cried, then came be-

tween them as they circled each other. Gabriel
dodged her to get in his punch but Edgar, perhaps due to whatever liquor he'd been imbibing,
was not so accurate.

He clipped Violet's shoulder and she fell back
against Gabriel. Every instinct in Gabriel to protect women, the job he'd been performing since
Sarah died, roared to life like a blazing furnace.

He eased Violet down against a tree trunk and
went after Edgar with every bit of violence in him
that he reserved for men who hurt women.

Violet wasn't unconscious but she was dazed
from the force of the blow and being thrown
against Gabriel. Her shoulder hurt like fire, but
as she groggily lifted her head from the tree trunk
against which Gabriel had so carefully braced her,
she realized the odd sounds weren't in her head.
Gabriel and Edgar were beating each other to a
pulp. The light from the closest bonfire let her
see enough to realize they were fighting in earnest.

"Stop," she said, but her voice was too weak.
She started to pull herself up, but Gabriel saw her.

"Stay down," he ordered.

She did, but only because she was disoriented
for a moment. As she braced herself to rise again,
Edgar went down beneath Gabriel's blows.
Gabriel followed him down to the mossy floor of
the willow grove and kept pummeling him, inches
from where she sat.

"Stop, Gabriel!" she said insistently, but he
seemed to be in another place and time. "Stop,"
she said again. He slowed and looked around,

blinking as if he'd been far away. But one fist was still in Edgar's hair.

"Gabriel, he's unconscious. Stop," she entreated, pulling at the sleeve of his shirt.

"He's . . . not . . . unconscious . . . yet," Gabriel said, panting from exertion.

"He doesn't need to be. Now stop. I won't have my friends fighting each other."

"He was going to hurt you, you naïve child," Gabriel said from between his teeth, but his hand relaxed in Edgar's hair. He eased the other man's head to the ground carefully.

Edgar groaned and began to crawl away. Violet started to go after Edgar, but Gabriel put out a restraining hand.

"He's hurt, he needs help," she said.

"So do I. He hit me first," Gabriel said in an eerily calm voice.

"You let him hit you," Violet said, recalling that sickening moment of impact. "Why did you just stand there and wait for him to land the first blow?"

She moved closer to where Edgar was pulling himself up from the ground.

"Later. Just let him go. He won't want your help now," Gabriel said.

She didn't believe him. Violet went over to Edgar. "Are you all right?" she asked, bending down.

Edgar staggered upright. Violet took a cautious step away. "I'm just fine," he snarled.

"Your lip is split," she pointed out.

"And my nose is probably broken too. D'you think I don't know that?" he growled. "Leave me alone." He stumbled out of the clearing without looking back.

Violet turned back to Gabriel, walking back to where he leaned against the tree trunk. "How did you know he would react that way?"

"Wounded male pride," Gabriel said, touching his face gingerly. " 'Tis universal."

"But *you* aren't shouting at me and telling me to go to the devil," she pointed out.

"I won," he said with such primal male satisfaction that she was torn between laughing and wanting to smack him for his pigheadedness.

"Amazing how the winner and the loser look so much alike," she observed tartly.

She turned. "Don't go, Violet," he said. Was he pleading?

"I'm just going to get some water for your cuts. I'll be right back."

He was drifting off when she returned, but he roused when she began to press the dampened cloth against the cuts and bruises.

"Did he hurt you, little one?" he asked in a low voice that seemed to vibrate through her arm from where she touched the cloth to his battered face.

"No, he didn't. I told you he wouldn't," she said with some exasperation.

He reached up and caught her hand. "Look at me, Violet," he said in a quiet voice that was underlaid with more steel than she had ever heard from him.

"No lies between us," he said.

Her cloth was going to drip on his shoulder. She tugged her arm away, and he let her. She concentrated fiercely on the cloth as she pressed it gently against Gabriel's cut forehead, avoiding his eyes.

"Violet?"

"I . . . yes, yes, you're right."

"Did he hurt you?" he asked, pressing gently for details. His breath was warm against her hand.

"No. But . . . but I was afraid he might." Gabriel turned his head into her hand, which had stilled again at his temple as they spoke. He nuzzled her hand gently, persuading her fingers to relax until the cloth fell from them. Then he kissed her palm, long and lingeringly.

"I was afraid he would do something stupid out of lust. I couldn't bear to see you mistreated," he murmured.

Violet held her hand against his clean-shaven cheek, her fingertips quivering over his skin in the lightest of caresses.

Gabriel struggled up against the tree trunk behind him, taking her hand in his. "Come here, little one," he said simply. "Let me hold you. I've wanted to all night." Her shoulder ached too, but she managed to crawl into his lap and rest her good shoulder against his chest.

His arms settled around her comfortably. They sat without moving, without words, in a silence as intimate as any time she had ever spent with him.

"Why did you let him hit you? To make it a fair fight?" she asked. "Edgar is heavier than you."

Gabriel sighed. "I said no lies, so I must keep my word as well. Although his words were crude, your Edgar was right. My intentions are exactly the same as his, though God knows I have tried to deny it and keep my hands off you."

Violet supposed she should have been shocked,

but Gabriel's words sent an odd, thrilling rush through her instead. Gabriel did want her, despite his careful treatment of her since that day on the riverbank.

"But you are different. Edgar wasn't giving me a choice," she said. "He just *assumed,* and then he acted on that assumption."

"And you resented his high-handedness, I know. But did he assume correctly? Was it just the way he chose to act that you objected to?"

"No. Yes. I mean, Edgar and I have been friends since we were little. We used to talk about getting married, but that was just a child's fantasy. I never thought he meant it."

"But what if he'd gone about courting you differently?" Gabriel asked.

"What do you want me to say, Gabriel?" she asked, exasperated. "Do you *want* me to choose him?"

"I am a damn fool, aren't I?" he asked with a chuckle. "Must have had some of the sense knocked out of me."

"I choose you," she said, her heart pounding. His barriers were down; she could be no less honest. "Is that what you wanted to hear? 'Tis the truth."

"No, that was not what I wanted to hear. And I am not asking you to choose. You shouldn't choose. Not Edgar, not me. Not yet, not now. You are too young."

"Are you saying I don't know my own mind?"

His head tilted back wearily against the tree. "Enough wordplay, Violet. I have a headache as it is."

"We should go inside then," she said, starting

to struggle up from his arms. "You can stay at Willow Oaks, that'll be best for you."

"I'm content right here. If you would mind not talking so much . . . I'm sorry if that doesn't sound polite, 'tisn't meant to be rude . . ."

"No, I am a chatterbox, I know it," Violet said, curving back against him again. She wasn't in a hurry to leave. Despite what he'd said, as long as he held her like this, nothing could be really wrong.

Gabriel nuzzled her neck with his lips. "I know a cure for chatterboxes." She turned her face toward him in inquiry, and his lips came down on hers in a leisurely fashion that nevertheless had her senses sizzling. Gabriel kissed her slowly, undemandingly, as if they had all the time in the world.

This was a kiss to dream about, Violet thought, feeling her body melt against him bonelessly. His fingertips stroked her cheek, ran gently through her hair, which had come down in disarray, touched her collarbone lightly. All the while his lips caressed hers, smoothed over hers, softly, gently, without the heaviness and urgency she'd felt from Edgar.

Her arms rose to twine around his neck, where she stroked the thick dark hair that tumbled near the nape into loose curls. Her breasts lifted with her arms and as she moved against him, his arms tightened around her. Then he slid his arms slowly down her back, beginning the same slow caresses with his hands that his mouth had been practicing on her lips.

Violet drifted, awash in sensation. Although she

had little experience, she'd never thought passion could be so sweet, so tender.

Gabriel kissed her cheeks, her eyelids, then slowly moved his mouth back to hers. "You taste of peaches," Gabriel said. "And something else."

"That's mobby," she whispered back. "Peach brandy. I only had a sip."

"Ah, I wondered." He ran his finger over the soft bow of her mouth. "And what is perry?"

"Pear brandy. Poire William, I believe you call it." Her lips vibrated against his fingertips.

"Mmm, we do. From the French," he agreed, tasting her lips with the tip of his tongue. "But you taste better, sweet Violet."

Her lips parted softly on a smile, and Gabriel slipped his tongue into her mouth. He heard the murmur of pleasure deep in her throat and brought his hands up to cradle her head while he explored the sweet inner recesses of her mouth. He explored every inch, every nook, every soft, smooth surface, every texture.

He kept his passion in check because this was for her, and, he admitted in the dark recesses of his mind, about removing any memory of Edgar and his sloppy kisses from her mind and mouth and body.

TEN

But when I saw thou sawest my heart,
And knew'st my thoughts, beyond an
  Angel's art . . .
              —John Donne, "The Dream,"
                Songs and Sonnets, 1633

Gabriel was reluctant to let Violet go. He would
just hold her until this yearning passed—this urge
to hold her, and, to be honest, be held. He had
the absurd feeling that she understood him. A
slip of a woman, barely more than a child—how
could that be?

Cupping her face between his hands, he pulled
back at last from the long slow kisses. She blinked
at him, her piquant face dreamy, her eyes dark
pools in the night.

"This is so different from the other time . . ."
she began.

"That was my fault, sweet Violet," he said, looking intently into her eyes. "These are my
amends."

He meant to stop there, God help him.

Then he felt the shudder pass through her

body. "Was something wrong . . . the other time?" she asked shyly.

Not if you were going to be my lover, he thought, trying to crush with his will the instant passion she aroused, even as his body decided it had had enough of restraint.

"No," he said with utter sincerity. He didn't have time to say anything else. With a wordless soft cry, she lifted her arms around his neck, brought his mouth down to hers, and launched the most innocently erotic kiss he had never imagined possible.

Her tongue twined with his, one hand found the sensitive nape of his neck, and the other slipped inside his shirt to explore his chest. She shifted in his lap and suddenly his hardness was pressed against her just where he'd wanted, but would never have allowed himself to initiate.

The almost inaudible sound of pleasure from deep in her throat undid him the second time. He pushed her gown off her shoulders, then down beneath her unbound breasts. The muslin gowns in fashion now did not need stays and she had the full advantage of it. He remembered the touch, the scent, the feel of her.

She did, too, because her nipples were already beaded into points by the time he kissed his way from her throat over the slope of her breast. Cupping her breasts in his hands, he lowered his mouth over them, kissing and suckling first one tip, then the other. Besides his own pleasure, his reward was the tightened grip of her hands in his hair.

She lay sideways within the circle of his arms now. He had unknowingly managed to position her perfectly for his mouth and hands to explore. Soon her legs shifted restlessly. She wanted a deeper caress, he realized.

"Gabriel, touch me," she whispered. Almost of its own volition or responding to the sound of her voice, he trailed a hand down the front of her gown, pressing the soft fabric against her belly and thighs as he smoothed the fabric against her body.

His hand slid into the sweet vee between her legs that held the center of her pleasure. He cupped her, watching her face in the dim light as he pressed against her softness.

Her eyes closed in bliss. He moved his mouth from her breasts back to her lips, pressing more deeply as he took her mouth in the first blatantly carnal kiss he had allowed himself since teaching her the lesson on the riverbank. This kiss he meant—he had meant the other too, but then anger had overridden his good sense—and he sensed that she would be a full equal to his unleashed passion.

Her body adjusted to his hands' presence. Lifting her, he raised his hand and let it trail down her thigh to her knee. Reaching her ankle, he lifted the light fabric and began a slow upward traverse over her smooth flesh toward the junction of her thighs.

Violet lay scarcely breathing and yet at the same time on fire. His hand was large and warm and yet so gentle as his caresses on her bare skin proceeded up her leg and past her thigh.

When he reached the unguarded curls, he sighed deep in his chest and kissed her again. "Do you want me to touch you there, Violet?" he asked. "This is the last time I will have the control for questions," he added in a strained voice. His hand hovered just out of reach, his knuckles brushing the soft patch that guarded her womanhood.

"Don't you know?" she breathed.

"I know what your body says, but I want your head to answer," he murmured.

"My body and my heart are saying the same thing. Don't . . . oh, don't stop," she said on a breath.

Then she might as well have been launched into the sky like one of the rockets. Gabriel stroked deeply along the seam, then slipped inside the folds. She was swamped by the sensation of liquid heat that slid through her.

Gabriel rested his forehead against hers, his breathing labored. His hand stilled. Violet wriggled, wanting him to continue the delicious exploration.

"Don't ask again, Gabriel," she said. "Please."

He laughed raggedly. "I wasn't going to," he confessed. "I was trying to slow down."

"Don't," she said, then angled her mouth to begin kissing him again.

Violet felt Gabriel jerk slightly in surprise as her tongue took the lead this time. His hand probed, exploring with light strokes, as sensations Violet could never have imagined coursed through her with every tracing, rubbing movement of his hand. Then she felt a pressure against her center.

This was the source of her moisture, and of her pleasure, too; he slipped into her with ease. She arched up against him with a wordless exclamation as he slid deeper.

"What you do to me, sweet Violet," he said into her ear. "I want to be in you, inside this snug passage that welcomes me so warmly."

In helpless answer, she clenched around him. His thumb stroked the nub of pleasure, as her muscles tightened in anticipation of the pleasure she was about to experience. But she didn't know that and it heightened her confusion. She moaned as the tension built.

"Shh, shh," he murmured against her lips, kissing her eyelids and her mouth. Her back arched. "Let it come. 'Tis all right. I'll catch you."

Then all the bright pleasure exploded within her, and she fell endlessly, bright sparks showering around her like the fireworks had earlier. He held her, and as she slid back down to earth, he caught her.

Violet sagged against Gabriel, the tightly drawn bow of her body relaxing. He was as hard as a rock, but said nothing, did nothing, as he slipped his hand from her and encircled her within his embrace.

She floated lazily, with a smile curving his lips that he could feel when he kissed the corners of her mouth. Gabriel stroked her damp hair back from her face, which was warm with exertion. He hated to break the intimate silence between them, and was quietly pleased that she seemed to share his mood, though he couldn't have said why.

He helped her sit up, slowly putting her garments back to rights as she leaned back and let him, her hair swirling around them both.

Violet was helping him, but he would have been the first to acknowledge the dressing was mostly an excuse for further loving touches and kisses on warm skin. He helped her to her feet, then brushed twigs and grass from her dress. He didn't want to see if grass stains decorated her skirt.

Clouds covered the moon, and no one would see her crumpled dress until morning. With the merrymaking, he was sure there would be few explanations needed. But the kiss-bruised lips and slumberous eyes—she was nearly asleep on her feet—those would have been more difficult to explain.

"Will you be able to get back inside your aunt's house?" he asked as they walked up the slope.

"Mmm," she affirmed. "The doors aren't locked." The sounds around them had lessened. There were other couples walking out of other copses or strolling away from the light of the campfire; they would not be remarked upon.

Gabriel held her hand loosely linked with his, marveling silently that he felt so at peace.

The closer they got to the big house, however, his emotions changed, a familiar weight settling on him again. The weight of responsibility, and of the watchfulness and tension that were a constant part of his life. Few saw it because he did not let them see it. But with Violet just now, it had all disappeared. He had been just a man with an open heart and a happy future ahead of him.

He tightened his grip on her hand briefly before letting it go. He was only pulling the wool over his own eyes. This night should never have happened, could never happen again.

And soon he would have to figure out some way to tell her. And yet, as they climbed the hill from the river, he offered her his arm. For the life of him, he could not regret what had passed between them tonight.

Tomorrow, in harsh daylight, he could regret that he had made love to her. Tomorrow, he could deny that he had forged a bond between them deeper and more powerful than what had begun at the river after their swim.

But not tonight, oh, not tonight. He tucked her arm into the crook of his elbow for the sheer joy of feeling her graceful hand on his bare arm below his rolled-up sleeve. Together they made their way slowly up to the house, the stars above glittering off the dark waters of the river.

When Gabriel returned to Williamsburg the next day, a letter awaited him. It was from Penelope, his most trusted companion, whom he had left in charge of his London establishment. He hadn't expected to hear from her so soon.

Once he'd read it, he wasn't sure what to make of its contents. She was trying to be reassuring but since he didn't know what had caused her concern, it was difficult to know how seriously to take the letter.

He had anticipated that his household might not feel safe with him away—he hadn't traveled outside Britain since his household became so large, but he thought he'd provided them with enough security not to worry. Something had to have alarmed them severely.

He swore softly under his breath. "Maximilian," he called. He dictated a letter to Penelope while he finished dressing. "Get this to the next ship leaving. Go to the Tidewater Nurseries dock, Harrison's Landing, to Yorktown if you must. Just get this on its way, please."

When Maximilian had left, Gabriel sat back in the Windsor chair in the room he used as a study, steepling his fingertips before him as he always did when concentrating deeply.

His next move with regard to Violet was even more uncertain. He had not come here looking for romance, far from it. Nor was he in a position to offer it. Yet no woman had tempted him or attracted him more than Violet.

He should end all this; kissing her at the July Fourth celebration had been a mistake. When he'd followed Edgar, he'd told himself it had been to prevent harm. But it had really been jealousy, he acknowledged now in the light of a new day. He'd refused to stay overnight at Willow Oaks or Oak Grove, and the ride back to Williamsburg over bumpy roads had been hellish. Yesterday had been lost to bruises and exhaustion.

Parts of his body that had taken a pummeling still ached like the devil, but his mind was clear. He wasn't going to take Violet's maidenhood. What would he be, what would his principles be, everything he based his life on, if he gave in to this sweet temptation? Whether he was falling in love with her was immaterial; it shouldn't, couldn't matter.

But, blast it, he should be honest with her. He didn't want to do her the disservice of pretending he didn't feel the attraction between them in order to end this. Nor would he resort to being heroic and so bloody noble that he hurt her while fooling himself that it was all for her ultimate good.

His actions had ensured that she would be hurt because she was sweet and young and impressionable. He would try not to make it worse by damaging her self-regard. She was beautiful and eminently desirable. She'd make some man—he refused to think about Edgar—a wonderful wife some day.

She deserved to know how he felt, not to have her innocent sensuality shattered by callousness or a lie that he wasn't attracted to her. Didn't he owe her that much, that she should know why?

Violet spent the next few days at Willow Oaks, helping clean up from the Independence Day celebrations and playing with her brother and cousins. Aunt Rose noticed that her mood was rather dreamy and detached, but she put it down to Edgar.

Violet didn't tell her otherwise. Aunt Rose had been asleep when they'd returned from the riverbank and since Gabriel hadn't stayed, no one had seen his bruises. Violet soaked her shoulder in a hot bath and was careful not to complain.

She had a feeling that her aunt would oppose a romance between herself and Gabriel. She knew that her aunt shared her father's aversion to aristocracy, although she wasn't entirely sure why. Gabriel was older than she was, but Uncle Peter was older than Aunt Rose by about almost the same number of years that separated her and Gabriel, so that didn't concern her.

What she imagined was that Aunt Rose would oppose her going to England, whether for a season or to live. So would her father. It was why she had planned to stow away, after all. She didn't think falling in love with a British lord was going to help her cause.

So there was no point in telling Aunt Rose that Edgar and Gabriel had fought over her, although she did wish she had a female friend her age in whom she might confide the thrilling and confusing events of the other night. But all her friends were boys.

Her thoughts turned again to Gabriel. Did he know what had sprung to life between them as a result of that night? She might be untutored in the ways of love, but she had been raised with the evidence of two great loves, her parents' and her aunt and uncle's, right before her eyes. She knew how to recognize true passion.

He'd shown her passion, and yes, lust, the day of their picnic, but Independence Day had been different. He'd been aroused then too, but that had taken second place to the breathtaking tenderness he'd displayed. There had been no intent to teach her a lesson that night, and the pleasure had been all for her.

Gabriel genuinely cared for her. Other than stating that she was too young to choose, which she found easy to dismiss—no one would tell her what she could or could not do—he had let down his defenses when he'd kissed her and held her so tenderly. He had been filled with yearning; with a longing that perhaps even he didn't realize was there. There was some hidden sorrow in his past, something that stood between him and how he felt about her.

And then passion had overcome them, and . . .

she hugged herself, remembering those moments in his arms.

Violet had the confidence of one young and in love. Given time, she knew she could overcome his reserve. She would draw out the cause of his private sorrow, and breach the remaining barriers around his guarded heart.

Penelope was frantic, but trying desperately not to show it. She'd sent her letter weeks ago, but knew there hadn't been time to receive a reply yet. Now her hand had been forced.

"We have to get to the docks, and quickly," she said to the other women clustering around. "One portmanteau each. Only take that which is most precious to you." Most of the women already had some sort of a bag ready. Many of them had fled adverse circumstances more than once.

Never in her wildest dreams, though, had Penelope imagined things could go against them this way. Gabriel traveled; it wasn't as if he stood guard on them night and day. But there had never been trouble before, not like this.

First Tessa had been followed, then had come the dreadful warning issued by the men who assaulted Diana, Cleo, and Athena when they had been out. If anyone recognized the signet ring or the men from the sketches Athena had drawn, no one had said so.

Penelope had looked carefully at their faces when they had shown the sketch around. All the women were afraid, but no one had turned white, fainted, or showed other definite signs of recognition.

That had been troubling. They couldn't help a woman who wouldn't volunteer what she knew. Assuming one of them did know who was after them. Others had been threatened before, but Gabriel or the very few men who knew the true situation and were trusted had always found a way to deal with threats and eliminated them.

Until now.

The rock had smashed through the drawing room window in the wee hours of the morning after the deadline for the unknown woman to return had expired. The mansion was set back from the street in its own park; the aggressor would have had to get past the guards at the gate or around the wall enclosing the park.

An elegant hand had written the crude message, "Come out, harlot. Don't make me come get you."

Most chilling of all, none of the men Gabriel had hired would admit to having seen or heard anything.

Penelope still suspected that the target was Lady Margery Bowers. But a tacit rule of the household was that no one inquired into anyone else's background. Apart from Gabriel, stories were shared only when the woman chose. Lady Margery's background was obscure. She said she had been raised far from London. Although they had seen each other at some of the same social events, Penelope did not really know her.

But Penelope would never force a confession. If she and Tessa were wrong, they might just reawaken old horrors and fears, and even worse, in the wrong woman. That would be the worst possible outcome.

No man, no matter how rich, how powerful—or violent—had dared to interfere with the Duke of Belmont's household before. It should not be different now. The mere absence of Gabriel should not have jeopardized them so.

Yet somehow, the extra guards Gabriel had hired for the duration of his trip had been suborned. They might be in the pay of the man searching for his runaway wife or mistress. They might merely have been paid to look the other way. Why they had failed was not nearly so important as the fact that they had, and therefore, the men could no longer be trusted.

Perhaps Maximilian had not had time to vet the guards himself; perhaps Gabriel's man of affairs had not been thorough enough. Or perhaps the men had been bought off only after they had been hired and Gabriel had left. Whatever the reasons, they no longer mattered. Their safety had been compromised and now the women must leave.

Penelope had not dared to send anyone with a message to Gabriel's solicitor. Alone or in a group, she dared not risk herself, or any of the women, even though both scrappy Tessa and fearless Diana had volunteered. She didn't know if Master Banks would be able to find a ship that would arrive faster with the news of their imminent arrival than they would themselves.

So she had scrawled a note and placed it on the hall table. If he came to check on them in a day or two, as was his wont when Gabriel was away, she hoped he would find it. That was all she had time to do.

Penelope didn't know if it was safe to take everyone to Virginia, but like the rest of them, she believed implicitly in Gabriel's promise to always keep them safe. He had never failed them. He would not do so now.

Therefore they would go to Gabriel. Where he was, there safety had to be.

If not, none of them would ever be safe.

ELEVEN

A fond kiss, and then we sever . . .
— Robert Burns, *A Farewell,* 1787

Maximilian left again a few days later. This time Gabriel had sent him on a scouting trip to South Carolina. The land Max had examined in North Carolina had been the subject of a scheme to drain the land in order to plant tobacco and hemp, but it had never come to fruition. If the swampland could be drained, it would be rich indeed, but there seemed to be no hope of that. So Gabriel sent Max further south. He'd read about the near-tropical climate in South Carolina and the exotic specimens it yielded, many difficult to grow in England or unknown. It seemed ideal.

If his report proved favorable, Gabriel would think seriously about establishing residence in South Carolina. It seemed from Penelope's earlier letter that he would have to bring his household here sooner, rather than later. Whether he did or not, or returned to England, his responsibility for those under his care would continue.

And Violet? She was young and beautiful and

innocent. He had no right to turn her life into a circus, just because his was.

He ran one hand through his hair, pushing away with his other the land reports he had before him from Maximilian's information-gathering surveys. He had to talk to Violet. To delay any longer would simply be cruel.

Riding out the next morning under a cloudy sky heavy with the promise of rain, his heart felt heavy too. A sense of foreboding dogged him. Yet all was as usual at the busy plantation. Violet must have spied him from an upper window because she ran out as soon as he reined up at the house. He dismounted and looped the horse's reins over the verandah railing.

"Good morning," she called out. She wore a simple but elegant gown of a robin's egg blue that emphasized her unusual eyes.

Those eyes.

Gabriel groaned inwardly. She had stars in them. This was his fault. But how to let her down gently, especially when everything in him screamed silently to keep her close and never let her go?

"There's a special place I like to go, usually to get away from the boys. Do you want to ride out there?" she asked shyly.

He looked up at the lowering clouds. "Is it outdoors?"

"Yes. Why?"

"I think we'll be getting rain presently."

"I don't mind," Violet said. "It doesn't bother the horses either. They shelter under the trees."

And his peace of mind—not that he had any—would be destroyed by the sight of her soaking wet again, her clothes molded faithfully to her delicate curves. Now that she dressed as a woman, he knew her shape all too well.

"Is there somewhere more sheltered? From the weather," he added hastily, lest she misunderstand.

Of course she would misunderstand, he berated himself mentally. The last time he'd been with her, he'd bloody fought over her honor, then held her in his arms with a tenderness he hadn't thought he'd had inside him, not since Sarah died. And then, he'd all but made love to her.

"The gazebo." She pointed to the white structure that stood amidst the dozens of rosebushes her mother had reclaimed from the original gardens and the dozens more that had been planted in the nearly twenty years since.

"That'll do," he said.

"There are even shutters my father built to block the rain." It turned out they needed them.

An hour later he stood with a stinging cheek once more, her final words ringing in his ears. As before, he hadn't defended himself. He deserved it. And more. If she'd been a man, she could have fought him. Just then, he'd have given her a sword himself and let her run him through. He hadn't told her how much he cared for her, but neither had he said he wasn't interested in her. He'd simply said it wasn't possible.

Gabriel winced. The storm was over, but even if it hadn't been, it was past time for him to go.

He would never forget what she'd said as she stood there with her innocent confidence in tatters.

"My father built this gazebo for my mother, just

like the one in her Williamsburg garden. Uncle
Peter built one for Aunt Rose at Willow Oaks, inside her knot garden."

Her husky, vibrant voice had trailed off to almost nothing. "In my family, the gazebo has always been a symbol of love."

Violet continued to sit in the gazebo long after
Gabriel had gone, long after the rain stopped
drumming on the gazebo's roof. She needed to
go in for dinner soon, but she didn't want either
Betsy or Mistress Steele to see her tear-stained
face.

What a fool she'd been. Imagining herself in
love with an English Duke, thinking he could love
her in return. How stupid could she be?

Beneath that charming exterior lay a will of iron
and a heart of stone. He was charming and light-
hearted to one and all—but nothing seemed to
engage his true affections. Least of all her.

She'd have been better off if she'd stayed
dressed as a boy.

That gave her an idea, and lifted her gloom.
She'd had enough brooding in the gazebo. Maybe
her life wasn't ruined after all, she thought defiantly. Perhaps she'd even make good on her original plan.

After all, hadn't she been interested in Gabriel
originally because he was the reason she was to
travel to England? He might have diverted her for
a while, she told herself, but she still wanted to
go to London. Didn't she?

Feeling better than she had all morning, she
walked slowly back to the house. She still had

most of the day ahead of her. Plenty of time to put certain plans back in motion.

What she'd thought was love was just infatuation. He was a passing fancy, just like she had been to him.

She was sure if she told herself this often enough, she would eventually believe it. The key was not to think of Gabriel. Not now, not ever.

"Will, would you ride over to Willow Oaks to see if Miss Violet is there?" Betsy asked him when he came in for dinner. The rain had brought a blessed breath of cool air with it, and Will had worked a little longer than usual directing the peach harvesting. As a result, he'd missed dinner at the big house, and had come directly to the little house he shared with Betsy near the gardens of Oak Grove.

"What, right now?" he asked, surprised. "I've got to go back to the south orchard. It'll be more than an hour over to Willow Oaks and back. Don't you think she just went over to visit the little ones and Mistress Rose?"

"I don't know. I mean, you're most likely right," Betsy said.

Will looked at his wife more closely. She wasn't one to dither. "That's the most sensible thing," she went on. "But you see, I saw the Duke and Miss Violet in the gazebo when the rain came down this morning. The Duke came out when the weather cleared, but Miss Violet stayed in there alone for quite a while. She didn't come to dinner. Mistress Steele served at one, like usual."

Will waited patiently. "Nothing I've heard

makes me want to saddle up for Willow Oaks, dear," he said. "Is there something I don't know?"

"Miss Violet hasn't been in her room. Malcolm says her favorite horse is gone from the stables, although nobody saw her leave."

It had been a long morning and Will was tired. "Can we discuss this later?"

"I just have this feeling that . . ."

"That what?" he pressed.

"That there is something wrong."

"What might that be?" Will asked in his most reasonable voice.

"I don't know," she fretted.

"I can't go chasing around after a feeling." Will sat down at the table. Betsy filled his plate with food, then sat down across from him. Immediately she got up again and began to pace.

Will threw down his napkin, not angrily, just resigned. "All right, Bets. I'll go. I know you're not the flighty sort."

She came over to kiss the top of his head. "Oh, you're a dear. You know I wouldn't ask if I didn't think there was a problem."

"I'll go now," he said, rising. "But don't you think Malcolm or one of the stable lads would have told us something if she went off in a huff?" he asked, reaching for his hat.

"Yes, I'm sure you're right. It's probably nothing, but thank you, dear."

Will rode quickly over to Willow Oaks. He soon learned that Violet had not been there. Remembering his wife's uneasy feeling, he took off immediately for Williamsburg in search of the Duke.

Once in town, he turned down Francis Street,

remembering the day he had first brought another English lord here. Then, it had been with the man he'd known as the fop Squire Adair Sotheby, who was really Adam Pearson in disguise. The Squire had intended to patronize the shop of Williamsburg's first florist, Lily Walters, to help establish himself in Tory society. Hard to believe that was twenty years ago now, and he had been the greenest lad imaginable. The shop was still there, with several employees who ran it on a day-to-day basis for Lily.

Around another corner, and he found the lodgings the Duke's man Maximilian had rented.

"Welcome, Will," Gabriel said, when the housekeeper showed him into the Duke's study.

Gabriel came to his feet immediately when he saw the look of concern on Will's face. "What is it? Has something happened to Violet?" he asked.

Will found the Duke more receptive to Betsy's concern than he himself had been at first.

"Were there any signs she was taken away against her will?" Gabriel asked.

Will was startled. "Why, no."

"Any signs of struggle?" he pursued.

"No."

"Did you find any of her clothes in unusual places?"

"No. Sir, what are you saying? What do you think has happened?"

"Probably nothing at all. But I have some experience with this sort of thing and . . ."

"What sort of thing?" Will demanded, his open, honest face taking on the beginning signs of indignation.

"Unusual disappearances," Gabriel said. No point elaborating; it would only shock Will.

Will look askance at him, but kept to the main point. "Do you think Miss Violet ran away?" he asked.

"Ah, Will, I hope not," Gabriel said.

"Begging your pardon, Duke, but Betsy saw you go together into the summerhouse. Would she, ah, have had a reason to be upset?"

"That is between me and Miss Violet," Gabriel said. Bad enough that he'd had to let Violet down so cruelly; he wouldn't humiliate her by discussing their private affairs.

Will looked like he wanted to argue the point, but Gabriel forestalled him. Remembering how he had met Violet originally, he asked if there were any ships leaving soon.

"Not from our dock," Will said.

"Even if you had a ship departing, I doubt she'd risk being seen so close to home."

"Do you think she might be running away?" Will asked worriedly.

"I think it's a possibility," Gabriel said, still determined to protect Violet's privacy as much as possible. "Where might she be able to find ships departing on a regular basis?"

"Why, that'd be Yorktown."

"Then that's where I'm going." Gabriel took Will's arm and escorted him out of the study.

"I'll come with you," Will said.

"No, why don't you search town for her here, just in case she's stayed closer to home. After all, she could just have come into town for shopping."

Will looked as doubtful as Gabriel felt. "Begging your pardon, sir, but she would have told someone if 'twas a simple explanation like that."

"I agree. She probably would have." Gabriel touched the other man on the shoulder. "But let's look for her here anyway, just in case we are fortunate and find that the explanation is a simple one."

"Aye, I'll look around Williamsburg," Will said. He opened the front door.

"Good man. I'll ride out to Yorktown." Gabriel took his hat off the peg in the hallway and called out to the housekeeper that he was going to the stables.

"Why do you think she might be in Yorktown?" Will asked, following Gabriel out the door.

Gabriel sighed. "The first time I met Miss Violet, she was dressed in boys' clothes and trying to buy ale in a Williamsburg tavern. She then planned to stow away on a ship to England."

"She didn't . . . she never . . ." Will sputtered.

Gabriel turned to look at him without breaking his stride. "Oh yes, she did. And she may again. Your mistress has a strong stubborn streak beneath that winsome exterior."

The men stopped to exchange a rueful look. "I honestly thought I'd dissuaded her from wearing boys' clothes," Gabriel continued, "but perhaps I didn't have sufficient influence."

"So you're saying I should be looking for a boy instead of Miss Violet?" Will asked, twisting the brim of his planter's hat between his hands.

"She did this when she was a child, did she not?" Gabriel asked.

"Yes, now that you mention it, sir, she did. She used to love to run around after the twins. But not in town, just out at the plantation. A harmless thing, really."

"When she was a child, perhaps. She's grown now, and her field of play is much wider," Gabriel said grimly. "And the adverse consequences, should any result, are much more severe." He picked up his pace and Will, though shorter by several inches, matched him stride for stride.

They quickly reached the livery stables. Will took the horse he'd left there from the boy and mounted.

The Duke was already astride. "I'll send word here and to Oak Grove if I find her. You do the same," Gabriel called over his shoulder as he rode out.

"Aye, my lord," Will replied.

During Gabriel's ride, his mind was filled with wild imaginings. Cases of women he'd helped came to mind. Not all had ended well. This was exactly what he'd feared since the first moment he'd seen Violet in her ridiculous get-up. If she'd dressed as a boy again, she was twice as vulnerable as when he'd first met her because now she was upset *and* alone.

And he had no one but himself to blame. He never should have gotten involved with her in the first place. He'd broken his own rules, the standards to which he held himself. Although he was loath to give himself such a prominent place in her life because he knew he didn't deserve it, he could have broken her heart. If her feelings were as strong as his . . .

As he thundered down the road, his horse's hooves churning dust beneath him under the hot summer sky, Gabriel tried not to remember the times that his attempts to help had failed. Intellectually, he'd known there was nothing he could have done differently in those cases, but that fact had done nothing to ease the sorrow, or change the fact that another woman had suffered. Suffered as Sarah had suffered.

Gabriel redoubled his pace. Finally, he saw Yorktown begin to emerge from the forest. The masts of ships spiked up on the horizon, standing straight and tall in the distance. The late afternoon sun sparkled on the water, giving the river a golden, tranquil appearance that was at odds with Gabriel's pounding heart and his fears for Violet.

The town was not large and the dockside taverns were few. Although there were no overt signs of rats, grime, prostitution, or the other sordid sights common around the London docks, Gabriel knew that sailors the world over could be a rough lot, as he'd told Violet before.

Gabriel hoped she wasn't in one of those dockside taverns, but he was afraid he knew better.

Stepping through the first low doorway, he ducked his head, taking a quick look around as he did so. He didn't want her to see him and then bolt.

Nothing here. He didn't know whether to feel relieved or apprehensive, and briefly he wondered if Will had located her. But his instincts, which had gotten him out of some tight spots before, were on full alert. He'd be very surprised if she were in Williamsburg.

It turned out his intuition was right. As he entered the second tavern, he spotted a slim figure at a table alone. The waistcoat hung loosely on the slender frame. It had to be Violet.

He advanced into the room, then slowed his steps. In profile, he could see that the person he thought was Violet appeared to have a mustache. But the old-fashioned queue kept his suspicions on alert. Hair was shorter on most men these days.

The figure was turned, back presented to Gabriel and the door. Not very smart, he thought, if she was supposed to be watching for pursuit. Hadn't he taught her to exercise even a little more care, a bit of caution?

Now he was angry. He walked up behind her quietly. No one else in the tavern appeared to notice anything out of the ordinary. She never heard him coming.

Gabriel tapped Violet on the shoulder. She whirled around, her hand flying to her mouth. Recognizing him, she relaxed. "Gabriel, you startled me," she said, her lips curving in a smile.

Then she remembered she was angry with him and started to turn away, ignoring him with her flawless little nose upturned. The first time he had seen her like this, he had been partly amused. This time, he wasn't. This time, he was going to blister her ears, if not her pretty little behind.

TWELVE

Wine, dear boy, and truth.
—Alcaeus, *Fragment 66*, c. 575 B.C.

Gabriel kept his hand on her shoulder, forcing her to turn back to him. "What in the great bloody blue blazes do you think you're doing?" he demanded in a low voice, incredulous. "Haven't we been through this before?"

"Have we?" she asked, looking at him impudently. With a sinking heart, he saw that Miss Violet Pearson had managed to buy herself ale. And from the unfocused appearance of her eyes, she'd either been successful at it for some time, or she had no head for beer.

Although it was probably the latter, it didn't matter which. Drunk and in a tavern. She might as well never have met him for all the caution she displayed. Which was none.

So much for the tender heart that he'd broken this morning. "Get up," he said, holding on to his temper with an effort. "This little adventure is now over."

"I think not, m'lord," she said. "I'm perfectly content here. I've booked passage on a ship leaving in," she swiveled around to peer out the window, "hmm, about two hours, when the sun goes down."

"In two hours, you'll be on the road home, if I have to stuff you into my saddlebag," he said. "In pieces, if necessary."

"Such tender concern, m'lord," she said. He winced at the mocking note in her voice, and the knowledge that he had put it there. "And here I thought you said we shouldn't see each other again beyond transacting Tidewater Nursery business."

"Violet, I know you don't believe me at the moment, but I do care for you. I always will."

"Don't call me Violet. I'm . . ."

"I know, Adam Pearson."

She looked around. "Don't use that name. I don't want to be recognized."

"Don't want to be recognized? How's this?" Gabriel reached out and stripped the old-fashioned queue ribbon from her hair. The rich mass tumbled down her back.

"Blast!" she cried. "How dare you?"

"You'll only attract more attention if you stay here now," he said. Already heads were turning to look at them.

"I hate you," Violet said in a low, passionate voice.

He took her arm to pull her up. "I know," he answered, refraining from pointing out that she had brought this on herself. But then, he was responsible for putting her in this rebellious frame of mind. This time, at least.

Violet stumbled as he led her outside. He knew she was in no shape to go anywhere. Horse or

carriage, she'd end up sick to her stomach. It was
likely that she would feel ill in the morning anyway, but that would be merely a hangover.

What a wretched mess. Thanks to him, young
Miss Pearson was tipsy, togged out again in boys'
clothes, and running away to boot. No one would
ever know how much experience he had in rescuing women from dangerous situations to judge
from this example.

Gabriel scrubbed at his face wearily as she hung
onto his other arm, swaying as if she'd already
boarded the damn ship. He'd been searching for
her frantically. The search for her, his fear for her
safety, the long ride to Yorktown, and his own lack
of sleep since the Independence Day celebration
meant he was exhausted himself. They could both
do with a good night's sleep. Starting this afternoon.

Violet lost her lunch, if indeed she'd had any,
behind the stables where Gabriel had gone to
fetch her horse. There would be no riding home
today.

He left the animal there, stabled with his own.
Given the few available choices, he quickly found
the best inn in town, and rented a room that
would normally have slept four or six men. The
room held two large mattresses.

Before entering the inn, he'd stuffed Violet's
hair up under her a cap and passed her off as his
runaway apprentice. That neatly explained the
hold he had on the back of her neck. In reality,
its purpose was to keep her upright, but the innkeeper had no need to know that.

After she tumbled into bed, fully dressed and
nearly insensate, he pulled a sheet up over her

and closed the shutters to darken the room. He stood over the bed for a minute, gazing at her pale face. Gabriel didn't know whether to spank her like a naughty child or hold her close and never let her out of his sight again. He had been so worried, and he nearly woke her up to tell her so. Remembering that he'd forfeited that right this morning, he sighed.

Closing the door quietly behind him, he went downstairs to rent a private parlor and eat a solitary meal. Later, he would bring her dinner, when she had sobered up enough to eat something and had a chance of keeping it down.

By the time he went upstairs again, night had fallen. Summer sounds of insects and night birds filtered in through the windows. Gabriel did not hold with keeping indoor spaces sealed and shuttered; he had read suspicions that it promoted disease. Opening the shutters, too, Gabriel let the moonlight and starlight in. He had also brought a lantern and a tray laden with a light supper.

Violet still slept. Sitting beside her bed with the tray, he prepared to waken her. But first, he had to get rid of that ridiculous mustache. It was charcoal, he noticed as he peered at her, but from a distance and in the dimness of a tavern, it would have passed muster as the dark fuzz a boy got when he first needed to shave.

She didn't stir as he turned her face towards him with a light touch. Before he had time to remember that touching her wasn't a good idea, he was bent over her with a damp cloth and the charcoal was coming off easily.

Soon, the only thing touching her face was his thumb, and it had wandered to her soft upper lip. He couldn't help tracing that soft curve and remembering the sweetness that lay within. His mouth hovered just above hers, his hand poised to stroke her cheek.

She opened those magnificent aquamarine eyes a moment later. Despite the unpleasantness of their last two encounters today, he smiled at her.

"You!" she said, batting away his hand. She sat up, clutching the sheet to her. She looked down. "Oh, I'm dressed."

"Disappointed? I didn't ravish you," he said, chuckling slightly.

"No, you just dragged me out of a tavern in front of a roomful of people, humiliating me and . . . and . . ." she spluttered.

"A roomful of strangers. Strangers who were drinking in the middle of the day. As you were, may I remind you," he said, folding his arms.

She glared at him. He didn't give an inch. Fine, so she was as stubborn as he was. He knew that. This was going nowhere. "How is your head?" he said at last, handing her a tankard of something cool that contained no alcohol.

"It's fine," she retorted. "Don't tell me you're concerned about how I am, after you told me this morning that we should no longer see one another," she said, then took a long sip. Her eyes continued to shoot blue-green sparks at him over the tankard rim. Gabriel prepared to weather the storm as best he could; after all, he had helped create it.

"Besides, who appointed you my personal moral advisor?" she snapped. "Do you intend to be around for every first experience of mine?"

"And which experiences would those be, little one?" Gabriel replied imperturbably.

"Well, for once I'd like to hear you call me by just my name." Gabriel set his tankard back on the table with a thud. When he called her by "just" her name, he wanted her under him, those magnificent aquamarine eyes focused on him as she reached the pinnacle of her pleasure.

The thought had predictable effects. Although his expression never faltered, Gabriel was glad his coat wasn't a cutaway. Despite their disastrous encounter this morning, his feelings for her hadn't changed. He knew he was in danger of crossing a line with Violet from which they could never return. Perhaps it was just as well she was spitting mad. He should keep things that way.

Stepping away from the bed, Gabriel gestured toward the food. "Have something to eat. Perhaps 'twill improve your mood." He spoke not a word while she ate her supper, although their glances crossed occasionally, hers fulminating, his outwardly impassive.

But his thoughts never strayed far from the young woman before him. For ten years, he'd been running his family's affairs since Sarah's death. He'd been surrounded by women—and almost nothing but women—for ten long years. He was jaded, tired, cynical, and inured to criticism. He did what he did, and no one else needed to know exactly what or why or how. He never explained himself. So why then did he care so much what Miss Violet Pearson thought of him?

Evening's shadows lengthened as the silence stretched between them. Violet appeared to be starved but seemed equally determined to chew every bite as if it were the last. Obviously, she didn't want to talk to him. Gabriel had tipped his chair back, leaning his head against the wall. He began to doze.

Violet obviously thought him asleep when she rose and picked up her boots in one hand. She tiptoed past him silently, heading toward the door.

He sighed. Gabriel's hand shot out and captured her wrist.

"Ow!" she complained as the boots fell from her hand, landing on the floor with a dull thud.

"Spare me the histrionics, Miss Pearson," he said. "Did you like that? I used your name."

"Hardly," she retorted. "You sound so very . . . stuffy. So British." She tried to pull away from him, but he rose from his chair and pulled her over to the smaller bed in the room.

"Sit down, Violet," he said in a peremptory tone. "I'm not your wet nurse, and I'm tired of pulling your pretty *derrière* out of disaster. You seem to have no regard for your own safety."

"I haven't been in trouble yet," she said defiantly.

"Thanks to me."

"Have I thanked you?"

"No, but perhaps 'tis time you did."

"You're threatening me? Then you're just another bully like the ones you've warned me about."

Gabriel went from slow burn to lit fuse. "I have never mistreated a woman. I never will." He dropped her hand and left her sitting on the bed. For all her provocations, she'd never crossed any important line before. And even through the irrational fury that threatened to swamp him, he knew that she had no idea what such words meant to him.

Will returned home by dark, hoping the Duke had fared better in his search. He was pleased to find a note waiting for him with news that Miss Violet had been found. Betsy said a lad from Yorktown had just delivered it. If it had come any earlier, she would have sent the boy on to Williamsburg to find him. He was ready to ride for Yorktown now but Betsy persuaded him to wait until morning. The Duke didn't need his assistance now that Miss Violet had been found, she said, and he let himself be convinced to stay.

Gabriel sat at the room's one table, writing in a journal by lamplight. He had neither spoken nor looked her way since their argument some time ago.

Violet had long since lost her anger. Her mother had always said she had a gift for understanding people. She was glad her mother wasn't around to see how badly she'd failed this time. Her mind was so clouded, in such conflict about Gabriel that she had not understood him as she should have.

Although she knew it would sound foolish if she said it aloud, she blamed being in love for her failed acumen—not that she would ever say so to Gabriel. Her foolish gibe about mistreatment had tapped some deep, deep well of pain and anger in him, and it went all the way to his soul. And for that, she was more than sorry.

She had seen his charm, his ardor, his pain, and now, his fury, and a cold thing it was, too, compared to his usual warmth. It felt like the temperature in the room had dropped twenty degrees, and it wasn't due to the advent of night.

"I'm ready to talk now," she announced.

"Are you?" he said briefly, his expression more remote than she had ever seen it. He returned his attention to his journal.

"You broke off our relationship this morning," she pointed out, keeping her voice level. "And without much explanation either. So what do you care what I do? Why should you have anything to say about it at all?"

He looked up, and she felt pinned by those unreadable silver eyes. So brilliant on the surface, so many uncharted depths beneath.

Gabriel rubbed at the nape of his neck, where his dark hair curled at the ends. He looked exhausted. "I felt . . . that I am responsible for your emotional turmoil. As I told you this morning, 'twas not a good idea to get involved. I am only here for a short time and you are a child . . ."

She glared. ". . . you are too young," he amended.

"I was enough of a woman for you to . . . for you to . . ." her voice trailed off as she blushed, grateful that the candle hid her face in shadow. She was flustered, which was not how she wanted to appear to him at all.

Gabriel looked up. He closed the journal and gave her his full attention. "In that way, you are fully a woman, Violet, and a beautiful one." His expression softened. "But you are young and innocent. You should and you deserve to remain that way until your marriage."

Suddenly his expression changed and the charming aristocrat vanished, replaced by a deeper, more serious Gabriel. Intuitively, she knew that this Gabriel wasn't going to let her latest adventure pass without serious examination.

She was correct. "But setting that aside—although do not think I am diminishing your beauty and charm, Violet, for I want you to have no doubts about yourself in that regard—I think it's time you told me more. 'Tis past time for you to tell me what scheme you had in mind that dressing as an unconvincing boy and sailing to England was supposed to accomplish."

Violet twisted her hands together in her lap. The metal bedstead she had curled up against was cold against her back. "I told you why I corresponded with you. I wanted to learn more about my family's business. I wanted to prove to them that I wasn't a silly girl who thought only about what sort of marriage she could make."

"Your aunt told me enough about the women in your family that I hardly think you would be treated that way, or that anyone in your family would think you chuckle-headed. Come now, Violet, did you really think you were regarded that way?"

His gaze was not quite relentless, but it was incisive enough to allow her no room for half-truths. "Mama and Papa don't think that way, that's true, and neither do Uncle Peter and Aunt Rose. The twins, however, are a different matter."

"Your older brothers? But they don't run the business, your father does."

"And my mother," she reminded him.

"And your mother." He smiled, and her heart turned over. She told it to stop, he didn't want her. But then why had he come after her, if he didn't care?

"Of course, 'twas her business first, you've told me. I did not mean to slight your mother's achievements."

"I've been afraid they would come back and lord it over me after they graduated from Harvard. Although I had plenty of schooling at home, women don't go to university here."

"I know," he said gently. "They don't in England either. But your father made provisions for you, did he not?"

"Yes, I know Latin and Greek and mathematics, not just French and embroidery and music. I can't complain about my education. But it isn't the same. Learning in a room at home, even with tutors to supplement my father and mother is hardly the same as going out into the world and experiencing adventure on my own."

"Is that what you've been after? Adventure?" He didn't sound judgmental now, just considering. She dared to go on and tell him her most closely held dream, the one she'd never told her family because she knew they would have said no.

"I have wanted to go to London and have a Season since I turned fifteen. But Papa left England to get away from society, and Aunt Rose came here because she was going to be married off to some horrid old lord. She detests the aristocracy too."

"So you think that they wouldn't want you to go to England, is that it?"

"That's right. All the English people in my family wanted to get away from their old lives. But it's half my heritage, too." Could he understand? He'd told her he didn't go to balls very often. He probably thought her frivolous for having such a silly dream. After all, Mama and Aunt Rose had wanted to be independent and run their own businesses.

It wasn't that she was uninterested in the family business, but she had wanted to go to London before she settled down. It wasn't even that she wanted a Season to look for a husband. She just wanted to see London, travel to Paris or Rome, meet new people, dance and dream in a wider world than the one in which she'd grown up.

"Your dream doesn't mean you're any less intelligent than the women in your family. And although I agree with your aunt, that she was wise to flee the marriage mart, I don't think you're frivolous," he said.

Startled, she met his intense silver gaze. It was as if he'd divined her thoughts. "I don't mean to sound like an older, overbearing brother, but Violet, I do think your family's right. London isn't a mythical dream kingdom. It's a real city with very real problems. English society is so stratified that anyone outside the aristocracy spends either all their time hoping to be knighted, like the growing merchant class that helped finance the war with America, or marrying into it. The poor, especially in London, live a hardscrabble existence. And unfairness is everywhere. There are few such opportunities as those that exist in America."

"We have servants," Violet pointed out.

"Yes, but the indentured can buy or earn their freedom after five or seven years."

"But we also have slaves in America. The tobacco plantations can't manage without them."

"You do have slavery," Gabriel acknowledged. "And that is a great evil, one of the few we don't also have in England. But that's not my point, Violet."

"You think I'm just a foolish girl. That's exactly why I didn't tell my family about my plans."

"I don't think that. But what were you going to do once you got there? Your grandmother, the Dowager Countess of Dalby, is elderly and doesn't venture out much anymore. Your aunt's mother is embittered about the match she failed to make for her daughter, your Aunt Rose. Rose is no longer in contact with her mother."

Violet made a startled movement. How did he know all that? Gabriel lit a candle from his lamp and brought it over to the little table at the bed where she sat. "London society is a very small place, my dear. I knew of your father's family, and after I talked to your aunt, I realized who her family was. You wouldn't have had an easy time of it without making any arrangements. You need a sponsor."

"But I could have made my own way. . . ."

Gabriel shook his head. "Violet, don't you listen to anything I say? You wouldn't have been able to travel safely alone. If you'd survived the crossing with your virginity intact. . . ."

"But aboard my uncle's ship I would have told them who I was," she protested.

"That was when I met you in Williamsburg, correct?"

She nodded.

"But this jaunt to Yorktown . . . you weren't going to board one of your uncle's ships from here, were you?"

She shook her head, feeling glummer by the second. "You'd have been lucky, as a young person alone, to make it to your grandmother's house in London safely," he went on inexorably, demolishing her dreams.

"But as a boy?" Violet said, still clinging to her disguise plan.

Gabriel put down the candlestick he'd been holding, then returned to the table across the small room and sat down again. He propped his booted feet on the table edge. "You could have been impressed into the Royal Navy."

"As young as you say I looked?"

"Cabin boys can be as young as eight. I am not going to recount what can happen to a pretty boy such as you appeared to be. But once your true identity had been discovered, as it would have been within seconds of a sailor assaulting you sexually, well . . ."

"Stop, that's enough!" Violet felt positively ill.

But Gabriel appeared determined to see this through to the bitter end. He continued in a low voice, ruthlessly thorough. "You'd have been fit only for a brothel if you'd lived the night."

She flew at him, pounding her fists against his chest. "You're horrid. Stop, stop it! You don't want me, so why should I listen to you? I'd find someone in London who would have."

Almost knocked out of his chair by her fervor,

the table legs thunked solidly back onto the wood floor as he grabbed her wrists. He rose, stilling her hands by covering them with his own larger ones. "Violet, please. It's not that I don't want you. I do, far too much. But I said nothing to you this morning when I changed my mind at the last minute. I had intended to, but thought it would only make you feel worse. Now I know I was wrong."

She looked up at him through lashes that trembled with tears, which she absolutely refused to shed. "I'm confused. You're apologizing for not telling me something you said you meant to tell me but you didn't. Tell me what?"

"Oh hell, what a cake I've made of this," Gabriel said, transferring control of her hands to one of his, while with the other, he raked back his tumbled hair. He released her, then set his hands lightly on her shoulders.

She watched his face, fascinated, as he made another transformation. Somehow he went from man to lord, just by the squared set of his shoulders and the change in his eyes from light to dark.

"Violet, I care for you. I am indeed attracted to you, and I can't imagine a reason why that would change. But I have responsibilities that do not allow me to form a romantic attachment."

He didn't sound like a high English lord very often, but he certainly did now, Violet thought. Was that just another way of keeping her at arm's length? Then what he'd said sank in.

"Are you married?" she asked, stepping back so that his hands fell away from her shoulders. Violet had a sinking feeling in her stomach that had nothing to do with her eventful afternoon.

Indeed, some part of her almost wished he was still chastising her for her foolishness or that her head was still befuddled with drink, because she hated the direction of this conversation.

"No. I have at least some honor, believe it or not," he said, frowning. "Although I suppose I couldn't blame you for thinking ill of me."

"I don't think badly of you, Gabriel," she said, clasping her hands behind her back. She stood back from him a step.

"You don't need to reassure me. I'm not here to justify myself, Violet. But I know that life can be difficult for beautiful young women, because of what happened to someone very dear to me. I will not let that happen to you. Gruesome as it is, I would much rather you hear the filth that could happen to you than to experience it. I couldn't live with that."

And that was that. Violet looked away in frustration. He cared about her, he wanted her, but he wouldn't do anything about it. Some mystery kept him from being free to court her. He wouldn't tell her what it was, but through his relentless detail of the horrors that could befall young women, he had managed to dismantle her foolish dream.

THIRTEEN

Suspicion is the companion of mean souls,
and the bane of all good society.
    —Thomas Paine, *Common Sense*, 1776

The next thing she knew it was morning. She'd fallen asleep on the other bed. At some point Gabriel must have covered her with a quilt. She vaguely remembered him giving her a headache powder in the night so she wouldn't feel the aftereffects of drink in the morning.

It had worked. Her head was clear. She looked over at the other bed. Gabriel had fallen asleep on top of the covers. The sunlight slowly edging into the room hadn't reached his pillow yet, but it was close enough to outline his clean, sculptured features, the long lashes beneath his strong brows, his firm mouth. Relaxed in sleep, he looked younger than his twenty-seven years.

Violet looked down at herself. She was still fully dressed. She felt almost absurdly disappointed, but told herself that it was better this way. He'd taken her dream of going to England from her. Not completely, of course, but she saw now she could never go as a boy.

She wasn't out of ideas, just because her chosen method of travel wasn't going to work. She'd write to her grandmother, so she would know in advance that Violet was coming. Perhaps she could arrange for another well-born lady to sponsor her. She could try to get her parents on her side. Something. Anything to take her mind off Gabriel Isling, Duke of Belmont, because he had made clear that she did not have a place in his life.

Fine. She would put him out of her mind and carry on. A flirtation, that's all this had been. She wouldn't remember his lovemaking, his kisses, the fascination of his active mind, her curiosity about his secrets, her intuition that beneath the surface he was a complex man whose dark past needed to be exorcised so he could love.

No, she had to stop. She wouldn't think of him. She wouldn't care for him. She wouldn't.

Oh blast, she wasn't even fooling herself. She couldn't forget. The feeling she had deep down inside was that she could be the one to bring his heart into the light, and that feeling would not go away.

She should get up and leave: there was nothing here for her now. But she couldn't make herself move. Violet turned her head into the pillow, willed her overactive mind to be quiet, and drifted back to sleep.

Will arrived in Yorktown early. Dawn had broken while he was on the road, and the cool of the summer morning was to be savored because it would not last long. It was landing day in Yorktown, and he would be able to purchase goods needed for the plantation right off the docks. It would be cheaper to buy supplies here than wait until they had been taken overland to Williamsburg or Richmond.

Will threaded his way through clusters of merchants and sailors, hogsheads of tobacco, and barrels of rum without hurrying. No matter how early he might be, a port town was always busy.

He knew which inn Miss Violet and the Duke were in from the note that arrived yesterday, but he reckoned they could probably both use their sleep. There was no need to rush over there. Betsy was firm in her belief that the Duke would not steal a march on Miss Violet's innocence, so he was not going to barge into the inn and demand to see them. Not if it would possibly embarrass Miss Violet.

No, he'd see what goods could be had, then go to the inn at breakfast time. He'd brought the carriage, so Miss Violet could ride home in comfort.

So it was that Will happened to be at the docks when several small boats brought in passengers from some of the ships moored out in the river. He had heard at least one ship was from London, and he waited to question a ship's officer. Adam Pearson's barrister often sent packets of legal papers and other items that needed the Earl of Dalby's attention.

Two boats were coming in from the *Mary Vinson*, one of the ships hailing from London, he was told. Will didn't notice anything unusual as the boats approached. A long boat was a long boat, after all. Then the boats tied up at the wharf, and the strangest sight he'd ever witnessed occurred before his very eyes.

One by one, the passengers were handed out of the boat, and the crowd began to stare. Three, five, seven. Whispers swelled to murmurs, murmurs to disbelief. Eight, ten. Will heard the speculation as it made its way through the crowd.

Twelve. They were all expensively dressed, they were all unescorted, and they were all women.

It couldn't be a bride ship. Some of the women were too old. Besides, that had been done in New Orleans, not Virginia. Some Catholic custom of getting convent-bred girls to marry the gentry, keeping the bloodlines pure, he had heard. There hadn't been *casquette* girls (so called for the small baskets in which they brought the gold and jewelry the church had given them for their dowries) in Virginia. They were too well dressed to be indentured servants. They were traveling together and they seemed determined to remain that way, although many a man was ready to offer employment of various types on the spot.

Will stood gaping as much as any man. A tall blonde woman gowned in champagne-colored silk seemed to be in charge. Another woman, whose voluptuous frame was only enhanced by her wealth of unbound red hair, stood next to her. A petite woman, whose glare seemed designed to keep the curious away, shifted restlessly, her arms cocked at her sides as if she meant to put up her fists if they were disturbed.

Two Englishmen were talking near Will when the spectacle engaged their attention. One turned to his companion as he recognized something about the group.

"I'll be damned," the first man, a portly, middle-aged merchant in burgundy broadcloth said to his companion. "I just came in yesterday off the *Laurel.* Do you know who that group of women is over there, Horace?"

"I came from Whitby on a collier headed for Boston. Storm blew us off course. We sprung some leaks and had to put in here. I'm not even supposed to be here, although 'tis good to see you again, Waldo. I haven't been in London in months, though. Who is who?" the other man, thin and balding, said.

"All the women over there. Haven't you heard of Belmont's brothel? Most notorious place in London."

"I, ah, frequent Madam Nicole's when in the city," Horace replied, glancing around furtively to see if anyone was listening.

Will knew how to be inconspicuous; he looked in a different direction. From the first mention of "Belmont" his attention had been riveted, but he wasn't about to show it. He had a very bad feeling about all this.

The heavy-set man guffawed. "Oh, very good, Horace. But those women aren't from your usual kind of brothel, my friend."

Horace blinked nervously. "But, Waldo, you just said . . ."

Waldo waved off the explanation. "I'd forgotten, you really don't get to town often, do you? Belmont's brothel isn't a house of pleasure. Not a normal one. It's reserved for one man. The Duke of Belmont."

"All of them? An entire brothel for one man?

Surely you mean he just bankrolls the establishment?"

Will listened in growing horror to the increasingly ribald description. "No, no. They live with him. The women aren't for hire either. Some perversion of the Duke's. He won't share 'em. None of 'em are allowed to go out. If they do, they've got guards with 'em, so they say. Some of the guards may be women, too. It's hard to tell with the ones who dress like men. Regular Amazons, some of 'em."

Women dressed as men? The very thing Belmont had said was dangerous for Miss Violet? Was he planning to kidnap her, force her to join this group of . . . fallen women, whatever they were? Will clenched his fists at his side. He had to get to Miss Violet. He suddenly doubted his wife's assurance that Miss Violet would be perfectly safe with Belmont overnight.

Who knew what could have happened to her since yesterday, especially since she had spent the night in his company? Sick fascination held him in place a brief time longer. Perhaps he'd learn something else, although he couldn't imagine anything worse than this.

"I just wonder what in the bloody hell they are all doing here," Waldo mused.

"Maybe he's tired of them and is going to pension them off," Horace suggested timidly.

"Pension them off? Did you see that flame-haired beauty? She's in her prime, that one. Now she was a courtesan, toast of the demi-monde. Never heard that about the rest. But then that one was known as the Incomparable Diana. Who could compete with that?"

Will had heard enough. Belmont's brothel? The Duke of Belmont who was Miss Violet's friend . . . business contact . . . or whatever he was. Belmont had come here to purchase stock for his conservatory, but he'd begun to talk of buying land—was it for this? To bring his trollops here?

The Duke had spent hours with Miss Violet, with all of them, discussing the nursery business, the available land, expanding his greenhouses. He'd never behaved in any untoward manner whatever, had seemed a perfect gentleman, for all that he was British. Mistress Walters had invited him for dinner, and Will had seen him hand Miss Violet into and out of coaches and boats with perfect decorum.

Yet this . . . these . . . his imagination failed to give him a more acceptable name than the one he'd heard that lecher Waldo use. The Duke's women didn't dress like doxies, he'd give them that, but who else could they be and what else could they be here for? Perhaps the Duke had a conservatory—Will could not say the man had no knowledge of plants and flowers—but he appeared to be transporting some very odd inventory to America indeed.

Will felt sick. He had to get to Miss Violet right quick. All the respect he'd had for the Duke of Belmont, for the man's easy ways, his lack of condescension and open, direct style, had vanished. He had visions of Miss Violet forced into servicing the duke, taken away from them and sent somewhere where the duke intended to set up his brothel. All that talk about moving his conservatory here, supplying American plants and flowers

to the Royal Botanic Gardens at Kew. That was all
a load of tripe.

Will shouldered his way through the crowd,
leaving a few bruised elbows in the process, but
the murder in his eyes and the set of his shoulders
must have persuaded the offended that he was
not to be trifled with. The waterfront tended to
be a rough place anyway and he hadn't bumped
into any ladies. Not that the women he'd seen
were ladies.

Patrons were in the taproom breaking their
fasts when Will walked in. He went to the bar,
picking out the heaviest man, correctly identifying
him as the owner. Tavern keepers usually drank
at least part of their profits.

"Did a man and woman check in yesterday?"
he asked with no formalities. "In two rooms?"
How stupid was he to assume that the Duke was
honorable after what he'd just heard, Will berated
himself mentally.

"Or in one room," he added.

"There are two married couples here," the innkeeper began, "in the same room, not that it's
any of your affair. Who the hell are you?"

"This is my affair. I'm from Oak Grove and I'm
looking for my master's daughter. I sent a man
after her I trusted . . . and . . ." What was he to
say? He didn't want to ruin Miss Violet's reputation right here; maybe there was still a chance he
could get her away with no scandal.

"Did your trusted man elope with her?" the
innkeeper asked, waggling his eyebrows and leer-
ing.

Will's hand shot out, grabbing the man by the

throat. He hadn't had this much violence in his soul since the war. "What's your name?"

"Tom," he croaked.

"All right, Tom. This goes no farther than you and me. Nod if you understand."

Tom's face was turning beet red. He nodded. Will released him abruptly. "My lady was running away, on her own. Or she was, originally."

"No runaway women here, sir," Tom said, rubbing his neck. A middle-aged woman came out from the kitchen with plates of food on a tray, but she studiously paid no notice to Tom's red face or red neck. She started to pass them, but Tom grabbed her sleeve.

"Take over," he said curtly to the woman. Wiping his hands on his apron, he came out from behind the bar. Then he looked at Will and motioned him over to a side door.

Will followed Tom into an anteroom off the inn's entrance where the man pulled out a ledger book. "Lemme see," he said, running his finger down a page. "There was someone who came in yesterday with a runaway apprentice, but 'twas a man who had a lad by the collar."

Will remembered what Belmont had said about Violet and her boy's disguise. "That'd be them."

The man looked at him oddly. "Thought you said you had a runaway lass."

Will ignored that. "The man was tall, had dark hair, and was well dressed?"

"Aye. A Brit, he was," Tom said.

"That's definitely him." Will reached into the pouch at his waist and withdrew a coin. "What room?"

"I don't give out that kind of information."

Will gave him a contemptuous look. "If that were true, you wouldn't have told me they were here. Now, which room?" He pulled a second coin from his pouch.

Tom took the coins, not bothering to show any more reluctance. He stuffed them into his own pouch. "Top of the stairs, end of the hall. My best room."

Will gave him another coin. "Don't interrupt, no matter what you hear. And clear out the front room so I can get my lady out the door."

"That apprentice is your lady?" the innkeeper asked, amazed.

"Shut your face." He was surprised at his own language, but he'd never felt so outraged and betrayed before.

He handed Tom a fourth coin. "You're getting damned expensive. I could just go back to choking you. I said no viewing, no questions."

After hastily tucking the last two coins in his pouch, Tom dropped all trace of reluctance. "See over there?" he said, pointing to another narrow door not in general use. "That door'll go into the kitchen. Get your lady down these steps and through that back door. Don't go into the front room. Go the way I said, and none of my patrons will see her. I'll make sure that none of my people back in the kitchen will comment on what they see or how she's dressed."

"Make sure of that," Will said, withdrawing still another coin.

The innkeeper held out his hand shamelessly one more time. "This is for the kitchen lads and lasses, not for me. His lordship already paid me a pretty penny for exclusive use of that room. All

I'm doing is telling you where it is. Go on now. I'll stand in the doorway outside smoking my pipe. I won't let anyone in the inn during the next few minutes."

Will had already started up the stairs when Tom hissed to get his attention. Will looked down at him. "Now don't be leaving any blood or broken furniture up there. Do you understand me?"

For answer Will threw another coin at him over the banister and kept on going.

FOURTEEN

Nothing is so firmly believed as what is least known.

—Michel de Montaigne, *Essays,* 1580

Violet had the shock of her life when Will Evans burst through the door. As if drawn to him by an invisible thread, her eyes met Gabriel's. She sat bolt upright at the same time he did. Later, Violet would realize that being in separate beds was the only thing that saved him from an ugly fight with Will.

Will wasn't armed, but his color was high and his fists were up. Violet hadn't thought Gabriel was armed either, but he withdrew a pistol from beneath his pillow. She was horrified. Why did Gabriel need to carry around a pistol? There were no highwaymen in Virginia.

No time to worry about that now. "Don't point that at Will," Violet cried. "He wouldn't hurt you." She had reflexively pulled the sheet up to her chin, but now she let it drop. She was dressed, after all, although her shirt was badly crumpled.

"Lucky for you that you're in different beds and both dressed," Will said in a deadly tone she had never heard him use before. He was addressing Gabriel.

"Will, what's happened?" Violet asked. "I've not been harmed. That's Gabriel."

"I know who this is, but I don't think you know his true nature, Miss Violet. This man has abused your trust and lied to all of us," Will said, never taking his eyes off Gabriel.

"What is it, Will?" Gabriel asked. He'd lowered his pistol as soon as he'd realized it was Will—or realized that Will wasn't armed. "I don't intend to hurt you, or Violet for that matter. Why don't you come in and shut the door?"

Hastily, Will shut the door. "Miss Violet, is she . . ." Will's tanned face flushed even brighter. "Is she still safe?"

"Yes, Will," Gabriel said quickly, interrupting him on a topic that Violet had no wish to hear discussed by either Will or Gabriel. "I give you my word that Violet is fine. What is wrong? You knew I was coming after her. I sent a message to Oak Grove yesterday that I had found her, but she was . . ."

He glanced at Violet, then back to Will. "She wasn't feeling well," he said. "I told you she would come to no harm."

"It wasn't necessarily harm I was thinking of, begging your lordship's pardon," Will said. Violet had never heard him use such a sarcastic tone before. Even his stance proclaimed distrust and anger.

Violet rose and began to tug on her boots. "I'm fine, Will, and if you mean did Gabriel ravish my virtue, no, nothing like that happened."

"Don't be making a joke out of something that

you don't know anything about, Miss Violet," Will said. Gabriel was fully dressed, too, and yanked on his boots while Will had turned his head to talk to Violet.

"I know Gabriel would never hurt me, and you know that too," she said. "He has been our guest a dozen times. What on earth is the matter with you, Will Evans?"

Never in her life had Will ignored her, but he did so now, turning back to Gabriel. He even turned his back away from Violet as if he didn't want her to hear what he had to say next.

"Belmont, a ship came in for you. You were expecting it, I imagine?"

"A ship?" Gabriel said, not comprehending. Violet didn't understand either.

"What do you mean, a ship?" she echoed.

"Your belongings that you left in London? Surely you remember them?" Will said, still in that peculiarly angry, taunting voice. "Get your things, Miss Violet, we're leaving," he said over his shoulder, without ever taking his eyes off Gabriel. "Thank God I brought a carriage so prying eyes don't have to see you."

"I'm going back with Gabriel," Violet said in her most reasonable voice. "My horse is here; we can ride back together." She would have been happy to go with Will after the strange night she'd passed in Gabriel's company, but Will's accusations had put her back up.

Perversely, she'd found herself defending Gabriel. He'd broken her heart, but Will couldn't know that. So what was he trying to accuse Gabriel of doing? This wasn't the time or place to sort any of this out.

"We can tie your horse to the back of the carriage," Will said. "I don't want you going anywhere with him, ever again."

"Will, what do you mean 'my belongings'? I didn't order any of my furnishings sent here," Gabriel said to Will, still looking puzzled.

"Were you planning to take her with you?" Will asked bitterly. "That doesn't make sense, why bring them all here? Unless you were going to take all of them off to wherever that man of yours is buying land. Was that your plan?"

"That's enough, Will. Stop talking in riddles and tell me whatever it is that has you upset."

"I don't want to say it in front of Miss Violet," Will said stubbornly.

"Then *you* try and get her to leave without giving her an explanation," Gabriel said, throwing up his hands.

"Miss Violet, I want you to go down to the coach and wait for me," Will said.

"No, I won't. Why should I? Gabriel is right. I won't leave until you tell me what is going on," she said. "I'm not a child. I will admit that I was upset when I quarreled with Gabriel yesterday, and he was quite high-handed coming after me the way he did, but everything's fine now."

She moved toward him. "Why won't you tell me what has happened, Will? Why are you being so curt to the Duke all of a sudden?"

"You had to learn sometime, I guess," Will said, sounding defeated. "Just remember that I'm sorry to be the one who says this." The three of them stood in taut silence in the room while Will searched for whatever words he intended to say.

"Your precious Duke here is a whoremonger."

Violet gasped at the crude word. Whatever she'd thought he might say, that certainly wasn't it. His expression was pained, but Violet sensed a certain satisfaction in the words. This wasn't like Will, she thought. What was going on?

"What the devil?" Gabriel swore. "How dare you say something like that in front of Violet?"

"And I suppose you weren't going to make her part of your brothel, your lordship," Will said again in that mocking voice.

Violet watched Gabriel. His face cleared and paled all at the same time. He clearly now knew what Will meant, although she was as much in the dark as ever.

"Did you receive a letter from London about me? It's likely to have been filled with lies," Gabriel said.

"No, you have a delivery out there," Will said, jerking his head in the direction of the river, and still in that acid tone.

"Speak clearly, man," Gabriel said at last. "You won't get Violet to leave here short of shooting her or kidnapping her, so. . . ."

The word kidnapping seemed to set off Will in an alarming way, because he didn't even allow Gabriel to finish his sentence. He lunged at the taller man, who met Will's blow with a parry of his arm. He could have hit Will back, but didn't. He clearly wasn't going to allow Will to hit him as he had with Edgar, however. Violet was relieved to see that. Gabriel had nursed a tender jaw for a week after the fight on Independence Day.

What was she doing watching this as if she were made of stone? Violet tried to dart in between the men, but neither would let her.

"Stop," Violet said, raising her voice when Will continued his assault. "Both of you, stop!" Gabriel was maneuvering to keep from being struck, but he did nothing to take the offensive against Will. All he did was parry his blows.

"That's enough," Violet shouted. "If you're so concerned for my reputation, Will, then stop fighting. 'Twill bring the whole inn down on us."

That seemed to reach Will; he stepped back. Gabriel remained in a defensive stance, but made no move to step in under the other man's guard.

Will was breathing heavily with the exertion. "Was that your plan," he panted, "to kidnap Miss Violet, you scum? To make her part of your traveling whorehouse?"

"Will!" Violet was shocked beyond belief. "You can't speak to Gabriel that way. He's a duke, and a visitor here. He is my friend."

"He's no friend to you, I can tell you that," Will said.

This time Gabriel cut her off when she began to protest his language again. "Quiet a moment, Violet."

He looked at Will steadily. "I understand. They're here, aren't they?"

Fists still clenched furiously, Will nodded. He looked like he was about to have apoplexy.

Gabriel looked tired and tense. "I'd had a letter. They thought there was a threat. It must have gotten worse. Damnation." He seemed to be talking to himself now because Violet had no clue what he meant. And although Will knew something, whatever Gabriel meant, Will was as confused as she. It was also clear from Will's scowl that he wasn't interested in hearing any explanations about anything from Gabriel.

Gabriel looked at Violet. "I tried to spare you this, Violet, when I ended things between us, but perhaps 'tis just as well. Will has made the same judgment about me that most people do. I could tell him that this isn't what he thinks, but truly, there would be little point."

Gabriel bent over and picked up his saddlebag. While Will turned to open the door, Gabriel walked over to her. He bent toward her upturned face, but kissed her forehead instead of her lips. Violet was trembling. There was something so final about him now.

"I will explain it to you later, if you like," and he gave her a smile that was ineffable in its sadness. "I pledge my honor on it, should you ever come to me to ask." He glanced at Will briefly. "I owe no one an explanation, but you shall have one," he said to Violet, "if you wish."

Gabriel moved; his lips were now very near her ear. "I care for you very much, Violet, but you will soon see why I cannot let myself love you," he said in a voice too low for Will to hear. He straightened and headed toward Will.

"Where are they?" he asked as he reached the door.

"They came in on the *Mary Vinson*," Will replied.

"Thank you," Gabriel said, stooping to pass through. Will said nothing as Violet watched Gabriel walk out the door.

"Well, there's good riddance to bad rubbish," Will said with malevolent satisfaction.

Violet stared in bewilderment at a man she'd

known all her life, and one she now barely recognized. "What are you talking about? What has happened to make you so hostile to Gabriel?"

"He said it. You'll see," Will said ominously. "I am sorry that you will have to, but 'tis clear you won't believe me otherwise."

It was a short walk to the waterfront, but Gabriel knew what he would find when he got there. To say he was surprised was an understatement, though God knew Penelope's letter should have warned him. Something must have happened to make them flee, though. There had been no hint of that in her letter.

Or maybe there had been, but he'd been too distracted with Violet. Well, he needn't worry about that anymore. Will would happily destroy whatever capital he'd built up in Violet's eyes. But wasn't that what he wanted—to keep her from falling in love with him? This would do it more effectively than any words of his. And yet there was no solace in the thought, none at all.

When he arrived, the women appeared to have backed into a defensive formation, circling around together. Tessa had her fists cocked in her usual fighter's stance, although her size was more nearly that of a sparrow than a hawk. Penelope and Athena appeared to be negotiating with the driver of a dray and a couple of sad-looking mules. From the expression on the driver's face, Gabriel could guess what the terms were going to be. Sailors sidled around the edge of the group, like lions seeking to cut frightened gazelles from the herd.

Looking around, he realized that the way people reacted to him and his household in England had been transplanted here to America. It was no doubt due to the other passengers on the ship. Someone had recognized them, or heard the gossip.

They could have come less publicly. They must have been truly frantic. Penelope probably hadn't had the time to see his solicitor. Banks could have helped them to charter their own ship, but haste could have spoilt that plan as well.

Ah, well. If he'd entertained hopes that he could remake his destiny anew, he'd been proven wrong. His destiny had sailed to meet him, and it didn't include Violet Amanda Pearson.

"Penelope," he said, raising his voice to divert the attention of the growing throng. They saw him, his height, his deliberately exaggerated air of authority, and he hoped they didn't see how wrinkled his shirt was under his coat. Sleeping in one's clothes didn't make for the appearance of an imposing peer of the realm.

He closed the distance between them, stepping forward briskly to take her hands in his. "My dear, are all of you well?"

Penelope took her cue from his coolly formal voice and graciously inclined her head as he bent low to kiss her hand. "Yes, Your Grace," she replied. "Now that we are here with you, all shall be well."

Gabriel prayed he'd elevated the tone around them. Now he just had to get them out of here safely. The closed carriages he'd ordered from the inn's stables on his way here rumbled around the corner moments later.

"Where are we going?" Athena asked in her clear, precise voice.

"Let's get everyone settled first," he said, not wanting to give up any privacy they could gain by leaving this situation behind.

He squared his shoulders, and keeping Penelope's hand upon his arm, moved forward. The crowd parted, but not without muttering and hisses. That was nothing new either. So much for the New World, he thought briefly, with uncharacteristic bitterness. He hadn't realized how attached he'd been to the idea of a fresh start.

He was in the middle of helping the women into the coaches when two figures on horseback came around the corner.

The noise around them roared dully in his ears, then stopped. As if they were the only two people in the world, as if this were the intimacy of a hushed bedroom, he looked at the woman he wanted to love.

Gabriel met Violet's stunned gaze, saw her eyes widen as she took in the remaining women clustered around him, and Penelope's hand on his arm. For a moment, he thought she might ride up to them and demand to know what was going on with the fiery impetuousness he'd come to know so well, but Will Evans reached for her bridle and brought the horse's head around.

"Have you seen enough?" Will asked.

Violet nodded and let him lead her horse in the opposite direction. But her stricken gaze over her shoulder followed Gabriel until they turned the corner and rode out of sight.

He had never seen her look like that. He would never forget it.

"Do you know her?" Penelope said softly. Gabriel handed her up into the carriage without answering. She stood on the step looking down at him. Her gloved hand touched his cheek briefly. "We'll talk later."

Gabriel turned away. There was nothing to say.

Violet, too, had nothing to say on the long ride home. The hurt was so vast that she thought it might swallow her up. Had everything he'd told her been a lie? She chewed on that a little while as they rode along.

Before long, innate honesty forced her to correct herself. She didn't know that everything had been a lie. In fact, he'd told her very little about himself.

Her thoughts raced faster than the horses' hooves. Gabriel had never said he wasn't married. He had only acted that way. Had that beautiful blonde woman been his wife? No, Will had called them his "brothel." There had been so many women. He couldn't have a wife and mistresses all at the same time, could he? Not in the same place. What woman would stand for that?

And what of everything that had passed between the two of them? Gabriel had all but made love to her, acted as if he'd cared. He had even *told* her that he cared. And all the time he'd had this household . . . these harlots . . . those women . . . whatever they were. Were they why he wasn't free to form an attachment?

Will had enough sense to keep quiet, too, because even if he'd been right about Gabriel, she was still angry with him.

The ride from Yorktown had never seemed so long.

FIFTEEN

Lovers' quarrels are the renewal of love.
　　　　　　　—Terence, *Andria,* c. 159 B.C.

"Violet, would you like to talk? You seem so list-less," Aunt Rose said, bringing lemonade out to her on the second floor gallery. In the afternoon shade, Violet sat in a rocking chair sewing a dress for Cathie's favorite doll. The girls were napping and the heat had felled even her energetic little brother. He was asleep in the relative coolness of the house. He'd fallen asleep in his room, the guest room, while she read him a story.

"I'm fine," she replied. " 'Tis just the heat."

Her aunt sat down and handed Violet a lemon-ade while she took a sip of her own. Violet pressed the cool pottery mug to her flushed cheeks, think-ing longingly of a cool swim in the river. But she hadn't been in the water since that day with Gabriel and. . . .

As always, thoughts of Gabriel sent a sharp stab of pain through her. She looked at her aunt, afraid she knew what question was coming.

"Violet, I don't know how to say this, so I'm just going to go ahead. All right?"

"Of course."

"Darling, is there any chance that you might be with child?"

"What?" Violet was shocked. Her aunt was a plain speaker and could be quite direct, but she'd never imagined her asking that question. "Oh no, not at all."

"Are you sure? I mean. . . ."

"Aunt Rose, I grew up on a plantation. I know what procreation is. And since I haven't uh, partaken of that act," she said awkwardly, finding this incredibly difficult with her aunt's blue and concerned eyes upon her, "there's no possibility."

"None at all?"

"None at all," Violet affirmed. "Why, did you and Uncle Peter . . . ?" It was wicked, but it was the first spark of mischief she'd felt in days.

"Oh, no you don't. You're not getting that kind of information out of me," she said, breaking the awkward moment with a laugh. "Your mother will be appalled enough that I've let so many family stories out of the bag while she's been gone."

And on that note, Violet wormed a few harmless stories out of Rose, feeling pleased that she had diverted her aunt's attention. She got up to take the empty mugs to the kitchen, intending to see if Cook would have peach cobbler for dessert. Martha had told Violet that cobbler was the price of the little girl's nap because she was too old for them. Aunt Rose had something more to say before Violet's errand.

"If there is anything you want to talk about, Violet, please don't hesitate to talk to me. Especially if you don't feel you can say something to your mother."

"Thank you, Aunt Rose, but I'm sure Will told you. The most serious thing I did in Yorktown was lie about my sex and I had a bit to drink. I got sick and Gabriel . . . the Duke . . . didn't think we should ride home when I felt sick. He was the one who made sure I was safe, you know. He rented a big room and we slept in different beds, fully clothed. That was how Will found us. You can ask him," she added with a touch of defiance.

And that was all Violet would say about that morning. She didn't know what Will had told Betsy and Rose about Gabriel, but neither woman had asked why he no longer came around. Let Will say whatever he wanted, Violet thought defiantly. She knew the truth.

"All right, dear, I won't push. And I do believe you. Just remember that I'm always here if you want to talk, won't you?"

Violet nodded. After a couple of days, she was well rested and was tired of moping. She didn't want to confide in her aunt about her broken heart, nor did she want to go home and see Will's pitying or sympathetic looks. Or see Betsy's or anyone else's, for that matter.

"Do you know, I think I will go into Williamsburg," Violet said. "Mother has a big wedding in September, and I promised I would check on whether the grosgrain ribbon she ordered has arrived at the milliner's. There was a special shade the bride wanted woven into her bouquet. The milliner had ordered it from London."

"I will ask Will to escort you," Rose began but Violet cut her off.

"No!" Violet said, not knowing who was more startled, herself or her aunt. "I'm sorry, I didn't mean to sound so ill-mannered, but I don't need a wet nurse or a bodyguard. I don't want Will either."

"Now, Violet," her aunt began. "You know he was only doing what he thought best."

"Please don't talk to me like one of the girls," Violet begged. "I've always liked the way that you treated me: as a person and not a baby. Don't change now, Aunt Rose. I've only suffered a bruised heart, you know, not a death wound."

"You aren't going to . . ."

"To see the Duke? No, I imagine he's quite busy getting his household settled."

Rose put her hand over her heart and laughed lightly, the short sleeve of her yellow muslin dress fluttering with the movement of her hand. It certainly wasn't from any actual wind, although breezes came in fitfully from the river. Violet smiled uncertainly in return.

"What did I say that was so amusing?" Violet asked, a little bit startled to hear her aunt laugh right now.

"To be honest, little love, it never occurred to me that you might go see the Duke," Rose said. "I was more worried about you running away again."

Violet smiled, despite her generally low spirits. "Do I need a bond for surety?"

"No, dear, although I wouldn't mind having you give me your word." Aunt Rose looked so grave that Violet was sure she absolutely meant it.

"You are serious!" she exclaimed.

"Quite," Aunt Rose said with the determination Violet knew she used to manage her house, her husband, and her occasionally unruly children.

"You don't think I'm really going to run away, do you?" Violet found she was actually beginning to feel offended. She put the mugs back down on the tray her aunt had brought out, putting her hands on her hips.

"What makes you think I would do that again?"

"Yorktown wasn't the first time, was it?" Aunt Rose returned, all trace of humor gone.

"Who said that—Gabriel? Why would you believe him after his deception and lies?" Violet was beginning to work up a good measure of indignation. If she was angry at Will, she certainly wasn't any happier with Gabriel.

"Will told me. Just after your parents left. You went to Williamsburg to try out your disguise, didn't you?"

"Did Betsy say that? Is everyone going to betray my confidences?" Violet said, closer to tears than she wanted to be at the mention of Gabriel's name.

"Just a moment. You may be seventeen, but both your mother and I were in our twenties before we did outrageous things. You have some growing up yet to do."

"Gabriel took care of that for me."

Rose looked alarmed. "Violet, I thought you said he hadn't . . . ."

"He didn't. That's not what I meant. I just meant I may only be seventeen but I've already had my heart brok . . . bruised, and it does make a person grow up faster."

"Well, that's true. And it is one of life's more painful lessons. But young lady, you stop trying to change the subject again. How do I know you won't try some ridiculous stunt again?"

"Are you going to tell my parents?"

"That depends on the reason you tell me for doing it." Aunt Rose looked behind her, perhaps expecting one of the girls to stumble in sleepy-eyed from her nap. No little girl appeared and she turned her attention back to Violet.

"Don't you know already?" Violet asked.

"All I know is that you went. I don't know why." So whatever Gabriel had told Will, he hadn't revealed her secret. Violet was grateful at least for that.

She took a deep breath. "I wanted to stow away and go to London."

Aunt Rose didn't seem particularly surprised. But then, as Violet had learned only recently, Aunt Rose had done the opposite—fleeing England to come to America.

"And you were going to go as a boy?" she asked.

"Yes," Violet said, prepared to be defiant if she had to.

"Well, that's a sight more daring than I thought of." She leaned over and took Violet's hand to soften her belligerent stance. She urged her to sit down again.

"Just what did you want to go to London for so badly that you ran away not once but twice?" Rose asked after a moment.

All right, this was the moment of truth. Pray Aunt Rose didn't burst out laughing, Violet thought. "I wanted a Season in London. Not to find a husband. Just to see new places, travel, see where you and Papa grew up."

There was nothing but silence from her aunt for a moment. "Oh, Violet. Sometimes it seems like each generation wants the opposite of the one before. Did you know I *fled* London because of the marriage mart? I had not one but two disastrous Seasons."

"You don't talk about it much," Violet said shyly.

"Because I came here and met your Uncle Peter. There was nothing to remember, truly."

"Westminster Abbey? Going to Vauxhall Gardens? The theater?"

"Mmm, yes. London isn't all bad. I know you are half-English. Your father and I don't talk much about England because our experiences there were so unhappy. Your father's mother was almost as difficult to please as my mother. And both he and I found our hearts here in America."

She looked closely at Violet. "I thought for a time that you had, too. I am sorry, Violet." When no response was forthcoming, she sighed. "I'll talk to your parents when they return, dear. Perhaps something can be worked out."

Violet thanked her, then finished off her lemonade. As she bent over the tiny stitches of the doll's dress again, she realized that the prospect of London didn't hold quite as much appeal as it had two months ago. Not without Gabriel.

Who'd have thought that the egalitarians who had overthrown a king could be so narrow-minded, Gabriel reflected. They weren't even in Boston, which he knew was still dominated by the rigid attitudes of the Puritans' descendants. Sadly, the residents of Williamsburg were proving to be similarly self-righteous.

"Max, did you have any luck?" he asked as Maximilian entered the morning room, which this early in the day, he shared with only Penelope and Tessa. His rented town house was filled to bursting, but Maximilian had been unable to procure another.

"No, Your Grace, no luck at all. Although I do not think luck even begins to enter into it."

Gabriel put down the *Virginia Gazette*, grateful that the town's newspaper had yet to run a story on Belmont's brothel, but it was about the only good thing that had happened so far.

"We're being ostracized," he said to the women.

"What?" Tessa said.

"Shut out," Penelope said succinctly. "Doors closed."

That Tessa understood. In response, her colorful oath questioned the legitimacy of these Virginians' ancestors.

"Is there no vacant mansion owned by a planter gone bankrupt or one confiscated from a Loyalist who fled the war?" Gabriel asked.

"Confiscations ended in 1790, Your Grace," Maximilian said.

"All right. We're going to have to make the best of this," Gabriel said. "I hate it when you call me that, you know," he growled at Max.

"I know," Max said. "You are the Duke, however," he pointed out with perfect equanimity.

"Thank you for reminding me of that," Gabriel said, letting his frustration seep into the sarcastic remark.

Max inclined his head politely, the perfect, discreet manservant.

"Gabriel, we need to find some place to go," Penelope said. "You're being horribly cramped, and we're all restless without our usual tasks and routines."

"But until we determine who was threatened, or how many of you, I cannot parcel you out among taverns and inns," he replied. "That assumes I even deem such an establishment safe enough for a group of women on their own. The easiest solution would have been to lease a house but either Williamsburg has none at present, or refuses to make any available."

"What about that place we landed—York something?" Tessa asked.

"That town is even smaller than Williamsburg. The best tavern is one I couldn't return to anyway."

Tessa started to ask why but a glance from Penelope quelled her. She'd no doubt fill her in later, Gabriel thought. He had missed Pen; she'd been his confidante for years, even though she was three years younger than he.

But as much as he cared for Penelope, for them all, in fact, nothing replaced the rapport he'd been building with Violet, the stimulation of her company and the excitement of a growing passion unlike any he'd ever experienced.

Penelope shot another glance at Tessa and both women rose. "Poor Gabriel," Penelope said. "Here you sit trying to have your morning coffee, and you can't even be alone with your thoughts."

Tessa was already out of the room, but Gabriel put out a restraining hand toward Penelope. "Pen, do you have any idea who the men were after?"

He pulled out the chair next to him and motioned for her to sit. Penelope picked up her plate and poured herself a cup of fresh coffee from the silver coffeepot at Gabriel's elbow.

"Diana, Tessa, and I think it's Lady Margery, but she didn't so much as give a guilty start when we showed everyone Athena's sketch of the signet in the house in London."

"I didn't recognize the crest, either, but then I hardly know the insignia of all of the lesser nobility," Gabriel said. "If 'tis Lady Margery, do you think she is clever enough to hide her emotions so well? Remind me what her story was, Pen. Neither Max nor I had time to confirm the full details before we left for America."

Penelope dissolved a second lump of sugar in her coffee. "Margery said she fled because she had been beaten by the man with whom she became involved after her elderly husband died. Her husband had no fortune, so she was nearly penniless. Gabriel, she didn't seem that high in the instep, but her clothes certainly befit an heiress. She seemed too quiet to have been a high flier. But she was obviously deeply afraid of someone. She had bruises up and down her arms that she hid from us as best she could, so in the end, we didn't question her further."

"Could she have invented all that?" Gabriel asked quietly.

"The story, certainly; the bruises, no. I've asked myself that a dozen times since the trouble started." Penelope had been picking blueberries out of her scone and dropping them on her plate instead of eating them. "It's hard to say for certain, Gabriel," she said, watching the scone collapse into a pile of crumbs. She pushed her plate away.

"You know we all come to you with defensive behavior we've adopted to stay alive or to keep our sanity," she said with a detachment that only several years away from the period of her own abuse could have given her. "One woman may show fear to appease her abuser, while another may have developed an utterly calm demeanor. I don't know Lady Margery well enough to know what her reaction is to distressing events. She didn't show any signs of falling apart more than anyone else over this. Cleo was the most afraid."

"That's not surprising. Cleo is only sixteen," Gabriel said, thinking that when she first came to them, she had reminded him of a terrified child. He still thought of her as a child. Violet was only a year older, yet she seemed so much more mature.

"I know she's young. But sadly, with Cleo's mother still alive, I don't think her father is likely to come after her. And certainly not now, not here in America."

Gabriel, veering away from Violet mentally like the reaction to probing a sore tooth, had another thought. "Is there any possibility she is but a stalking horse for someone else?" he asked.

"Margery, you mean, not Cleo?" Penelope asked. He nodded.

"You think that someone might have been deliberately placed among us to find out more about the woman who is the real target?" Penelope asked. "I have to say, that particular idea never occurred to me."

"Trust me, it takes years of this before one's

thoughts become so devious. 'Tis not a condition devoutly to be wished, I can assure you," Gabriel said with dry humor.

Penelope sat down again and they ran through all the women, with Gabriel questioning whether there had been any odd behavior at home since he had left. They concluded they simply did not know who had been singled out, and whoever she was, the woman thought she was safer in not confessing her identity.

"Perhaps whoever 'tis is afraid that she may be asked to leave," Penelope said, taking the last sip of her coffee. She declined Gabriel's offer of a third cup.

"I don't know how to get the truth out of her, whoever she may be," he said, rubbing his hand through his hair slowly, as he did when deep in thought.

"Oh, you do, dear friend. You just don't want to use those methods."

"What, interrogation?" Was Penelope suggesting what he thought she was suggesting?

"Or what amounts to it," she agreed. " 'Tis unpleasant, but I don't think you have a choice."

"Pen, I'm surprised at you. What if Margery is innocent? What if she is not the victim? I would have just added to whatever horrors she has already suffered."

"If she is who and what she says she is, then she should do all in her power to cooperate," Penelope said. "I would."

"You always were my staunchest supporter," Gabriel said ruefully. "Sometimes I wish I had as much confidence in me as you do," he said.

"You do. You are just tired and distracted. Buck

up," Penelope said with a smile. "We all feel much safer here. After all, what kind of trouble could follow us here? We're on a different continent, for mercy's sake."

Gabriel and Max exchanged glances as the blonde woman with the bearing of one to the manor born left the room. Even wise, cautious Penelope hadn't thought about their pursuer being fanatical enough to cross the ocean. Sadly, water was not enough of an obstacle to prevent a man from chasing after his obsession, Gabriel feared.

If one of the women in Gabriel's care had inspired that kind of fanatic quest, through no fault of her own, then another ship could already be on its way here or had perhaps already arrived.

Gabriel wasn't about to scatter the group or put them in a position that would be difficult to defend, not if his worst fears were about to be realized. His scruples forbade him to interrogate a woman, even if all the lives in his household were at stake. A woman who feared to come forward, even in the safe and secure atmosphere of his household, was a frightened one indeed.

SIXTEEN

Chords that vibrate sweetest pleasure,
Thrill the deepest notes of woe.
  —Robert Burns, *Sensibility How Charming,*
  1787

"Your parents will be on their way home soon, Miss Violet," Betsy said, entering the morning room.

Violet looked up, but not with a great deal of interest. She'd been toying with her food, pushing eggs around on the plate with her fork because she wasn't hungry.

"Will's received a note that came with some cloth your father purchased up in Boston, along with some new glass for the greenhouses," Betsy continued. "And this is for you," she said, holding out a sealed letter.

"Thank you, Bets," Violet said. The toast hadn't been any more interesting than the eggs. After returning from Willow Oaks yesterday, she found that no matter where she was, she still couldn't stop thinking of Gabriel.

Violet broke the letter's seal, opening to find it

half-filled with her father's bold script, the other half with her mother's graceful curving letters. They had written it as soon as they had arrived, and it had still taken weeks to get here. Their expressions of love made her feel guilty, as if her deceptions had hurt them, even though they didn't know about them.

There had been no harm done, though, she told herself firmly. Nothing visible, anyway. Her heart might be broken, but that had been entirely her own fault.

She folded the letter back into thirds. "Well, Williamsburg it is," she said brightly. "The boys are all well, and so are Mama and Papa. She bids me look sharp for that ribbon the milliner was importing from France."

"Why?" asked Betsy in what sounded like a suspicious voice.

"For the September wedding," Violet explained.

"No, I mean why must you go into Williamsburg?"

"Betsy, I already told Aunt Rose I'm not going to run away. Nothing ever happened between me and the Duke, and nothing will happen now that his . . . family is here."

"Family?" Betsy snorted in a most unladylike way. "Is that what he calls them?"

"I don't know what he calls them, Bets, because I haven't asked him. And I don't intend to." She threw down her napkin and rose.

"Now don't go bouncing out of here in a huff, Miss Violet," Betsy warned. "We are still acting in your parents' stead, you know."

"And you've been doing a wonderful job, Betsy,

you and Will," Violet said, hoping to placate Betsy.

"I don't know about that, seeing as how you've run away twice."

"I talked to Aunt Rose about all that and promised I won't do anything like it again. I wanted an adventure, it wasn't home I was running away from. Certainly not from you and Will. And besides, with Gabriel coming after me that second time, I learned a lesson. You do trust me, don't you?" Violet asked, aware that her narrowed gaze was probably sending out sparks hot enough to burn Betsy.

"Miss Violet, that isn't my place and well you know it. But I love you and I don't want to see you unhappy. If he's the reason you're unhappy, then why would you go into Williamsburg and risk running into him?"

"I still have a life to lead and I'm not going to let a failed romance—no, flirtation, it wasn't even enough to be considered a romance," Violet said, crossing her fingers behind her back, "drive me away from town or anything I usually do. I did do some foolish things earlier this summer but I'm over them now." She treated Betsy to her best imploring gaze.

"Don't go turning that charm on now, you'll be just like his lordship," Betsy said, then put out a hand when Violet dropped her gaze.

"I'm sorry, Miss Violet, I didn't mean to upset you. I wasn't thinking when I said that about the Duke."

Violet forced a smile. "I'd be a poor excuse for a woman if I let the mere mention of a man's name upset me, now wouldn't I?" she asked, producing a grin she hoped was sufficient to fool Betsy.

"That's right," Betsy said approvingly. "You just keep that spirit. You got that from your mama, you know." Betsy had now evidently decided an outing was just what Violet needed. Soon Violet found herself outside with a list from Betsy of a few items she wanted from Williamsburg, and an escort in the form of Malcolm and his son with Aunt Rose's maid, Eunice. Malcolm ran the stables at her aunt and uncle's, but Stephen, who was just a year older than her brother Peter, was going to Williamsburg to be apprenticed to the blacksmith.

Violet suspected that Will Evans had foisted father and son on her, but Malcolm, a big, strapping fellow, was such an agreeable sort with a guileless brown gaze, that she swallowed her objections. The son had the same cocker-spaniel eyes; Violet had often seen little Peter and Stephen together at the stables pestering Stephen's father.

Will might have had an ulterior motive of keeping an eye on her, but one look into the father's eyes and she knew he did not. Moreover, Will was nowhere in sight.

She did ask Malcolm and Stephen to step outside, however, when they went to get the horses. She dashed into the empty stall where she had stowed her clothes behind a plank, and when she came out, she had on her boys' clothes again. Malcolm showed neither surprise nor displeasure.

Instead, he grinned. "I remember when you first wore breeches. You were just a little bit of a thing. 'Course, you still are, not much taller than my Eunice. You used to drive your brothers crazy

trying to beat them during their riding lessons,"
he reminisced. "Miss your brothers, do you, Miss
Violet?"

She smiled. She supposed she did miss them,
in the way of a little sister missing the big nui-
sances that had dominated her life since she
could first toddle. But if Malcolm wanted to think
she was wearing these clothes out of nostalgia, she
had no objections.

"Oh yes," she replied. "I miss them like a bad
tooth. Once it's pulled, it stops hurting. And the
tooth is gone."

Stephen blinked at her slowly. Malcolm just
laughed, and then helped her to mount. "I know
it's a sight easier to ride astride and you can't do
that in your gown. Don't forget to bring your
dress, now," he said, "and you can change at your
mother's shop."

Violet stuffed her hair under a wide-brimmed
planter's hat and shrugged. "It's in my saddlebag," she said. She had no intention of slipping
away from them, running away, or tasting forbid-
den liquor. She just wanted to prove that no one
could completely dictate her life—not Aunt Rose,
not Betsy or Will Evans, and most especially not
Gabriel Isling, Duke of Belmont.

"Bloody hell, Horrid, how much longer do we
have to spend in this stinking backwater?" Brick
complained from their post inside a small house
across the street from the Duke of Belmont's
rented home.

Big and blond, Nathaniel was called Brick not
only for his beefy frame but because his skull was

as thick as one. "Those women ain't ever coming out of there."

"Come on, Brick, buck up," Horrid Harry, his thin, wiry fellow henchman answered. "They can't stay in there forever. There's too blame many of them, for one thing."

"I wonder how many of 'em he can fit in bed at one time," Brick said in a thick voice.

Harry boxed Brick's ears. "None of that, me lad. No swiving 'til we get back to London and get the rest of our payment. You know what Lord Albie said. The woman is his. Anybody who touches 'er besides 'is Lordship gets his bollocks cut off. Besides, you don't want a lady of quality. They just lie there, I hear tell, thinking of their duty. You want a nice lusty tavern wench with something to squeeze."

"This isn't helping, Horrid," Brick complained.

"You're the one who started it. Keep it in your pants. I'll go get us summat to eat from Chowning's down the street." Scratching at what passed for side-whiskers—his inability to grow decent face bristles through the acne scars that pitted his face had given him his own nickname—Harry sauntered off down the street toward Chowning's Tavern.

If anybody got a turn at the woman, it would be the men who had put up at Raleigh Tavern, his lordship's salaried men. Hoity-toity Nicko and Dan would be taking the credit for it all. He and Brick were only the muscle. Just like when he'd told Brick where to throw the rock and risked the women calling the watch, since they'd had to get so close to the house. It was Nicko who rightly said the women would be too scared. But Harry and Brick had done all the dirty work, like usual.

But even the smarter men hadn't predicted the damned women would all go haring off to America! Harry scratched at his cheek, causing a fresh pimple to pop. Unlike Brick, he had ambition. He didn't care how beautiful Lady Margery Bowers was; he wasn't going to risk losing his big score.

Daughter of a widow who'd fallen on hard times, "Lady" Margery had been Lord Albie's find. He'd made her into a lady and sent her out into society. Seems he'd promised his wife he wouldn't take up with any more whores and risk a disease that might prevent the conception of Lord Albie's heir. The rest of his wife's money was in trust for a future son, since Lord Albie's father-in-law had known too much about his son-in-law's habits.

Get a baby, get the money. Except Lord Albie couldn't keep his hands to himself. If he didn't have a woman to slap around, he'd get ugly with the wife. And if she complained to her papa, he'd be out on his ear. So Lady Margery had occupied him on both the slap and tickle fronts after he'd had ten minutes of jabbing his poker into his wife.

It beat Harry why Margery had wanted to ruin her cozy life. She'd had a nice set up, a house, a made-up background as the widow of some obscure baron. Until the wench had gotten the notion that she was better than her creator and was entitled to a life of her own. It was one of Lord Belmont's women that had put that notion in her ear, someone she'd met at a Royal Society lecture.

Athena, that was her name. Athena had helped Margery "escape" from her own house.

And Albie couldn't get to either woman. He'd exploded in frustration after Dan and Nicko warned Athena and her companions to tell Margery to leave and the slut hadn't. Belmont had snugged those women up tighter than a mole in a hole.

Harry smiled as he handed over the blunt for their lunches, causing the serving girl to shudder in revulsion. Harry knew what sort of effect he had on people. As long as he had enough of the ready to buy a woman, he didn't really care what she thought of him.

He reviewed the situation as he walked back. Dan and Nicko had received a note from the captain in Yorktown, who wanted to sail within the week. That meant the pressure on him and Brick had increased. If the women weren't coming out, they'd have to go in.

But how the bloody hell were they going to do that? The women had to be so tightly packed in that house that they were sleeping four or six to a bed. No way he and Brick could get in and out of that kind of situation unnoticed. Some of the women had already seen Dan and Nicko in London. No one was going to open the door to any of them.

Harry came in the back door and tossed the packet to Brick. That was Nicko's problem, coming up with the plans. All he had to do was wait here and snatch the woman if she came out. He had her description; he even knew Lord Albie couldn't bear to part with anything that he considered his.

"Horrid, did I say I wanted mustard on this?" Brick whined. Harry boxed his ears again, then settled down to eat his own lunch. He gave a loud, satisfying belch in the empty house. There was nobody here to complain about what he and Brick did or didn't do.

If the right woman never came out, it wasn't going to be Harry's fault. He'd already thought of setting a fire to literally smoke them out, but knew he'd have to see Dan about that idea. None of them were to damage the woman; his lordship's orders had been very strict about that. It just wouldn't be possible to control a fire once it had been set. If he or Brick hurt the wench, they'd pay with their lives.

After making sure Violet arrived at Lilies of Francis Street safely, Violet was grateful to see Malcolm and his son ride off on their way to the blacksmith's shop. She'd have a little peace and quiet now.

But her mother's shop was bustling, and she had a dozen questions to answer for the workers who had seen her on Independence Day with Edgar. She was thankful Edgar had gone home without another confrontation. Violet wouldn't have minded staying friends with him if he behaved, but she thought it might be awkward for a while after his crude attempts to court her. Besides that, it might take a while for him to get over the black eye she was sure he'd gotten from Gabriel.

No, she said patiently, she was not walking out with Edgar and no, she hadn't heard he'd run into a tree that night during a pause when the fireworks weren't flashing overhead. A shame, she agreed. He'd broken his nose, too? Oh dear. That must have been quite a tree.

Poor Edgar, she thought fleetingly, but after his I-know-best treatment of her, she really didn't have too much sympathy for her would-be beau.

Then she listened as wild speculation ensued about Gabriel and his bevy of women. Most of the workers didn't know about her relationship with Gabriel, so she just listened, rather disgusted with the lewd tone of the gossip.

After an hour, her teeth hurt from smiling. She escaped to the milliner's only to endure a similar set of questions. More chattering ensued, until finally she left with the grosgrain and a promise to return soon. Malcolm was expecting her back at her mother's shop for tea, after which they would ride home around four.

Violet walked slowly once out of sight of the milliner's, in no great hurry to get back to her mother's shop. For some reason, wearing the boy's clothes didn't give her the secret thrill it had before. She'd been served liquor in York-town, after all, and that had been her main goal. Twice Gabriel had stripped her of her disguise, so it was just pure deviltry that had made her wear it today.

But the familiar excitement of striding along in trousers and having her hair in a queue died abruptly. She turned a corner and almost ran into a bevy of women standing on the sidewalk arguing about which general store, Prentis or Tarpley's, was closest.

Violet felt butterflies invade her stomach suddenly. She recognized the woman with the flame-red hair from that day on the waterfront at York-town. She was not as tall as Aunt Rose. Her hair was a deeper shade of red, bordering on russet, and her figure was even more voluptuously curved than her aunt's.

These were some of Gabriel's women. They had seen her and it was too late to back away. If she left now, she'd look like a baby who was scared of women.

A woman whose slim figure was topped by a cap of daringly short pale curls, called softly to her. "Would you help us, please?" Violet feigned looking around as if there were someone else be-ing addressed but the woman, whom the others called Cleo, asked her again in a polite voice.

Violet stuck her hands in her pockets and saun-tered up to the group. She'd forgotten the char-coal for her mustache, she thought, cursing her luck. She said hello in her deepest voice.

The red-haired woman was staring at her rather strangely. "Do you live here?" she asked.

"Yes," Violet said gruffly, trying to look unin-terested.

We are looking for the Prentis store," the vo-luptuous woman began.

Another woman interrupted. "Or Tarpell's store."

"Tarpley's, I think 'tis," the woman with the short silvery-blonde hair said.

"Tarpley's," Violet affirmed.

"Which store is closer to where we are now?" Cleo asked.

"To here?" she replied, scuffing her boots in the dirt.

No answer. She looked up to find the entire group of six women regarding her thoughtfully.

The red-haired women named Diana drew her into the group a little way so she was less visible from the street. "You're not a boy, are you?" she asked.

"What?" Violet said, trying to look incredulous.

A woman standing at the fringe of the group spoke up. "We have at least one friend who wears trousers sometimes." Heads swiveled to look at her, but she didn't seem aware she'd said anything unusual.

"That's Tessa's decision, whether to share that or not," Diana said to the dark-haired woman, who was wearing a beautiful gown of violet-colored silk that complemented her eyes. They were a shade of bluish-purple that looked like the periwinkles her mother grew, although Violet suspected they would look blue in a blue dress.

Violet took a closer look at the woman who seemed to be half in and half out of the group. Diana noticed her looking too. "You and Margery could be sisters," she said. But the sadness in Margery's eyes was something Violet hoped never to see in her own.

Diana paused, as if suddenly aware that talking in a public place might be dangerous. Just ahead, Duke of Gloucester Street was full of people, horses, and wagons. "But what are we doing standing on the sidewalk like this? We're too visible," she said, which Violet thought a very odd thing to say. They'd been in full view at Yorktown.

"Is everything all right with you?" Diana asked, taking a measuring look at Violet. "You aren't running away, are you?"

"Oh no, nothing like that," Violet assured her. "I have twin brothers and we used to dress alike sometimes. I just rode in from our plantation and I like riding astride."

"If you were as boyish as all that," Diana said astutely, "You wouldn't be looking at Margery's dress with such longing."

"It's the most beautiful gown I've ever seen," Violet said honestly.

"Is there someone who wants you to dress as a boy? Or do things you don't like?" Cleo asked shyly. "We can help you, if you're in trouble."

"Help me? I'm fine. My clothes are at my mother's flower shop just down the way. Good day, ladies," Violet said, suddenly wanting to get away from this group of women who had some strange tie to Gabriel that consumed his life. She'd thought she wanted to know what it was, but now she wasn't so sure.

Diana put a hand on her arm. "Cleo is right. If someone is hurting you or taking advantage of your youth, we could help you." She named a street and number, and asked Violet if she knew where it was.

"I know the house. It's the Duke's," Violet said, then clamped her lips shut as the circle of women went utterly silent.

"Are you a friend of his?" Diana asked, real caution in her eyes, taking her hand away from Violet's arm.

"He came here to buy some of my family's stock for his conservatory." She met Diana's gaze squarely with her own and changed the subject. "If you want to cause fewer problems for Gabriel, you should travel in smaller groups."

"We would if we could," Cleo answered. "But we are fleeing trouble ourselves, and Gabriel has warned us not to go out alone."

"Trouble?" Violet said, puzzled.

"Cleo, hush," another woman said.

"No, I think this lady knows Gabriel well, don't you?" Cleo asked in a kind voice. She was easily the youngest of the group and had an almost ethereal air about her.

"I do. I did," Violet said, then to her consternation found tears beginning to fill her eyes. "But then you came," she said, her gaze taking in the whole beautifully appointed group.

"Excuse me," she blurted out, then brushed past the women and turned in at a side alley that ran between a set of houses. She hugged the paths that ran behind peoples' gardens, staying off the main streets until she came to the yard of her mother's and Uncle Peter's old house, which still housed the shop.

She entered by the back gate, knowing no one would see her out here. No one picked flowers this late in the day, and the employees inside would be putting everything away for Monday.

Like a magnet, the gazebo drew her gaze. The graceful white structure that her mother had loved and her father had rebuilt at Oak Grove still stood, serene in the garden's center. Violet went there, sinking onto the bench in the dappled sunlight, and let the tears come at last.

SEVENTEEN

Was ever woman in this humor woo'd?
Was ever woman in this humor won?
  —William Shakespeare, *King Richard III,*
    1593

Gabriel could not have been more flabber-gasted if told that an angel from heaven had descended to bless him.

"Violet Pearson wants to see me? Am I reading this note a-right?" he asked Maximilian. His imperturbable butler nodded.

"Wait, don't show her in." Gabriel ran his hands through his hair, desperately trying to think. There were women everywhere. Where could he possibly talk to her?

Max raised an eyebrow. "She isn't here, Your Grace. She asks you to meet her at this address tomorrow, after services at Bruton parish church." Max showed Gabriel the address.

"Oh, I see. Very well. Fine." Casting a narrow-eyed glance at Max, he wondered if his redoubtable manservant was about to smile at his master's evident mental disarray.

Gabriel prayed that no one would enter the

room now or he'd have to thrash Max. He couldn't believe his first thought had to been to receive Violet in here. This tiny room he'd stuffed himself into was little more than a pantry. In fact, he suspected it was the pantry, although Max refused to confirm it, probably to salve his ego. Gabriel called it his office, just to get a modicum of privacy.

He had about as much privacy as he had space in here. Gabriel was seriously considering chartering a ship for them all to sail up and down the Virginia—Carolina coast just to get out of this house that had become too small.

Max appreciated being in his employ far too much to laugh at him. He just raised that damned eyebrow as he left.

Tomorrow. What could Violet want?

Tomorrow. Was she crazy? Violet wondered. Why would she risk her heart again? She wasn't, she told herself. She wasn't going to Gabriel to rekindle a romance, just to offer those women, whoever they were, some assistance. They had talked too much of danger and their eyes were the saddest and wariest she'd ever seen. She didn't know exactly how they had come to live with Gabriel, or what they had suffered, but something in her told her that they were frightened. There was plenty of space on the plantation; that had to be better than cramped in a Williamsburg town home surrounded by less-than-friendly townspeople.

She'd sent a note home with Malcolm that she was staying in town and would go to church on

Sunday at Bruton parish in Williamsburg. When she was home, she usually went to the chapel at Westover, upriver at the Byrds' neighboring plantation. Since Will had not come thundering after her, she assumed Aunt Rose and Betsy had accepted her assurances and her request for them to trust her, as she had asked.

Will would be unhappy if he knew she was going to see Gabriel, and Betsy would no doubt try to dissuade her, but Violet knew things were not as they seemed to the others. They couldn't believe what she knew deep in her soul. Gabriel was no perverted monster. Nor was he a lecher. She didn't care what gossip and rumors swirled around him.

And those women weren't harlots or experienced jades. That young woman Cleo had been near her age. It wasn't that she had a lot of experience with trollops, for heaven's sake, but that intuition her mother had always credited her with had come into play again. Something in Cleo's eyes and Diana's caution—and that woman who had stood half in and half out of the group—told her that they had all been hurt in some profound way that didn't show on the surface. There was an echo of it in Gabriel's eyes.

She wasn't going to throw herself at Gabriel either. She didn't know why he couldn't be with her because of those women, but she had heard her mother's stories of intolerance. When the townsfolk in Williamsburg had thought she'd gone over to the loyalists. The rock through her shop window, the snubs.

Violet had spent enough time in town to hear what people were saying. Many of them knew that

Gabriel had visited at the plantation and several had met him on Independence Day, the ones who had plantations up river as well as houses in town.

They hadn't ostracized her, Adam and Lily Pearson's daughter; they'd been more interested in gossip, at least the ones she didn't know well. The milliners and her mother's employees were too well mannered. They had only been interested in Edgar. Since no one here had connected her with Gabriel romantically, they had thought she'd be interested in all the salacious speculation that had come to town with this so-called Belmont's brothel.

The church bells tolled after the service at Bruton parish church, where the faithful had begun to return. The Anglican Church had severed its association with the British crown and memories of the war had begun to fade. Gabriel had attended the service, which was nearly identical to that at home except that the king was not mentioned or called the Defender of the Faith as had been the case in England since Henry the Eighth had defied Rome in order to marry Anne Boleyn.

And he'd gone alone. He had offered to accompany any of the women but they had all demurred. There had been a late afternoon service on Saturday that was less well attended. Perhaps they had gone then. No one in Williamsburg was going to stone them, but they went out only in small groups and they tried to be as discreet as possible. Some of the women were chafing, he knew, because they'd had more freedom in London, but until he knew who was after them and

whether they were safe here, he couldn't allow
them the freedom they normally enjoyed.

But usually at least Penelope accompanied him
to church. He hadn't even seen her this morning,
only Tessa who habitually rose early, but who was
quite emphatic that she never planned to set foot
in a church again. Knowing Tessa, it probably involved some bishop's silver candlesticks, and that
meant it was better not to ask. So he hadn't expected her company, but he was surprised not to
see Penelope.

"Is she well?" he had inquired of Tessa.

"Aye, she's fine," Tessa had replied. A swift unreadable glance passed between Max and Tessa,
and he had the uncomfortable feeling that his
meeting with Violet was the reason Penelope
wasn't attending church.

He looked at Tessa who shook her head firmly.
Her look said she wasn't going to answer any
questions, so he shouldn't bother.

So he didn't.

Maximilian had the good sense not to even lift
his eyebrow as he closed the door behind Gabriel.
A glance between them confirmed that Max remained armed and would throughout the duration of the emergency that had sent his entire
household to America.

Since the ladies had arrived, he'd found solace
in the quiet ceremony at church, but not today.
The high box pews had prevented him from seeing whether Violet had also attended the service,
but he had the address tucked into his pocket.
He did have time to reflect that what unsettled
him so this morning was not merely anxiety at
seeing Violet, whom he'd not seen since that

dreadful moment at the wharf in Yorktown, but that for once, he was not in charge. She had requested the meeting, she had arranged the time and place.

After so many years of doing for others, he was quite unused to having any matter taken out of his hands. He hoped that didn't mean he was getting old and crotchety.

Directly after communion, Gabriel quietly left the church without waiting for the service to end; he'd not wished to be ostracized by the clergyman or any of the good people of Williamsburg. He was certain that only the size of his expenditures and the solidity of his currency—he used silver in a country surfeited with poor paper notes—kept doors from being shut all over town.

He wanted no rocks thrown through his window from the townspeople here. Nothing that might confuse the issue of whether one of those he sheltered was still a target.

Was that Violet up ahead? he wondered, catching a glimpse of rose-colored silk as a woman turned the corner. He had seen Violet so rarely in womanly clothes that he couldn't remember if she owned such a gown.

Gabriel fisted his hand against his side in frustration. He was acting like a boy. Mentally he told himself to settle down. Violet had asked for the meeting, so he could assume she would be there.

Turning onto Francis Street, Gabriel soon found the building. A sign painted with a large white lily and golden letters that read "Lilies" made him smile at the play on words.

This was her mother's shop. He saw nothing through the large front windows as he knocked.

Then a flash of rose at the window, and there she was, opening up the door to him. A ribbon in the same deep shade of rose wound its way through her hair, which she'd pulled up in a style reminiscent of Cleo's, except hers was longer.

He bowed. She smiled briefly, although it looked strained. "Come in," she said. "This is my mother's house, where she and my uncle grew up."

" 'Tis still her shop?"

"Yes, although she doesn't come here so often anymore. I stay here when I am in town."

Doffing his hat, he held it under his arm as he followed her to the back of the house. She had set the sturdy trestle table for tea with a set of the Chinese design called Blue Willow.

"Will you have some?" she asked, turning to a kettle that hung over a small fire burning in the center of the large hearth.

"Thank you," he said. She gestured for him to sit as she poured hot water into a teapot from a kettle that she must have set out to heat before going to church. The back door to the garden stood open, preventing the heat from becoming stifling. Butterflies flitted among hydrangea bushes and crape myrtle that were in bloom. A white gazebo, similar to the ones he'd seen at Oak Grove and Willow Oaks stood in the garden's center.

As she finished preparations, he looked around the interior, noting herbs hanging from the rafters, along with bunches of roses and other flowers in various stages of drying. The summer roses must have been recently hung, because they were still vivid in color and scent. He inhaled their fragrance, watching her graceful motions as she prepared the tea.

"You don't drink coffee?" he asked as the steeping tea added its subtle aroma to those around them.

"We do, and I do, but with an aunt and a father hailing from the mother country, I grew up with tea. I found that I actually prefer tea to coffee."

"How English of you," he said, essaying a faint teasing tone. She looked at him, smiled, then swore as a bit of water splashed out from the teapot and onto her hand where she hadn't guided the kettle carefully.

"Let me," Gabriel said, instantly beside her. Although he was sorely tempted to take her finger and kiss it, he lifted the kettle from her with its towel wrapped around the hot handle and finished pouring the water into the teapot. He swirled the tea leaves around, closed the teapot and covered it with the towel to steep.

"For a man who lives in a household full of women, you're quite good at that," she remarked, holding the fingertip, which had turned faintly red, up to the air.

"I sometimes think tea is the social glue that holds England together," he said. "We've all taken tea to each other on many a dark night of the soul."

As if he'd said too much about himself and his household, he abruptly moved back to his place and sat down. Violet nursed her finger and appeared to be wondering where to begin.

In the end, she just began. "Gabriel, I want to offer you a place for your . . . your household. Temporarily."

He couldn't help himself. He stared. "Why would you want to do that?"

"You have nowhere to go, do you? At least not immediately."

He inclined his head. " 'Tis true. No one wants us, and it takes time to arrange the purchase of property. But why would you want to help us?"

Her expression was faintly troubled. "I don't really know myself. Despite what people are saying, I don't believe your entire household could possibly be composed of doxies. I don't believe that of you."

She looked at him over the rim of her teacup. "Am I wrong?"

Reaching for her free hand, Gabriel enclosed it within his own larger one. "No, you are not wrong."

She pulled her hand back. "I met some of them on the street the other day." She paused, looking uncertainly at him.

"Their stories are theirs to tell, I'm afraid," he said. "I can't break their confidence."

"I understand." But she didn't, not really, he could tell. And that made what she was doing even more generous. Taking him, taking them all, on trust.

"I am still mistress at Oak Grove for a while longer," she resumed. "And while I am, I can at least offer you makeshift space while you decide what to do and where to go." Her gaze dropped as if it hurt too much to meet his eyes.

"Violet, this is far too generous of you."

"I am sure I will be told so." She reached for the teapot, but he got there first. He poured her a second cup as she looked on.

"There is a small house near the fields I showed you the first day. It's the largest of the houses the indentured servants stay in for a time when they've finished their service. There's no one there now. It won't hold all of you but it can take a half-dozen, and the rest can stay here in town with you. . . . If I. . . ."

"No," he interjected. Her eyes went wide with astonishment at the interruption and the abrupt rejection. He tried to reach for her hand again but she kept both of them firmly wrapped around her teacup.

"I don't want to spurn your generous offer, Violet, but I can't allow the ladies to be separated, nor I from them," he explained. It wasn't much of an explanation, though, and he knew it.

"They are not your mistresses?" she asked.

Good, they might as well get that out of the way. "No, they are not."

"Then what difference does it make where they stay? You have to be packed in there so tightly that women are sleeping on the floor," she pointed out.

"That's where Max and I have been sleeping," he said ruefully. "And one or two of the others. Yes, the quarters are very close. Much more so than anyone has been accustomed to," he confessed. "My house in London is quite large."

"I inquired about the house across from you," she said. "My mother's friend Mary lives in town, and had told me 'twas vacant. When I looked into it, I was told it's been rented."

His brows flicked up. "I tried as well. So I know of at least one place that wasn't denied to me out of spite."

"I'm sorry I couldn't help. You can show yourself out then." Her lashes veiled her eyes but he knew he'd hurt her. *Again,* he thought savagely.

No, he wouldn't let it rest this way. Not this time.

EIGHTEEN

Stay, O sweet, and do not rise!
The light that shines comes from thine eyes.
　　　—Anonymous, *A Pilgrim's Solace*, 1612

This time when he reached for her hand, he nearly had to pull it off the teacup. "Violet, listen to me," he said, turning her palm over and resting his other hand on top so that he enclosed her hand between both of his. "My household all came here the way they did and as suddenly as they did because of a threat to one of their number."

Skepticism warred with interest on her expressive face. Curiosity won out. "What kind of threat?"

"The women who share my household have all had a rough time of it in life," he said. "Men in their lives have hurt them, mentally, emotionally, physically, sometimes in ways that I would repeat to no one on this earth willingly. English law lets men treat women as property. Though I sit in the House of Lords, I cannot change the law and I cannot change attitudes there. So I do what I can; that is how they all came to live under my protection. And although I do everything in my power to keep them safe, it isn't always possible."

He was leaving out a great deal, but he'd hurt her feelings and he didn't know how much longer she'd listen to him before tossing him out on his ear. So he had to make his words count.

"Something happened after I left London. There were threats, then an attempt to frighten and perhaps even kidnap one of them. The additional guards I'd hired were compromised or bought. So Lady Penelope, who is my good right hand, decided that their best hope of safety lay in coming to find me. And that's what you saw that day in Yorktown. They had just arrived."

"So you didn't know they were coming?"

"No, not at all. That's why I reacted to Will so oddly. Penelope had sent me a letter with her early concerns, which I did receive. But soon after that, the situation escalated and not long after she had dispatched a second letter, she felt that it would be more dangerous to stay than go. They arrived before the second letter did."

"But everything is all right now?"

"We hope so. But I have not been able to discover who was the object of the threat. Until I do, 'tisn't safe to divide them or leave some on their own."

"How can you not know which woman is the one they want?"

"A signet was shown to one of them in London. Athena, who has excellent drawing skills, did a sketch of the ring, but no one recognized it—or claimed to recognize it."

"But what about the woman who was the target?"

"If she recognized the ring, she did not come forward," Gabriel replied.

"Can't you ask them? Doesn't she endanger everyone in your household by not admitting that she is the one sought?"

"Penelope suggested much the same thing. Sometimes any move that frightens a woman who has been ill-treated can drive her back into her shell or evoke the memories of what she suffered. I can't mistreat them, not when they have barely begun to trust a man again."

"Why would you have to mistreat them to ask a question, a simple question?" she asked.

"It might seem a simple question to you or me, but the woman who has been damaged may find it far more frightening or even threatening to whatever well-being she has been able to restore in her soul."

Violet extracted her hand from between Gabriel's, pushing an errant curl back into place. Gabriel longed to tuck it behind her ear himself, but knew he didn't have the right. He poured another cup of tea for himself instead, and stirred in several lumps of sugar just to give his hands something to do that didn't involve Violet.

"Why would asking them who is looking for them qualify as mistreatment?" she asked in a reasonable voice.

To hell with the sugar. Gabriel reached out to soothe the frown from Violet's brow. "The chief rule of my household is that no one is forced to divulge their story until they wish to reveal it. Some have never been able to talk about what happened to them; some, especially those who were hurt as children, cannot remember. That may be a blessing. For some, that lack of memory is the only defense available to them, to retreat somewhere where the bad things can't pursue them."

"Do you mean it is possible that the woman doesn't know she is the target?"

" 'Tis possible," Gabriel said, "but not likely. I think it more likely that she is simply too frightened to even come forward. She may fear that she will be tossed out, back into the streets, or into the gilded cage that holds so many upper class women. The terror and the misery is the same, no matter the station in life."

Violet sipped the last of her tea, refusing a third cup when he offered. "But now that everyone is here in America? Surely they are all safe?"

"Perhaps. But this sort of obsession doesn't easily fade. If a rich man is after one of the ladies, then his resources would enable him to cross the water."

"I see now why you didn't like the solution I proposed," Violet said. "Until you know if there is still a threat . . ."

"Exactly."

"But in the meantime you are all shut up in a house that is too small, with no one knowing whether 'tis safe to venture out." Violet rose to set the teacups in a bucket of water.

She turned back to him, her rancor gone now that she understood. "This place isn't as pleasant, but not far from the houses I spoke of, there is an old barn. Haying is over and it's still too early for tobacco, so it is empty. I wouldn't vouch for it through a cold winter, but for a few weeks in good weather, it should serve. I'd offer the main house, but you'd still have the problem with splitting people up."

"If there is any danger, the last thing I want is to bring it to you and yours. Not your house, Violet. No, we aren't that proud, not if safety comes with it. This barn, how far back on your property is it?"

"Well away from the main house. You would bring no danger to us, I think."

"What about Will?"

She hugged her elbows, looking down into the dying embers of the cooking fire. "I'll speak to Betsy. She'll bring him round. But I would still stay out of Will's way, were I you."

He rose, moving to stand just behind her. Putting a hand on her shoulder, he squeezed lightly. "I have no words to thank you for this generous offer. By all rights, you should be angry, and yet. . . ."

"Don't say anything more. I still am angry at you. But there was something in those women's eyes. I just wanted to help." He was looking at the nape of her neck, where curling strands nestled against the back of her head, beneath the pulled-up hair. He wanted to bend and kiss that tender spot. Yet he had to make reason prevail over lust, sense over sensuality.

He stepped back. She turned to face him. "One thing, Gabriel. I've had word that my parents are on their way home." She laid a hand on his sleeve. "Will is certain to have a few things to say about you, and even though I could tell my mother that this all makes sense, it would take my father a bit longer to understand. He's a bit . . . irrational when it comes to me."

"I can see why. You are his only daughter," Gabriel said, unable to resist the stray lock that danced against her cheek. He smoothed it back, letting his fingertips linger there lightly.

Her eyes took on new depths as sensuality stirred in them. Then she seemed to remember where they were and what had happened between them. She tossed her head back so her hair was out of reach. "But you had best not be here when my father arrives," she said. "He may act first and ask questions later, depending on what Will tells him and whether I am able to see him first or not."

Did she think he was going to abandon her? Before outrage welled up and spilled over, he realized she was simply trying to protect him.

He smiled and covered her hand with his own. "Don't unman me, sweet Violet. Everything I have to answer for, I shall."

"Except the things you won't answer." She was still hurt, but not vindictive. He admired her tremendously for seeking him out and making the offer that she had, despite what had passed between them only a few days ago.

But the meeting was at an end, now that the business she had in mind had been transacted. Her replies turned cool and perfunctory.

And so there was nothing left to say. He arranged a date with her, saying that they would gather their belongings and as much furniture as he could take from the house and hire carts to transport it to Oak Grove.

She would make a far better businesswoman than she knew, he thought, as he turned onto Duke of Gloucester Street. She had ended their conversation almost immediately after her remark about his being the one who would not answer questions. She had also kept her composure, a remarkable thing for one so young.

But at least she was speaking to him. That should have felt like a victory after the way they had last parted. But somehow, the loss of all the vitality that he associated with her, and the special awareness of him that had suffused her eyes, made him feel lonelier than ever.

Women surrounded him, and the one woman he wanted, he could not have.

After meeting with Gabriel, Violet went directly to Malcolm and told him what kind of help she needed. She told him only that the women worked for Gabriel and that they had all been rescued from dire circumstances in England. Will had apparently said nothing to anyone at either plantation beyond his wife and her aunt, for which she was grateful, because it made her task now easier. There was no negative sentiment to overcome. No one had seen Gabriel for a few days, but neither had they heard the gossip or Will's condemnation.

Malcolm assured her that he could round up a half-dozen more workers. After she had secured his help, she went to Aunt Rose.

"They have been terribly mistreated," Violet said to end her explanation. "I don't know much about their stories, though, because Gabriel wants to protect their privacy."

Her aunt frowned. "Then they're not fancy women?"

"No. Or if they were, someone forced them to be, and 'twas never Gabriel. He rescued them."

"That's quite an undertaking. I wonder if his sister's death had anything to do with his cause. I vaguely remember hearing that she had died in childbirth. That was—and is—a common enough event that it would not occasion talk. But although her husband had been prominent in society, he went abroad afterwards, to Italy, I think. I never heard that he came back, although I was living here, of course, in later years."

Niece and aunt looked at each other. "Do you think something happened to Gabriel's sister?" Violet asked.

"I don't know. I never heard anything like that, but as he said to you, such things are not often spoken of, especially among the upper classes. Something about his sister's life could very well have influenced him on the unusual course he took when he came into his title. How extraordinary for someone as young as he was then—he couldn't have been more than fifteen or sixteen."

Violet left with her aunt's promise to send workers over. They didn't have long. Gabriel wanted to move as soon as possible. She had said to give them two days.

"Horrid, they're leaving," Brick roared from the front room. Harry, who'd gone to have a lie down on the mattress in the back, sat up with a start.

"What do you mean, they're leaving?" he called out.

"I mean they're carrying out satchels and what not."

"All of them?" Harry said as he stuffed his shirt back into his trousers.

"Here, look for yourself," Brick said.

He lifted the curtain, and then started swearing a blue streak. "Bloody hell, this ain't good. This ain't good. Brick, run down to Raleigh Tavern and tell Dan and Nicko."

"What if they leave before we get back?"

"I'll follow them. What else can I do?'

"Brick," Harry called as Nate prepared to step outside. "Remember, go the back way to the tavern. Don't look conspicuous now, mind."

"Conspicuous?" Brick said.

Harry groaned. It was a four-syllable word and beyond Brick. "Try not to let people see you're in a hurry."

"Oh, yeah, right, I remember."

"You big stupid lout. Just don't forget."

"I won't."

While Brick lumbered down the road toward Raleigh Tavern—inconspicuously, Harry hoped— he thought hard. Was now the time to try to get the wench his lordship wanted? He didn't think they were headed home to England; they hadn't been here that long. Probably they were going to a bigger house—Lord knew they needed it. Maybe it would make it easier if they had a larger house, they wouldn't be crammed into a few rooms.

But what if it were more remote? Then what would they do?

If he pinched the girl himself, he could get all the credit. Hell, if he bundled her up and out of here, he could get to a ship and set sail for England by himself. He wouldn't have to share the bonus with anyone.

The carts pulled up to the barn. They were in a remote part of Willow Oaks, at the edge of the tobacco fields. Uncle Peter had planted these fields for Aunt Rose, Violet knew, when he was trying to help her secretly. Giving her a cash crop so that if her attempt to run the plantation failed, she would not be alone and without resources.

The day was hot and sunny. Birds called in the trees. No one was in sight.

"This is . . . well protected," Diana said dubiously, looking around. Gabriel, who sat next to Penelope, driving one cart, squeezed her hand.

"Ladies, this isn't London," Penelope said, making an effort to be more positive. "And yes, it's a barn. But at least we will have more space."

"Are we going to sleep in the hay?" Tessa wanted to know.

"Tessa," Gabriel said warningly. "This isn't helping."

At that moment, a door opened, a smaller door set within the larger door that opened wide to admit horses, carts, and crates. This was a normal doorway. And in it stood Violet.

"I know this isn't much to look at," she said. "But at least you will have more room. Please come in," she said, stepping back.

Gabriel walked in, expecting a few mattresses scattered around, and the hay and old tobacco leaves swept into a corner. What he saw astonished him. Someone had built rooms here. Someone had laid a wooden floor.

He turned to Violet. "What happened here?"

"Some of those here who have been indentured servants, some deported for the crime of being Scots or Catholics or whatever other reason, were happy to help turn this barn into a temporary home."

"I can't begin to thank you enough," Gabriel began, wishing he could simply sweep her into his arms.

She looked up at him, reserve in every word and movement of her body. Then she smiled and became almost the Violet he'd known.

"Don't thank me. Thank them," she said, and a dozen people poured in from a door that opened at the end of the long hall that ran most of the length of the barn, past the rooms that had been turned into bedrooms, past the foyer in which they stood. They opened a door into a wide room that had space for everyone to sit and was more than decently furnished with chairs, divans, screens to separate the spaces into smaller groupings, a spinning wheel, even an old harpsichord, paints, brushes, and canvas.

The women moved down the hallway to greet the people who awaited them. A general rush of self-introductions followed. Gabriel turned to Violet who stood watching the greetings, the smiles, bits of conversation, and hesitant laughter.

"I can't believe you had all this done in such a short time," he said. "Or that you did it at all."

"You thought it would be a pile of mattresses and the smell of tobacco?" she asked with a smile. "I don't know that we can ever get rid of the tobacco odor, but we put down bunches of herbs and lavender before laying the floor. I think it helped some, don't you?" she asked, sniffing.

"I think it's wonderful. How did you get people to do this?" he asked, as the men moved out to the carts to help unload them and bring in the women's belongings.

"I talked to my aunt, to Betsy Evans, and to Malcolm who is married to Aunt Rose's former maid Eunice. They knew people who had been in similar situations and who were glad to help. I'm glad we could do this for you."

Gabriel knew then that he would not return to London with the women to live. They wouldn't stay here forever, of course, in a converted tobacco barn on Violet's family's property. But now that he knew there were people in America who could provide this kind of welcome from the generosity of their hearts, he would seek it again.

If some of them wanted to return to London, of course they would be welcome to do so. He would extend the shelter of his home in London, and keep the conservatory there and at his estate in the country. But he was going to move the household to America permanently. He resolved to tell Maximilian to take the property in Charleston.

NINETEEN

You can never plan the future by the past.
— Edmund Burke, *Letter,* 1791

The day after they moved in, one of the field workers delivered a note to Betsy Evans, who brought it directly to Violet. Written on it in an elegant feminine hand were the words "Miss Violet Pearson." Violet looked down at it, thinking that if it had been shown to Will, he needn't have worried that it was a billet-doux from Gabriel. Not that she expected one.

She opened the mysterious note and found she was invited to Aunt Rose's gazebo at dusk, after the workers had gone in from the fields. Mindful of her promise, she shared the note's contents with Aunt Rose. After her meeting with Gabriel, she had told her aunt some of what Gabriel had told her. Violet wasn't surprised that Rose's heart went out to them. She'd made no objection at all to the living quarters. Moreover, she'd searched the plantation high and low for extra mattresses, linens, and furnishings such as tables and chairs.

So at seven in the evening, Violet walked over to the gazebo built for her aunt, patterned after the one at Oak Grove, which in turn was modeled on the original building in her mother's Williamsburg garden so long ago. Gabriel's lady couldn't have known what the gazebo meant to Violet and the women of her family. She was probably just looking for a discreet place to meet to avoid drawing attention.

Waiting for her in the gazebo was the tall woman who seemed to have been in charge that day in Yorktown. She moved toward Violet at once, shaking hands in a direct and friendly fashion. "Penelope Henley," she said. "We met briefly yesterday, Miss Pearson."

"Please, call me Violet. What can I do for you?"

"I want to thank you for lending us so many of your belongings and making a place for us here."

"I was happy to help. You would have been more comfortable in the small houses but Gabriel said you shouldn't be separated."

Penelope looked alarmed. "Oh, not like that."

"I know there isn't anything, ah, romantic, between you. Or if there was with some of you, there isn't now." Violet hoped this wasn't too personal a thing to say to a woman she barely knew.

Penelope nodded. "Did Gabriel tell you all this?"

"Gabriel? What do you think?"

"I think you're a very unusual young woman, Miss Pearson."

"Violet, please. I like ceremony no more than Gabriel, though my station in life is not so exalted—and annoying—from that point of view."

"Still, this can't have been easy for you . . ." Penelope said.

"I will own that you've caused quite a stir in

our little town," Violet said. She wondered if Penelope knew how much of an understatement that was.

"We didn't want to, believe me. We were quite happy in London for the most part."

"Until you were threatened," Violet said. Would Penelope tell her anything more?

"You know about that?" Penelope sounded surprised.

"Even Gabriel had to tell me something."

Penelope laughed briefly. "Yes, even Gabriel. But we would not have accepted your offer unless we were sure it would be safe."

"Did Gabriel tell you that?"

"Why do you ask?"

"He said he wasn't sure if the threat was still active, and that none of you was sure who was the target—except perhaps the woman herself, and that she might be too frightened to come forward."

"That's the most Gabriel has ever told anyone outside our group about it."

Violet couldn't summon up a lot of pleasure from the thought. "He had to tell me something, didn't he?"

"As you said, this is Gabriel we're speaking of. No, he didn't have to tell you anything. It's one reason why there is such gossip. He thinks once explanations or defenses start being given out, they will never stop. You already know that he believes in protecting our privacy and if that means never explaining his actions or intentions, he has let his reputation hang, as London cant would term it. The fact that he told you so much means. . . ."

"Absolutely nothing," Violet said firmly.

"That's not true," Penelope returned. "I think he loves you, Violet."

"Surely not." Loved her? After ending whatever it was they'd had between them? No, it couldn't be possible. She wished her heart wouldn't leap about so hopefully in her chest after a statement like that. It couldn't be good for her.

"After what we have experienced, few of us take conversation lightly. I am perfectly serious," Penelope said, and Violet knew she meant it. "There is something between you, is there not?"

"There was," Violet said, finally sinking down onto the cushioned bench in the gazebo. Honeysuckle bloomed nearby, its sweet perfume wafting through the wooden structure with the slightest breeze.

"Oh, dear," Penelope said, seating herself next to Violet. "I think I can guess this part."

"Why?" Violet asked, her heart now tripping into double time. "Has it happened before?"

"No, because it has not."

"I don't understand," Violet said, perplexed.

"Violet, Gabriel is a complex man who is not easily understood. He seems light and charming on the surface—and indeed, he is a most charming man—but there is a strong reason behind everything he does."

"I know he is dedicated to all of you," Violet said, hoping her voice didn't sound too wistful.

"He is. He has literally saved our lives, several of us. It probably seems extraordinary, even obsessive, to you."

"He said someone he knew had been hurt. I assume in a similar way to what some of you had suffered."

"Yes, but it's much more personal than that, even more deeply felt than just someone he knew," Penelope told her.

"Then we're back to Gabriel not telling anyone an important part of his story," Violet said with a sigh.

"I'm going to break his confidence and tell you this, Violet, because . . ."

"Oh no," Violet said, "don't jeopardize your relationship with him on my account."

"It won't. His future and yours hang in the balance. I thought loving you was too important for him to risk losing you, but this sense of honor runs so deep, it is hard for him to acknowledge that he has a right to personal happiness himself, not just trying to see to ours."

Fireflies began to glow around them as the night deepened, and in their short-lived light, Violet watched Penelope's face. "I don't think you should tell me, Penelope, truly," she said. "If 'twas important enough to Gabriel, he would tell me."

"But that is my point. It is important and you should know, but the man is too blasted stubborn—or noble—to tell you."

"It's all right. Someone he loved was hurt and it compelled him to start rescuing women. I really don't need to know more than that." She laid her hand over Penelope's.

"Very well," Penelope said, defeated. "But what about you and Gabriel?"

"There is no me and Gabriel," Violet replied. "He doesn't have time for anyone in his life. At least not anyone he hasn't rescued."

"That's why he needs you," Penelope said, conviction making her voice seem to ring out in the small space. "Someone has to break through that wall. He does need a life of his own, desperately. No one interested him until you. I can't bear to see him lose a chance at such much-deserved happiness. Or you, for that matter."

"But he's not a child, Penelope, nor someone to be led to such a decision," Violet answered.

"I don't think he's ever been a child," she replied softly. "We can leave, that might help."

"What, and have him worry about you?" Violet asked, shocked. "Of course not. That's not an option for him."

"It's not like we've been with him forever," Penelope told her. "I have been with him for nearly four years, but the others mostly come and go."

"Some of them are able to make lives for themselves, then?" That was hopeful, Violet thought.

"Oh yes, certainly. Gabriel will find employment for them or send them to contacts he has in other places, and more could set up on their own with a bit of nudging. Once they change addresses or use new names—he knows people who can help with that too—they are difficult to trace."

"Gabriel has always sufficiently convinced the men it is not worth their while to pursue these women. His position in society coupled with his wealth usually proves convincing. For the husbands and fathers of poorer men, money is usually enough; for those in society, the threat to ruin them socially usually does the trick."

"What happened this time?" Violet asked.

"The lord who wants our lady back has to be pretty deep in the pockets, because we believe that the extra guards Gabriel hired were bought off. The Belmont residence in London is set back from the street, so 'tis impossible that they knew nothing of how the vandal who threw a stone through our window was able to approach the house so closely. In addition, a few of the ladies had been out intending to take tea after a lecture, and two men approached them on the street with a knife and a signet ring. Both messages were the same: the unknown woman should give herself up."

"I can understand why you fled," Violet said with feeling. "How frightening. But you are safe now?" This was really the crux of the matter.

"We hope so, although we don't know for certain. But there have been no signs of further trouble since we arrived in Williamsburg. Except for the trouble that we have caused you." She squeezed Violet's hand.

"Really, Penelope, do not trouble yourself on that account." Violet was sincere. She was heart sore, but she liked this woman. "Gabriel had told me even before you came that he wasn't free. At first I thought perhaps he was married to one of you, then I realized that it was something about your group of women, that you had all been hurt in some deep and terrible way."

Perhaps sensing that Violet wasn't going to budge, Penelope let the subject go. "What I really came for was this." She withdrew her hand and reached for something beside her.

"This is for you," she said, pressing a large, fragrant bundle into Violet's hands.

"What is it?" Violet asked, feeling the silk

through the light covering. The scent of lavender wafted up from the tissue that wrapped it.

" 'Tis the dress you admired on Lady Margery that day we met you in Williamsburg. What better for a Violet than violet?"

"This is that beautiful violet dress? Oh, I couldn't take this," Violet said immediately.

"Of course you can. It's the latest fashion, from Paris before all hell broke loose there with their revolution."

"But Lady Margery?"

"Has others, she assures me. She says she doesn't need so many formal gowns now that we are in America."

"It's too nice," Violet said.

"Nonsense," Penelope said. "You've done a very generous, gracious thing. We have little enough to thank you with, so please take this with our thanks."

With that, Violet knew she had to stop protesting. So she thanked Penelope again, and the two women parted.

Violet was taking a ride around the plantation early the next morning. Her parents would be home soon, and she didn't want them to think she had neglected the business. The peaches needed harvesting and the grapes would be ready soon. She would speak to Will later. She needed to breach the reserve that had grown up between them after Yorktown. Will was a reasonable man, and Betsy should have helped convince him that the idea of Gabriel and a brothel was a foolish one.

But she soon ran into Gabriel, who had crossed from Willow Oaks into Oak Grove's territory. He probably wasn't aware of it. With a wave at her, he reined in his horse next to hers.

" 'Tis a beautiful morning," he greeted her. "With the scent of flowers in the air, and the bounty your family has cultivated with nature's help, Oak Grove proves every statement William Byrd made in his writings about America as Eden, don't you think?"

"Aye," she said, looking around at the dew-laden grass and trees. The August sun had not yet burned off the night's moisture, and birds cheeped in the trees as they woke and began to move about. For the first time, Violet had doubts about her plans.

Seen through Gabriel's eyes, her family's lands were indeed beautiful. She knew she hadn't fully appreciated them, because for so long she'd had other vistas in her mind's eye. Just now she could not summon up a mental picture of London that she usually conjured with longing. She only saw Gabriel, his coat off, his sleeves rolled up as he was now, surveying a land blossoming with flowers and trees, satisfaction in the relaxed stance of his body and his ready smile.

Silence fell between them. Gabriel didn't want to say anything to break the moment of fragile accord. Violet looked at him after a minute. "You said in Yorktown that you would explain if I ever came to you to ask. Well, I'm here now and I'm asking. Will you tell me? All the truth?"

What a magnificently brave woman she was, Gabriel thought in admiration. Not one society woman of his acquaintance had ever thought to disbelieve the rumors. Truth be told, he'd found to his horror that it titillated a lot of them. That was one of the many reasons he'd stopped going to society events unless he was there to observe a situation in which he might take a hand to rescue someone.

"Yes, of course I will tell you," he said, he who'd never told anyone the full story, not even Penelope. "Why don't we sit?" They dismounted and put the horse's reins over tree limbs at one edge of the orchard, and the animals began to graze.

They found a fallen tree to sit on. Violet looked at Gabriel expectantly, and he took a deep breath.

"I had one older sister, Sarah. My mother had miscarried several times after Sarah was born, and there was a stillborn child. She had given up hope when she began to carry me. Her term was difficult and ultimately, and she died of childbirth fever shortly after I was born. Sarah was eight years older than I. She was my mother, my best friend, my playmate, everything. Our father the Duke saw my mother's death every time he looked at me. He was never warm.

"He died when I was nine, and control of the fortune passed to Sarah until she should marry or I came of age. She was seventeen then, but persuaded the trustees that she need not marry and risk the fortune—and that seemed to be all they cared about.

"I went up to Oxford at fourteen. Sarah married soon after but she would never tell me whether the trustees had changed their minds or whether she had fallen in love with the Marquis of Wingate. It didn't matter to me—she was certainly entitled to marry and be happy, and I didn't care about the money." Gabriel pulled a violet from the plants growing in the grass around the old tree.

"He seemed pleasant enough at the wedding but there was something about him I didn't like. He seemed cold to me, and there was a hint of some underlying coldness or contempt toward Sarah. But what did I know? I was a boy and Sarah revealed nothing to me.

"I came home for a visit the next year, and did not notice anything amiss, although Wingate was never about and Sarah never mentioned him. Aristocratic marriages are often for convenience and mutual advantage; my parents' love for each other was somewhat unusual, I learned." He offered the violet to Violet, but she shook her head, intent on his story.

"I only learned what it was when I came home for a visit after hearing that Sarah was carrying Wingate's child. Because of our mother's troubles, I knew she would be afraid. So I came down from Oxford to be with her when her time came." He continued to pick violets from around them, slowly and methodically, creating a small bouquet. He was scarcely aware of what he was doing, so lost was he again in those dark days.

"What I found shocked me. Sarah was in childbirth, and had been for far too long. She was too weak to get the babe out, and too hurt even if the child had not been so large for her. I also learned that she was covered in bruises, and that Wingate had been beating her since their marriage."

"My God, why did she stay with him?" Violet asked, appalled.

"I asked myself that more times than I could count. I was only thirteen, I was naive, a child. I just assumed that the match was a good one. Sarah never told me any differently.

"It turned out that Wingate had gotten Sarah alone at a society event and compromised her. To avoid having her reputation smeared through the mud of tattletale journals, to avoid tainting the family name, she agreed to marry him. Of course that was his plan all along." He crushed the violet he had just plucked, forgetting to transfer it to the other hand.

"And once he had her, and control of the funds and lands that were not entailed to me, he used them, spent lavishly, and abused poor Sarah.

"The doctor told me that she would have had a difficult delivery anyway. But she was so weakened by the beatings, and had possibly suffered some internal damage, he said that the child's health was compromised along with her own.

"I wanted to kill him but Sarah forbade me," he said almost matter-of-factly, while a chill ran down Violet's spine. She clasped her hands around her knees, resting her head on them, looking at Gabriel sideways. Now she saw for the first time the source of his hidden sorrow. He was lost in his history. She wondered if he even knew the violets were growing limp in his strong grasp.

"She didn't want to be responsible for my having to go to the continent in exile," Gabriel continued. "All she asked was that other women not suffer what she had. I swore that oath rather than the one I wanted—which was to kill Wingate. And she made me promise not to kill him, although that was perhaps the hardest promise I ever kept.

"So instead, I became this odd sort of Robin Hood, providing a haven for women who had been abused in various ways—through physical violence like my sister, or others who were playthings for sexually sadistic men. Some suffered emotional abuse—their parents or husbands never touched them physically, but through their belittling words wore their confidence down and broke their spirits."

Gabriel paused. "It's been ten years, and the world never seems to make an end to victims." She put her hand over his, moved almost beyond words.

He handed her the violets, giving her a rueful glance. "These are rather bedraggled, no match for your beauty."

The gallantry was so typical of him, Violet thought. And all this time, all those years, he had been keeping this pain and anger to himself.

"And will you do this forever?" she asked, filled with sorrow that his burdens were so enormous. "Haven't you done enough already, for so many others?"

He gripped her hand so tightly she felt her bones shift slightly, but he was unaware of his own intensity. "It can never be enough," he said. "No woman should have to suffer what Sarah did. I won't let anyone else, knowingly. I can't."

"But when do you have a life of your own? You can't save the world, you know that, don't you?"

"Of course I know, intellectually. Emotionally, that's a different story. Sometimes I feel I can never stop. Who would help them if I don't?"

"I see." And she did, though it made her sad far beyond her years. If he could never stop, he would never have a life, never know any joy of his own.

"Do you? You are the first woman who has not experienced the same suffering they have who has ever made an effort to understand. I've never understood why."

"Others probably don't want to think it could ever happen to them."

"You really do amaze me, Violet, to understand so much when you are yourself so young." He looked at her next to him on the log, his gray eyes warm. "I want to thank you for being so kind. Would you consent to hear a concert with me in Williamsburg tomorrow night?"

Violet hesitated. "Why?"

"We can't be friends?" he asked.

"Do you really want to be my friend?"

"Do you really want me to answer that?" he returned.

"Yes."

"You are my friend, no matter what else may be between us." His eyes told her a different story about his feelings, and on the strength of what she saw there, she agreed to go.

As they rode home, Violet found she wasn't quite ready to give up on Gabriel. Not after what Penelope had said. Could Gabriel really be in love with her?

Then her hopes deflated. Even if he were, what good would it do? His will was so powerful, his hurt so deep. He'd see making love to her as a betrayal of his principles.

But he cared for her, it wasn't just words he

said to get rid of a pesky younger woman. She had felt the attraction between them, felt it even now, as she sat beside him on the log. She wanted to comfort him but she knew deep down in the feminine heart that had only recently woken to life in her, that he would not accept anything routine or pro forma. She would have to give him herself, and as he made her his, she would make him hers. She hoped.

TWENTY

O that the beautiful time of young love
Could remain green forever.
            —Johann C. F. von Schiller,
            The Song of the Bell, 1799

Gabriel and Violet walked back to Gabriel's rented home after the concert, enjoying the night air scented with jasmine and honeysuckle as they passed tidy gardens along Duke of Gloucester street. He offered to escort her to her mother's house, but she said she wasn't ready to go.

Knowing he was flirting with temptation, he brought her inside and poured her a glass of sherry. Their light talk gradually became more personal and intense.

"I have to ask you something, Gabriel, after our conversation yesterday. Did you come after me in Yorktown because you cared about me?"

"Violet, I. . . ." he said, his gaze troubled. Now he was in deep water.

"Or was it because I was another rescue project, another poor woman you didn't want to see in trouble?"

"Is that bad?"

"Not if I were just another woman in trouble. But I wasn't in trouble, Gabriel."

"You were going to be," he said firmly.

"I wasn't in trouble yet," she continued, "and I don't want to be one of your reclamation projects."

He continued to look at her, not understanding. "Do you think I see women as kittens to be scooped up before they climb a tree they can't get out of? That would be insulting to your sex, not to mention each and every woman I've ever helped."

"No, I didn't mean that. Your motives and your actions are honorable—almost too honorable, Gabriel." She reached up suddenly to touch his cheek. "You don't have a life of your own, my dear lord, and heaven knows you're entitled to one."

Had she been talking with Penelope? Or was her insight so strong that even at her tender age she could see him so clearly?

He turned his head to kiss her palm, knowing he was going under. He deliberately lightened his tone. "Ah, Violet, you undo me. You are so young and yet so . . ."

Beginning to feel on firmer ground, she smiled and ran her finger across his lips. "So beautiful? So fair?"

"So spoiled? So compliment-seeking? So shameless?" he returned in the same style, his voice vibrating across her finger.

"Yes, but you like it," she said teasingly.

"I like you," he said emphatically in a tone that suggested far more than friendship. He captured her finger, kissed it with his lips, then allowed the very tip of his tongue to give it an extra caress.

Violet felt that caress in an instantaneous line that ran from her lips down her arm, through her breasts and into her belly, where desire began to uncoil.

"Your eyes turn turquoise when . . ." he said softly, taking her hand in his and kissing the suddenly sensitive palm.

Violet closed her eyes and felt desire lick through her again with his kiss, followed by the gentle brush of his tongue in the centermost spot on her palm.

"When what . . ." she said languidly, having trouble making herself speak. She just wanted to feel his touch again.

"Open them first," he suggested. "So I can watch them change color."

"My eyes change color when what," she managed to say, feeling the melting sensation steal through her body. She swayed on her feet.

"Your eyes go turquoise when you feel desire," he said. "Come here." Keeping her hand in his, he walked into the study that had been converted into a downstairs bedroom after his household's arrival.

He walked over to a full-length oval looking glass, turning her to face the mirror, while he stood behind her. Lifting both hands up under her hair, he dislodged the pins, and curls began raining down upon her shoulders. He began to rub her hair, his fingers pulling gently and massaging her scalp. Violet arched back against him. She'd never felt anything half so sensual in all her life.

"Open them," he said again in a deep, richly compelling tone. She did. "See how blue they are now?"

Violet only saw Gabriel behind her, his broad shoulders extending beyond hers, watching as he brought one hand around to caress her neck and throat while with the other, he continued to massage her hair.

She leaned back, luxuriating in the sensation. She heard a little moan from Gabriel and deliberately swayed her hips back against him because she knew what had made him groan.

"Look at you," Gabriel's voice, dark and warm, came again. "You know what you are doing to me, don't you?"

She tilted her head back so it rested in his cradling palm. "No," she admitted.

"Open them," he said again. "Look."

Gabriel looked at her eyes in the mirror going slowly a deeper blue, while Violet was transfixed by the sight of his hand traveling ever so slowly down her throat, caressing her collarbone, then dipping lower to the neckline of her gown.

As she pressed back against him, feeling the hard ridge of his manhood through her thin skirts, he deliberately trailed his hand down to the curve of her breast.

"You're watching now too, aren't you?" he said against her ear.

"Yes," she whispered, wondering suddenly how much longer she'd be able to stand up. As if he'd heard her thoughts, Gabriel slid his hand from her hair, down her back and around her waist. His firm grip helped keep her upright.

His other hand slowly danced and retreated,

danced and retreated around the curve of her breast with such maddening deliberation that she thought she might scream if he didn't cup and cover it with his whole hand.

He chuckled softly against her ear. "Like that?" he asked mischievously.

"No. Yes. Oh, Gabriel," she said, arching her back out and up so that his hand would slide over her breast, and finally, he obliged.

"Now they're going dark," he said. Violet was so entranced by the sensation of Gabriel's hand covering her breast, where her nipple had instantly peaked into his palm, that she'd lost track of what he'd been talking about

"What's dark?" she murmured.

"Your eyes, sweetling. Now they're going dark with passion."

Violet looked in the mirror. "Yours, too."

He'd been watching her so intently he hadn't looked at himself. Now he looked up and met her eyes in the mirror. His hammered silver eyes had gone gray. He bent his head to kiss the side of her neck, but they both watched as his hand moved up and over and slid inside her bodice. The contact of warm flesh to warm flesh was too much for Violet. She swayed against Gabriel, feeling weak and wanton and wanting, all at the same time.

He kissed his way up her neck to her jaw, then angled his head to kiss her lips. She turned her head toward him, her lips seeking his blindly as her eyes closed, so awash was she in the powerful sensations that swept her body. His tongue entered her mouth, gently exploring, his hand moved to her other breast, and they stayed locked in that embrace for what seemed an enchanted eternity.

Her other nipple had already peaked before his hand arrived and she felt his smile against her mouth. He deepened the kiss, fondling the taut nub with his fingertips while the hand at her waist slid slowly down over her belly.

Violet pulled herself up on tiptoe by twining her arms around Gabriel's neck. She gasped and he moaned as his hand made contact with the secret place between her legs that had known his touch only once.

There was too much cloth covering her to suit her. She wanted him there again. Again he seemed to divine her thoughts because he allowed the hand at her breast to join the one at the junction of her thighs.

He turned her to face him, his hands lifting her skirts from front and back. He cupped her buttocks and lifted her up against him. She knew what pressed against her, and that he was hard for her, but now he had too much clothing in the way.

She tilted her head back. "Gabriel," she said on a breath.

"Do you want me to stop?" he asked, breathing hard, but his hands stilled on her bottom and he started to let her slide down from his body.

"No, oh no," she said, the air on her naked bottom feeling deliciously cool and naughty. "No, I want to touch you," she said, "but you have on too many clothes."

"Ah," he managed, understanding when she pressed against his rigid manhood, sliding herself towards him from the shelf of his palms holding her up.

"For that we'll need a bed." She nodded her understanding.

He laid her on the bed and rested one knee on the counterpane while he undid the buttons of his trousers. His manhood sprang free of its confines and the stab of desire that flared through Violet was more intense than anything she had ever known. At the same time she wondered how it would fit.

"Does it frighten you?" he asked gently.

"Mmm," she nodded an affirmative. "A . . . a bit."

Instead of coming down over her, he stretched out beside her and propped himself on one elbow.

"We'll take it slowly then. I can't guarantee his patience, but," and he guided her hand toward him, "he's certainly happy to get to know you."

Although she laughed, she touched him timidly. Gabriel reached down, wrapping her hand around him. She gasped. He was hard and soft at the same time, steel under velvet, and she watched his eyes close as she tentatively slid her hand up his length.

He bent over her until she saw only his handsome face above her, his silver eyes smoky and intense. "I won't hurt you, Violet, and you won't hurt me. Go ahead and explore."

As her hand made its first tentative exploration of his length, his size and hardness, and the various textures of him, he began to kiss her again. Deep kisses that rekindled the link between her body and her feminine core, that made her want to have him touch her. But he held himself back, letting her hands go where they would while he did nothing more than kiss her.

Finally she no longer felt afraid that something frightening or sudden would happen, and she missed his touch on her body.

"Touch me, Gabriel," she said when he ended a kiss to place his lips against her throat.

"Where?"

"Everywhere."

He laughed shakily. "Be careful what you wish for, darling. I've never wanted to touch a woman like I want to with you. I want you to feel my touch everywhere, my lips, my hands, on your body."

And while she still held him, hot against her palm, he brought one leg up between her thighs and lowered his mouth to her breasts.

A sudden madness seemed to seize both of them. His hair brushed her chest as he suckled one nipple, then the next, pushing her dress below her breasts fully to get better access to her. She tugged at his trousers.

He sat up, pulling her up with him and tugging the dress from her body and off over her head. She dragged his shirt off him and he lifted up to remove his trousers.

This time when he bore them back down to the bed, he was naked and so was she. He settled himself over her and she sighed with the unbridled rich luxury of feeling his warm firm flesh pressed against her from shoulder to leg.

He cupped his hands around both breasts and resumed kissing them. The suckling increased until every time he pulled a taut nipple against the roof of his mouth, the sensation went straight to the place between her legs. The need for his touch there grew until she opened her legs and he slid in between them to press his hardness against her softness.

He was nudging her legs apart when she felt him pressing for entrance against her portal. "You aren't afraid, are you?" he asked.

She shook her head but he felt her muscles tighten. He rolled to the side again, not completely off her, but enough to allow his hand to roam from her breasts to her thighs. This time when he took her with a deep kiss, his hand slid between her legs and he stroked deeply in rhythm with his tongue in her mouth. The excitement mounted quickly again and she forgot her fear as his skilled hands made her pliant and wanting again.

Parting her gently, he slid a long finger into her. Then, slowly, another. Having been touched by him like this before, it was a welcome intrusion and one that she accommodated with no pain.

"I need you to open wider so you can accept me, love," he said in a low voice. He gently pushed her thigh wider with one hand, beginning a deeper rhythm that soon had her writhing. When his mouth moved from hers to cover one breast, she arched up and into his hand and with a spasming glory, feeling pleasure rocket through her. She felt it everywhere, felt him everywhere, from her breast in his mouth, to her womb against his hand.

Before the glory had quite finished, he rolled, putting himself where his hand had just been and nipping gently at her breasts.

Since she was still contracting in pleasure so intense that it curled her toes, she hardly felt him push through her maidenhood and seat himself in her.

She only knew that his body was in hers, they were one, and when he flexed inside her, touching the entrance of her womb, it sent her higher until she cried out incoherently.

He thrust in her and the pleasure went up spiraling out of control again before she'd even recovered from the first. Her eyes opened wide, seeking him blindly and he watched her. She knew he was looking at her eyes as he lifted on his elbows until only his manhood was in her and then he too was crying out, her name on his lips as he began his own climax.

She scarcely noticed that he had left her until she felt the dampness on her belly. He clasped her closely, his manhood throbbing between them, his face buried in her hair.

He turned sideways to face her, their mouths an inch apart, his arm around her waist to keep her close to him. "Now I've seen your eyes blaze incandescent with passion," he said into her ear. "And I have never seen anything so beautiful."

Hours later, he made love to her again, deep in the night. He withdrew as before, but she was so involved in the wonder of his touch and the exquisite pleasure that she hardly noticed. She was weak and limp when they finished. Gabriel kissed her tenderly, then rolled with her to one side, fitting himself against her and nestling like spoons.

"Sleep," he soothed, brushing her damp hair off her forehead. She knew her hair brushed his chest and wondered if he was hot. Then suiting action to thought, even though she had not expressed it aloud, she felt him do up her hair swiftly in a long braid. She reached back sleepily. It was perfect, not too tight nor too loose.

"I hope we have girls," she murmured sleepily. "You do that so well, you can braid their hair at night." Then she drifted back to sleep, unaware that he had gone rigid at her side.

When Gabriel finally slept, nightmares plagued him, fear consuming him with memories of his sister's death in childbirth, and the story of his mother's death while giving birth to him. Gabriel had withdrawn from Violet both times, but that was never foolproof. And he had broken his cardinal rule.

No, that wasn't true, he thought, feeling the gentle rise and fall of her breath beside him. She wasn't one of those he had helped. Violet had never been abused; she never would. She had a loving family.

She also had a father who would kill him if he knew what had just happened to his unmarried daughter. As if guilt had suddenly entered the room with the thought, he found he could no longer sleep. Sliding his arms gently from around Violet's soft, warm flesh, he rose and grabbed his clothes. He lay her dress carefully over a chair back so it wouldn't be crumpled.

When he'd dressed and shaved in the other room, he came back in, intending to leave her a note about seeing her later at Oak Grove. The sight of her, asleep so trustingly in his bed, was almost more than he could take. They couldn't go backward, but how could they possibly go forward?

He groaned softly. "Oh hell. This should never have happened," he whispered into the silent room just lightening with dawn's pale hues.

Violet was no longer sleeping deeply, and she had heard him. She started up, furious, the bed sheet clutched to her throat. "How can you say that?" she demanded, without even a good morning.

"No, sweetling, that isn't what I meant," he said, putting out a hand toward her.

"Oh really," she said, hands clenched on the sheet. "What did you mean exactly?"

"Violet, I love you, but this isn't fair to you. There can't be the kind of love you need, you deserve. Not while I'm . . . not as long as I have the . . ."

"Your charity work?" He'd said he loved her, she thought dazedly, yet they were arguing.

"That isn't fair," he replied. "You know what they have suffered."

"Yes, I do, and I don't mean to be cruel to them, but Gabriel, when will you have a life of your own?"

"You sound like Penelope," he said.

"Well, she's right. You could spend your whole life like this and never get over the guilt of what happened to your sister. You couldn't have saved her. You know that, don't you? You were a boy. Just a boy."

Her anger had melted away with his declaration. She didn't even think he'd intended to say it. There was only love in her heart for Gabriel.

He loved her too, but it clearly wasn't going to solve anything.

Violet lifted her arms to Gabriel, fearing that she had already lost him. He stepped into her embrace, and as if it were the most natural thing in the world, began to kiss her.

His arms went around her neck, working his fingers into the braid he'd created last night, undoing it as deftly as he'd made it. As her hair cascaded around them both, Violet leaned into the kiss and gave him everything she could that didn't involve words, because words took them nowhere.

Violet let her kiss tell him of her love, her respect, her desire. In that kiss, there was joy and despair all mixed into one. Gabriel tasted of their lovemaking and the masculine scent that was his alone, even through the spicy bay rum he'd splashed on after shaving.

Gabriel lifted his head, looking down at her silently. She sat up but he made no move to pull her back into the kiss. In that moment she knew she had lost him. "You can't leave them, can you?" she asked sadly.

"Give me time, love," he said, stroking her hair. She had never heard him plead.

"I don't think time will make any difference. Goodbye, Gabriel," she said.

He turned away, finding his way down the steps by feel, because his eyes were touched with sudden moisture. The weight of his responsibilities pressed down upon him as never before.

What he'd seen in Violet's eyes had been love tempered with sorrow, but she saw him as a man. In the eyes of Penelope and her sisters in misfortune, there was absolute trust and acceptance, but to them, he was larger than life. He had become the powerful protector; he had saved women from his sister's fate. But he had also bound them to him, he realized.

It wasn't just that he wanted a life for himself now; it wasn't just that he wanted to love Violet. Penelope had been saying he needed a life for himself for years now. Between Violet's comments and Penelope's, he saw for the first time that some of them might never lead independent lives if they didn't get out from under the shelter of his wings.

As he walked down the street, he never saw the curtains twitch open, then back in place, in the house across the way. He was too preoccupied to notice, too tired and heart-sore to maintain his usual level of alertness. Besides, he had no reason to think there was a threat here, and if there were one, it would never occur to him that it could be directed at Violet.

So he strode on, oblivious, while the pink streaks in the sky faded like hope before the reality of a relentless, burning sun.

TWENTY-ONE

. . . never doubt I love.
—William Shakespeare, *Hamlet*, 1601

Harry was astonished. They had retreated back here, him and Brick, while Dan and Nicko decided whether they could get the woman out of that barn they'd rigged up over at the Pearson plantation. It was a piece of damned bad luck. The house here had been jammed, but out there the very lack of neighbors made it impossible to approach the place without giving themselves away. The duke and those women of his were far too chary to let four strange men in their door.

Harry and Brick had kept up the watch at the Duke's house, just in case. That poker-faced manservant of his might be somebody to follow.

Instead, look what fate had given him. The Duke and the woman, Lady Margery, had come back from somewhere last night, just the two of them, right here in Williamsburg.

Even better from his point of view, they'd spent the night here, and Belmont had left early. Albie wasn't going to like the fact that his woman and Belmont had spent the night together, but Albie didn't necessarily have to know that. The Duke had left early, which left the woman alone. Dan and Nicko were at the tavern, so it was just him and Brick.

There was no point double-crossing Brick, not when he was right here. If the big man had been out, Harry would have had a go at it alone, but Brick could be counted on to lift the struggling woman to get her into a carriage. He was a far sight stronger than Harry. So he'd split the bonus, Harry thought with a mental shrug. It was still more than the nothing they would have gotten had Dan and Nicko found her first.

Brick had taken night watch, so he was now snoring in the back room while Harry watched the house.

"Brick," he called softly, knowing the big man would wake without much difficulty. "The bird has landed in our very laps, lad. We're going to get her ourselves and head back to London without our quality friends."

Brick was up and at his side in a minute. "I'll go get a closed carriage," he said, for once not needing to be told what to do.

"That's it. Hurry though, because we don't know how long she'll be in there."

"I'll hurry," Brick promised, heading back the way he had come, in order to exit by the back door.

Staring numbly at Rose Walters, all Gabriel could think was, *not again*. Violet was gone. She'd disappeared. Again? He could scarcely think of anything else. After everything that had happened, she had gone ahead again with her foolish scheme. Damn it, he wouldn't go after her again.

"Gabriel, no, wait, you don't understand," Rose Walters said. "I don't think she's gone off again in boys' clothes. For one thing, I've found her clothes, the boys' clothes she used to wear."

It felt like his heart had suddenly plummeted to his heels, leaving him hollow inside. "Did she have more than one set?" he asked.

"Not that I know of. They were her brothers' old clothes that she had rescued and stuffed in a trunk."

"I took her to a concert at the Capitol last night. She was going to stay at her mother's old house." Had she noticed he'd said "was going to"—since she hadn't?

"Yes, she often does that when she's in town," Rose said. Nothing seemed amiss in her expression.

"I was supposed to go back to my house. I didn't want to ride all the way out here late at night and leave Violet alone in town. If Violet hadn't decided to stay in town, I would have escorted her back here." And God help him, he blushed.

If Rose Walters noticed, she said nothing.

"When did you come back?" Rose asked.

"This morning." Violet had been in his bed at dawn, curled up like a cat after cream. Then he'd uttered a stupid sentence, and things had blown up between them again. In a sense, he wasn't that surprised that she'd disappeared; the words they'd exchanged had seemed so final.

He didn't know if Violet had risen immediately or if she'd taken her time. The original plan—to the extent that either of them were thinking last night—had been for her to stop by her mother's store later and do some errands in Williamsburg. Maximilian wasn't home, and the housekeeper wasn't due until tomorrow, so he had no reservations about her falling asleep again and waking up later to find herself in an awkward situation.

But now night had fallen and Rose had come to the barn in person.

"You are really worried, then?" he asked. "She wouldn't have stayed over for another night?"

"Normally, no, I would not be concerned. But her parents have arrived in Williamsburg. Lily wanted to check on some things at the shop, and Adam and Peter had ordered some items in Williamsburg to be ready upon their return."

"They didn't know Violet was going to be there, so they didn't expect to see her. But when we sent word back that Violet was in town, and they couldn't find her, they sent another message back. It was brought to me. Of course, she wasn't there and once I went over to Oak Grove myself, and found that she wasn't there either, I began to be concerned myself."

"I can guess what happened next. Will Evans rode for Williamsburg."

Rose, normally so composed, twisted her hands together, giving him an apologetic glance. "If I'd had any idea that Violet wouldn't be there, believe me, I would have gone over myself, but. . . ."

"No, no, 'tis all right, Rose," he said. "Please come in. This is all my fault. Fortunately for me, I am not going to have time to visit Violet's father because I have to find out what happened to her."

He looked directly at her. "I do know where

she was until this morning. She was with me last night."

The look he received in return was distinctly cool. "I thought as much. What happened? Did you make up and then quarrel again? I thought you said you were not free."

"I won't excuse my behavior, madam, but neither will I explain it," he said, drawing on all the gravity he could muster. Rose Walters might be her aunt, but Violet was still owed her dignity and her privacy. He would not breach it, even to her aunt.

"Suffice it to say that as far as I know running away to England dressed as a boy was not a factor in her thinking. Not when I left." He did not say they had quarreled; but suddenly Gabriel worried that Violet had gone off again on her scheme after what had passed between them. He'd told her that he loved her, but he had not been able just then to offer her a future.

"And when did you leave her?" she asked, her voice icy.

"This morning," he admitted, his gaze unblinking.

"That's how you know she wasn't planning on running away. Things had reached a satisfactory stage? . . ." she asked, letting the unfinished thought linger unpleasantly in the air.

He ignored the insinuation. "I must return to Williamsburg at once. I will search my house, because I believe that is the last place she would have been found." His grim expression alerted her to the possibility of something more serious than a lover's spat because she reached for his arm, suddenly seeking reassurance.

"What is it? You fear something has happened to her?" she asked.

"Unfortunately, I do. Someone was after one of the women in my household. I believe Violet told you that, did she not? And that this was the reason they all came here so suddenly."

"Yes, she did tell me that," Rose admitted.

"Her sudden disappearance, I fear, could be an indication that the pursuer is still after that woman, and may have mistaken Violet for her. Something bothered me last night. Let me fetch someone. Will you wait a moment, please?" He asked her courteously to sit on a bench just inside the door while he went down the hallway.

A few moments later, a tall blonde woman came down the hallway after Gabriel.

"Lady Penelope, when was the last time you saw Violet?" he asked.

"The day before yesterday. I gave her a present from us."

"What was the gift?" Gabriel asked in the cool, clipped tones of the English aristocracy that Rose hadn't heard in years. He sounded every inch a peer of the realm.

Penelope looked surprised but obligingly supplied a description of the dress. "You are taller than Violet. You haven't been here long enough to have the dress made. So it belonged to one of you?" Penelope nodded.

"Then to whom does the violet-colored dress belong?" he asked.

"Why is that important?" Penelope asked. " 'Tis what we all agreed to give to Violet."

"Yes, but whose was it?" Gabriel continued implacably.

Rose was puzzled and opened her mouth to speak, but Gabriel turned to her with a brief gesture while waiting for the other woman to reply.

" 'Twas Lady Margery's dress. Oh, Gabriel, no, do you think . . . ?" Penelope said, leaving her sentence unfinished as she gazed at Gabriel with stricken eyes.

"I do," he said, then turned to Rose. "Violet was wearing Lady Margery's dress last night," Gabriel said to Rose. "I thought there was something vaguely familiar about it, but I couldn't place it."

"But what is the significance?" Rose asked, wondering why both Gabriel and Penelope had gone so pale.

The tall blonde woman, Penelope, looked at Rose somberly. "We believe that Margery was the one being sought in London. We were attacked and our security was compromised. 'Tis why we came here."

"No!" Rose cried, her hand going to her mouth to contain a sob.

"Yes, I'm sorry, Rose," Gabriel said. "Do you think you can keep Adam Pearson away from me long enough so that I can get to Williamsburg?"

"Not once he hears this."

He inclined his head. "I understand that, and I won't hold you here. I just need time to get to my town house and search it. Violet's father can take the next ship if he wants, but I will not be hindered until I can determine what happened. And I do think I have a better chance of finding out than he. No disrespect intended, but the man has lived here for twenty years. I know present-day London far better than he."

"No, no, I understand what you're saying," Rose said. "This concerned your household long before it concerned our family. Adam Pearson will not be pleased that the two have mixed, however, and he will not be held off. However, he is not yet alarmed, just curious as to where his daughter is at the moment."

Her frank gaze met Gabriel's. "I can tell you that he will be alarmed as soon as she sees me, though. Even were I to lie about what I know— which I shall not do," she said, her expression resolute, "he is too insightful not to see my concern at once."

"You will not have to lie, madam," Gabriel said. "I need five minutes with Lady Margery, then I will ride to Williamsburg. I will send Maximilian to Yorktown now to find me a ship, and I promise you I will leave immediately."

"Adam may be on the next one after that," she said. "Your chances are better than his because you know now who the enemy is. Yes?"

He nodded in assent.

"And Adam has not been to London in ten or more years." Rose took Gabriel's hand. "One question more? Do you think she is alive?"

"Absolutely," he said, squeezing her hand in what he hoped was a reassuring manner.

"He wants her back alive," Penelope said.

Rose sent her an anguished look. "But Violet is not the woman sought, is she? Therefore she will be a great disappointment to this man . . . this whatever he is."

"Captor," Gabriel said. "Jailer."

"This is not relieving my mind, Gabriel," Rose said.

"I am sorry. I will retrieve Violet, my lady. You have my word and my life on it."

"You may be certain her father will see to that if you do not. Godspeed, my lord. You will need it." Rose clasped his hand briefly. Then drawing her shawl around her, she left, escorted by Malcolm and a servant who had waited out of view and out of earshot just beyond the converted barn.

"Slap and tickle?" a voice above her asked hopefully. Violet had dozed fitfully, the pain in her head from the fall she'd taken trying to get away from these two men still bothering her. Her arms, which had been wrenched behind her back, ached as well. She remembered they'd mistaken her for one of Gabriel's women and hadn't bothered to listen, so eager were they to get her to a ship. Then the big man, who was called Brick by his disgusting little companion, had gagged her so she couldn't scream in the carriage, although she'd been so dazed, she doubted she could have.

Now her mouth was free, and her hands, and she lay in a narrow bed. But the rising and falling motion told her what she'd already sensed while recovering consciousness. They were at sea, so what would be the point of escape? She didn't even know how much time had passed since they'd grabbed her as she stepped out of Gabriel's town house in Williamsburg that morning.

At least she had all her clothes on. So far, at any rate, although the big, beefy man seemed interested in raping her. Violet tried not to show her fear.

"No slapping," the man called Horrid said. This man wasn't as big as the other one, but he seemed to have the only brains between the pair of them, and he'd said nothing was to happen to her. An unlikely savior, but she would take what she could get.

"Tickle all right then?"

"No, Brick, you have to leave 'er alone."

"Why?" the big man asked, a frown knitting his brow.

"Don't you remember our orders? We're to leave Lady Margery alone. Alone means we don't hurt her. No slapping unless we have to keep her in line and no swiving her. None at all."

Brick's face fell. "No fun?"

"Didn't you have wenches in that town?" Harry demanded.

"Yah, but that was a week ago."

"So? This trip will take six weeks, five if the tail-winds are good. It could be two months. You find a sailor who wants some company or you go be alone with your right hand."

Violet was horrified, although she supposed she should be grateful that she was off limits. To Brick anyway, not that she trusted the scarred-face man much either. But the instruction to go find a sailor? That was sodomy.

He must have noticed the revulsion on her face. "Oh, look," Harry said, "we're offending her ladyship. We'll leave you to your delicate thoughts then, my lady. Have you forgotten Lord Albie so quickly? From what Nicko and Dan said, you're not no stranger to some of this. You wouldn't know about sailors and buggery, I s'pose. But His Lordship has some peculiar tastes, too, I hear."

"I'm not Lady Margery," Violet said once again. Brick might be brutal, but he was more gullible than the one called Horrid.

Brick looked confused, but Harry just snorted. "And I am? You never told them who you were in London, from what I hear. Never told them you were the one Lord Albie was looking for. Clever, that, but it didn't help in the end. His Lordship is mighty particular about getting his property back."

"I am not Lady Margery, I am Violet Pearson of Oak Grove plantation," Violet protested again but they had heard it before and didn't believe it any more now than they had before.

"And we got 'er without Dan and Nicko," Brick gloated, as if she hadn't spoken.

"That bonus should be all ours, right and tight," Harry agreed. "Even if we gotta give some to the captain for leaving without Dan and Nicko. Now let's leave her ladyship in peace 'til her dinner, since she don't seem to like our company."

"Our cabin's not as nice as 'ers," Brick whined.

"That's because she's got Dan and Nicko's cabin. We still got the same one we had on the way over."

"Why didn't we get the good one? Look what we got. Dan and Nicko didn't pinch 'er, and we did."

"You gonna complain again?" Harry said threateningly. "You must powerful like your ears boxed."

Brick clapped his meaty hands over his ears and fled. Harry gave Violet a mocking bow. "Your Ladyship," he said, and closed the cabin door. She heard the exterior bolt slide home and despair settled over her again.

She didn't know what would be more horrible—to have those hired dogs assault her, or to endure what sounded like horrible perversions from this Lord Albie. Now she knew why Gabriel had said there were things he wouldn't repeat. She couldn't believe that this type of thing was precisely what some of the women he'd taken in had endured. Her esteem for him rose a hundredfold, even as her spirits sank lower. She'd thought she'd known and understood, but she realized for the first time that she knew nothing at all of the ways of men who were so depraved, so hateful.

No one knew where she was. How long would it be before someone missed her? With her past rash actions of this summer, her family would probably think she had just run away again. If they tried to look for her as a boy buying passage on a ship from Yorktown as her last escapade had been, they'd never find her. Or they would waste who knew how much time looking for her.

It could be worse, of course. Far worse. Those horrible men could be attacking her now. Instead, she was being saved for this Lord Albie. But the more time passed, the more likely someone was to rescue her. If only she knew how long it would be until someone missed her and investigated.

TWENTY-TWO

Do not put such unlimited power into the hands of the husbands. Remember all men would be tyrants if they could.
—Abigail Adams, *Letter to John Adams*, 1776

Penelope had disappeared while he said his brief goodbye to Rose. Now she reappeared in the hallway, indicating to Gabriel with nothing more than a nod that someone waited for him in the makeshift sitting room that he would have offered to Violet's aunt had she not been so concerned.

"Your Grace, I . . . I have to speak with you," Margery said as he came through the door. He motioned for her to sit down on the divan, although he remained standing. He was too tense to sit.

"I am sorry, so sorry." She was weeping. Most of them didn't weep, because they'd been beaten for it. It made him ill to see it, because it reminded him of what they had gone through.

"Shh, it's all right," he said. "No one can hurt you here. You have nothing to apologize for."

"Oh, but I do. I knew. I knew they were after me."

He'd rested an arm on a standing desk that held the plans to the property he was purchasing in Charleston, but now he turned to face her. "What do you mean?"

"That signet ring. In London. When Athena drew the sketch. I . . . I recognized it."

"Everyone looked at it. No one recognized it. I had decided the sketch must have been inaccurate, despite Athena's amazing ability to remember facts and images in her head. How did you know what it was?"

"It . . . it was made for me. It isn't a real signet, that's why no one could have recognized it or found it in *Debrett's Peerage*. He . . . the man who. . . ."

"You don't have to go into that," Gabriel said, interrupting. He wanted to know anything that related to Violet, but Margery did not have to retell what had happened to her. Sometimes just recounting their tales brought on nightmares.

"Very well." She cast him a grateful glance. "He invented a background for me. I was supposed to be a minor nobleman's widow, someone obscure enough that no one would investigate or really care. I lived quietly. He was married. He . . . he didn't flaunt me."

"Why didn't you come forward before?" Gabriel asked. He didn't care about her background; he never did. All he cared about was giving them the chance to make a new life. And keeping them safe. But now someone else was in danger, someone he loved.

"I was afraid," Margery confessed with her head bowed in shame.

"This is why we must all join together, and remain together," he said, willing her to look up at him.

"I . . . I know. But I was afraid," she said again.

"Your actions—or failure to act have endangered someone else. I can understand your fear, but. . . ."

"Do you?" she asked, bitterness creeping into her voice. "How can you? You are of the very sex that hurt me."

"I do not belittle your experience, but all men are not beasts," Gabriel said gently.

"So you say," she retorted. "My experience has been otherwise. But even though you are generous, you don't know what we experience. You can't. So you can't know what it is to be afraid, not like I do."

He inclined his head in acknowledgment. "I could tell you about my sister, but that still leaves me of the same gender as your abuser. And that is something that can never change. But I won't argue that with you," he said. "I've neither the time nor the inclination at present. I must find Violet."

Gabriel went to stand before Margery, who huddled on the couch. He bent his knees until his eyes were level with hers, so as not to loom over her. "History cannot be changed. The only thing that matters is what we do now. From this moment on and in the future. Do you understand that?"

She looked away. "Look at me," he said softly. "Did you give her that dress knowing that it would be identified as yours? Hoping that if these men came after you, that they would be diverted by the physical similarity with Violet and mistake her for you?"

Her gaze avoided his, dropped to the floor. He put his hand out, gently, under her chin, turning her face to his.

"Did you think that giving Violet your dress might make them mistake her for you?"

"I did," she said, fresh tears flowing down her face. "I wanted to give her something for being nice to us, that part was true. She also admired that dress when she met us that day on the street. But . . . it was Lord Albie's favorite. I didn't think anything would happen to her," she cried, "you must believe that."

"What did you think would happen?" If she'd known him better, she would have realized how furious he was, but he'd long ago trained himself not to show such obvious signs of emotion. All she heard was his quiet voice, felt his hand on her chin.

He dropped it now and stood up. That was a signal, too, another one she didn't realize meant she was in serious trouble. "What did you think would happen, Margery?" he asked, more steel in his voice.

"I didn't think anything would happen. I didn't know they were here, none of us did. But now that you are here with us again, I thought if anyone went after her, you were . . . are her friend, that you would be around to help her, to rescue her."

"Rescue her from what?" he asked, foreboding swelling in him like a rising tide.

"From being taken back there . . . to . . . to him."

"That's what they want?"

"I'm certain that's what they've been told to do," she said, sounding very sure of herself for the first time.

"How do you know that?" Gabriel asked.

"The message with the ring, and with the rock . . . it was to tell me to go back to him, that he would never let me go. And he hasn't . . . so you see now, don't you?" she asked pleadingly.

"Margery," Gabriel began. "Did you think we would ever let you go if you wanted to stay?"

"I didn't know. I. . . ."

"You didn't give us a chance. You didn't trust us to keep you safe, to tell us what kind of help you needed." He clenched his fists at his sides. Thinking of Violet with them was a roiling pain in his gut that threatened to make him ill.

Still he tried to speak gently. He knew she had suffered much, and that trust was almost impossible in her circumstances, with her history. But had she learned nothing from the women in his household? Usually just knowing that others had survived similar situations, and exchanging their stories comforted them, gave them strength.

"I was frightened," she said again.

"I understand that. But by not coming forward, you put everyone's safety in jeopardy."

"I'm sorry, Your Grace."

For once, he didn't care that she used his title. He hardly noticed, in fact. "So you think he wants you back, that is all?"

"Yes."

"Where will they be taking her?"

"The house I had in London was in St. John's Wood."

"What do you think he'll do when he discovers that Violet is not you?" he asked, his face grim.

"I . . . I don't know."

"Will he kill her?"

Her hand flew to her mouth, shocked. "Oh no, no. I don't think he would do that."

"Won't he be angry about the switch?"

"He'll be angrier at the men for making the mistake."

"Will he hurt her?" Gabriel asked, his mind racing. How fast he could get to London, how far behind them would he be? Could he catch them at sea with a fast ship and fair following winds?

Margery cringed at the word "hurt," then reached for his hand. He looked down at her, too preoccupied now to worry about towering over her. She rose.

"Your Grace, I . . . this is hard to say, but. . . ."

"Say it, Margery," he said, disengaging his hand. "I won't hurt you. You know that much at least, I hope."

"Yes. Yes, I'm sorry. The reason I'm so certain that he won't be angry is that he . . . he may be glad to have her."

"What do you mean?" Gabriel wondered how much worse this could get, when every fresh revelation was like a body blow.

"He may see her as . . . as another me. Someone who doesn't know him, doesn't fear him. In the beginning, he was quite charming. One of the things he liked most about me was that I was a virgin. Violet is even younger and innocent."

Gabriel didn't tell her otherwise. At least he'd

done all he could to make certain Violet wouldn't become *enceinte* from their time together. He didn't know how it would play with Albie. If he thought her a virgin, as Margery had been, perhaps he would take his time with her, pretend to court her, not hurt her. He might still have time to get to her.

On the other hand, if Violet was feeling defiant, as she was likely to, things could go very badly for her.

"Your Grace," Margery said, rising to her feet to face him. "I . . . I can come with you. I know his moods better than anyone." He looked at her, realizing that she was terrified, and that her offer was an act of great courage. It followed her exceptionally poor judgment, but it had cost her dearly to say what she had.

He patted her hand, squeezing it briefly. Now that he knew the situation, he had a tremendous desire to be away. "Thank you. I don't want you to come with me, Margery. You are better off, and safer, here."

"You'll still allow me to remain?" she asked, her expression heartbreaking.

"Yes," he said, although it cost him to speak gently. "I would be much angrier if I thought you had thrown Violet to the wolves deliberately."

The fear roaring in his blood filled him with a sense of terrible urgency. "You made several errors in judgment, but I do not believe you acted maliciously."

"I don't think I should stay. Everyone will hate me now," Margery said, her handkerchief damp from wiping tears from her eyes.

"That is up to you. Nothing you've said to me

need go farther than this room. Except to tell Penelope and Maximilian, who need to know the true situation since I am leaving to go after Violet. They will be in charge, as always. But other than that, there is no one who needs to know anything other than what you choose to tell them."

"You are too kind, Your Grace. I will tell them, anyway. I've kept silent for far too long." He agreed, but knew that it had to be her decision.

Now that he knew everything, much of the anger had drained out of him. Fear rushed in to take its place. "That's enough of the 'Your Grace,' Margery. I am just Gabriel."

"Godspeed, sir," she said. "Is there anything else I can do?"

"I would certainly welcome your prayers, and those of everyone here." And looking into her face, he saw that she knew he was deadly serious.

"Of course, I . . . we will," she said. "We will all pray."

He touched the top of her head briefly. "It will be all right, Margery. I know you didn't mean harm to come to her, or I would tell you to leave. But trust is essential. In me, in the other women, in Max. We will help you, but you can never be truly free until you are able to trust again."

"I know," she said sadly. He left the room, running as he neared the door. He had so little time.

When Penelope walked in, Gabriel was frantically writing instructions for Maximilian, who was due back tomorrow.

"Pen," he said, sensing her entrance into the room, "should I just let her father go after her?"

Penelope instantly knew the source of his frustration. He was in love with the girl and wanted to go after her, but his long commitment to them meant he felt he would be abandoning them when he left.

"Do not wait another minute, my friend," Penelope said. "She needs you now more than we do. And you should be the one to find her, rather than her father."

"Don't you think they will just release her when they realize she is not the one they were sent to find? Perhaps even before the ship sails?" He wanted reassurance that the delay in finding out what had really happened to her would not be harmful. Penelope knew she had to sound more assured than she really felt. She was cold inside with fear for Violet; she could not even imagine how Gabriel must feel, with the woman he loved having fallen into the hands of ruffians.

"They may not believe her, you know. She fits the general description of Margery. Knowing the nature of Albie's obsession, I am certain they are under strict orders not to touch her and to deliver her safely to him."

Penelope peered up into Gabriel's face. "You know all this, Gabriel. You know every delay is dangerous and they already have a head start."

"But how can I assure your safety here now that you have just arrived?"

"The only one they were after was Lady Margery. This America looks vast and wild but not, I think, unsafe. Not in the way London was. You are known here, and respected."

"I was until the ship arrived," he said matter-of-factly. Penelope knew he wasn't angry or bitter;

Gabriel had long since ceased to care what the world thought of him.

"What do you mean? What have we done?" she asked with a sinking heart.

"Oh, not you, my dear. None of this is your fault," he said, giving her a reassuring hug. "It was the damned gossip-mongers on board that have spread the 'Belmont's Brothel' stories. Americans are more open-minded than our countrymen, but there is a limit to tolerance."

" 'Man is born free, yet everywhere he is in chains,' " she murmured softly. "The chains of old attitudes and expectations."

"You sound like Athena, my dear, spouting Rousseau," Gabriel said in a deliberately light tone.

"Don't change the subject on me, Gabriel. The only threat I know about has been removed. You must go after her at once."

"What about her parents?"

"I'm sure her aunt will explain."

"He'll think me a coward for not being here to face him."

"When he knows you've gone to rescue his daughter? I think not."

The last time Gabriel opened the door that evening he regretted it for days to come. A tall dark-haired man in his early fifties who could only be Violet's father stood there, along with a blond man some ten years younger. Gabriel had no time to notice how much Violet's brother Peter Pearson resembled his uncle, before the older man clipped off two words covered with frost.

"Gabriel Isling?"

"Yes," Gabriel said, aware that Pen was coming up behind him at the sound of the knock. It distracted him just enough that he didn't see the blow coming. It connected solidly with his stomach and knocked him backward into Penelope, who caught and counterbalanced him.

"Wait, please," she cried. "You must be Violet's father and uncle."

"We are," said the blond man. He gave a crooked smile and nodded in Adam Pearson's direction. "We are apparently here to kill him, although I favored getting the story out of him first."

"No one is going to kill the Duke of Belmont." Penelope's smile was strained, but Gabriel knew her well enough to realize that she would continue to stand between him and them until someone knocked her out of their way. No one had ever broken Penelope's spirit.

"Please don't," she said. "Not only does he love Violet, but he knows who has her and he is to leave within the hour to seek a ship."

"A ship? Who has her, damn it, and where are they taking her?" Pearson growled, reaching for Gabriel. Penelope stepped firmly between them, as Gabriel sagged against the wall, the pain in his stomach keeping him from standing fully upright.

Peter Walters laid a hand on Adam's arm to restrain him. "Let's listen to the lady, shall we, Adam? I believe she has the information we need."

"Is she a lady?" Adam asked. Gabriel thrust Penelope behind him and prepared to avenge the slight on Penelope's honor, when Peter Walters stepped in the middle and raised his hands.

"That's enough from everyone. I never thought I would play peacemaker when you were around, Adam, but there is a first time for everything, I suppose. My wife tells me that you are Lady Penelope Henley," he said, putting out a hand toward Penelope.

She shook it firmly, grateful that one of the two had a cool head. "Time is of the essence, gentlemen, so if we could explain quickly, then Gabriel will be on his way and. . . ."

"He's not going after my daughter," Adam said. "He's the reason why she's disappeared."

"Adam, please. We are all going," Peter said. He reached out his hand to Gabriel, who proffered his own a bit warily. "I am Peter Walters, the uncle in question, and my wife thinks very highly of you. Otherwise I would even now be helping my brother-in-law beat you into a bloody pulp. My apologies," he said, with a slight bow in Penelope's direction.

"Gabriel loves Violet," Penelope interjected hastily, "and in no way had anything to do with the trouble that befell her."

"That's not entirely true," Gabriel said, not about to hide behind any woman's skirts. "Someone followed a member of my household to America. Violet was taken by this lord's servants because of her physical resemblance to the woman in question. I was just about to leave for Yorktown."

Adam looked like he had a hundred more questions, but again Peter Walters intervened. "We will have plenty of time for explanations once we are at sea."

"Why should I allow you to go with me?" Gabriel asked, astonished. "I thought you wanted to kill me."

"I followed my own future wife when she was kidnapped and taken off to London by her own brother. I lost three days' time while I sulked in an alcoholic haze because we had broken off our relationship. I got to England well after her arrival." Penelope was looking rather wide-eyed at this evidence that not all households besides theirs were unconventional.

"You say Violet has been missing only since this morning?" Peter continued. Gabriel nodded. "Well, I have a ship at Tidewater Landing. You will have seen the dock at Willow Oaks. It is mine, it is fast, and I was in the American Navy during the war. I know a thing or two about boarding ships. My ship is ready to leave now, with or without you. We may even be able to catch the ship from Yorktown that she's probably aboard, because it is likely to be heavily laden with tobacco or other cargo. We can move faster."

He looked at Penelope, smiled briefly. "I had to woo my Rose back from the clutches of her family. Her brother took her to England, which was his right, but 'twas against her will. This situation is similar and yet different, because these are strangers who hold Violet. I see no need for a light touch or for caution. We will outsail the ship and reach Violet long before she ever sees England's shores."

He turned briskly to Adam. "All right, old

man," he said with a wink. "Let's see if you can keep up. Shall we go?"

Peter looked at Gabriel next. "Are you ready?"

"I am," Gabriel said. He turned to Penelope, but she'd anticipated him.

"Your signature is on the papers, and Max will be back tomorrow. Don't worry, Gabriel, you are going after the threat, it is no longer after us. We shall be fine."

She surveyed the three tense men, then smiled unexpectedly. "Happy hunting." Her expression turned distinctly fierce. "Don't leave any of them standing."

Then the three men were out in the dark night, and Gabriel was nothing but relieved. They would save hours by merely riding to the dock at Willow Oaks to board Peter's ship. It would save him a trip to Yorktown and the negotiations to find a ship that would sail immediately. If her uncle was a good skipper, they might actually have a chance of making up time to catch the ship.

"Don't think this is over between us, Belmont," Adam said.

"No, sir, I shall not," Gabriel said respectfully.

TWENTY-THREE

Over the mountains and over the waves,
Under the fountains and under the graves;
Under floods that are deepest, which Neptune
  obey,
Over rocks that are steepest, Love will find out
  the way.
  —Anonymous, *Love Will Find Out the Way*

Gabriel, Peter, and Adam were boarding the ship to set sail in the middle of the night. Although the crew was tired from the trip down from Boston, they'd had the afternoon and evening to rest while Adam and Peter had begun the search for Violet.

They were just about to cast off, when torchlights appeared on the gentle slope down to the river. An older woman with Rose Walters beside her was in the lead. "You weren't leaving without us, I hope," she called.

Adam was too angry still to rise to his wife's attempt at lightening the situation, although he was not angry with her. "We are about to cast off," he said.

"I only need you for a minute. Step down the

gangplank, please, Adam," she continued. Rose had been searching the deck in the sporadic light cast from barrels of burning pitch on deck, while the sailors were rigging the ship.

She waved when she saw Gabriel. He returned the wave uncertainly, wondering what and how much she had told the men.

Peter Walters clapped him on the back. "Come on, Belmont. You need to meet Violet's mother, my sister Lily. She doesn't have time to give you a thorough examination, but she will pump Rose for information while we are away."

"That's what I'm afraid of," Gabriel muttered, but followed Peter down the gangplank.

When she met Gabriel, Violet's mother held his hand for a long time, searching his face, although for what he did not know. "If what Rose says is true, my daughter may have met her match in you."

"You can't know that on such short acquaintance," Adam said.

"Yes, I can," Lily said. "I knew with you, before I even saw your face."

"I know," Adam said, the anger gone from his voice. "I knew at once, too. It just took me far too long to admit it."

"A common male failing," Rose Walters put in, smiling at Peter. Each couple drew apart and whispered to each other for a few moments. As they kissed each other goodbye, Gabriel turned to walk up the gangplank.

Rose Walters stepped away from her husband and put out her hand. "I know you will find her," she said. "Don't lose her once you have found her." The others hadn't heard, but Gabriel nodded.

While Peter looked on, Gabriel bent to kiss her hand. "Adam will come around," she whispered as he straightened. "I know you love my niece."

The goodbyes were said, and kisses exchanged. There were a few tears as well. Then the three men trudged up the gangplank to begin their journey.

On their third day out, they saw a ship ahead in the distance. The weather had been clear with freshening winds, so they had made excellent time. Peter Walters sent his men aloft to unfurl more rigging, seeking to catch every available puff of wind to propel the ship onward as fast as possible.

"How do you know 'tis the right ship?" Gabriel asked.

Peter looked at Gabriel "We dispatched someone to Yorktown as soon as we talked to Rose. He got back to the house just before we left. It's what Lily told Adam before we cast off. The captain is competent and a good sailor. However, he's greedy, which is no doubt why he got mixed up with these ruffians. We might even make do without a fight if you offer him money to switch sides."

"What, and deprive the Earl of Dalby of his desire to take someone's head off?" Gabriel said. "If it's not going to be mine, the heads of the men who took Violet would be the next best thing."

"Aye," Peter said. "I can see where that would

be a disappointment to him in his current mood."
He pretended to punch Gabriel in the shoulder.
"Mayhap that will still be you."

"I'm not going to fight my future father-in-law,"
Gabriel said, appalled.

"From what I heard Rose say, wasn't that the
issue between you, that you couldn't marry?" Peter said, his stance at the wheel wide-legged and
steady. He kept his voice low to avoid attracting
Adam's attention, for which Gabriel was grateful.
If looks could kill, he'd have been dead where he
stood a dozen times over.

"That was before Violet was taken and I realized
I couldn't live without her," Gabriel said.

To his amazement, Peter smiled. "Don't look
puzzled, Belmont. Didn't I say I'd spent three days
with a bottle in a stupor because Rose and I had
quarreled? When her brother took her, I had the
same epiphany. Whatever we thought stood in our
way was not nearly as important as what we had
between us."

While Gabriel stood pondering those words, Peter changed the subject. "I need to see to the sails
if we are going to catch up to the *Sea Maid*. Take
a hand at the wheel." Then he was off, as nim-
ble-footed as any of his men.

That night at dinner, Peter explained that although they had made good time, they had at
least another day to sail before they could catch
the ship.

"Won't they suspect something if we come
alongside them?" Gabriel asked.

"No, 'tis common for ships that pass close to
one another to communicate, trade goods, ask

about spare parts, and the like. They'll have no idea of our intentions," Peter said confidently.

He thought he saw a skeptical look on Adam Pearson's face, but the older man said nothing. He was still tough and fit, and his energy never seemed to flag. He'd unbent somewhat around Gabriel but not to the point of warmth. Nor would he, Gabriel realized, until they had retrieved his daughter safely, and until Violet told him how matters stood between her and Gabriel.

Gabriel wondered himself how matters would stand when he saw her, and his thoughts kept him awake at night. He slept in the first mate's cabin that had been given to him, while Peter and Adam shared the captain's cabin. Adam had said the captain's cabin should go to Gabriel since he ranked higher in the nobility, but Gabriel had cut that short immediately, refusing to stand on ceremony. It had increased his stock with Peter, he could tell, but Gabriel couldn't read Adam's expression, with those aquamarine eyes so uncannily like his daughter's.

The next day dawned cloudy but the wind picked up, swirling whitecaps into the sea. "I don't like the weather," Peter said over breakfast, running his hand through tawny-colored hair that had yet to turn gray. They had come visibly closer to the ship they were following, close enough that the boy in the lookout could identify the ship from the description they'd had.

"Won't a storm make it easier to come up beside them?" Adam asked.

"This plan, such as it is, never depended on

stealth," Peter replied. "We were going to board, trade, ask some questions, and if all else fails through subtlety, made an outright offer to pay more than those louts were given to pay for Violet's passage."

"Then what is the trouble?" Gabriel asked.

"For one, the wind may blow us off course. The weather, if it turns to a storm, may make it difficult to come alongside and board. It would be highly unusual to attempt to do so in bad weather, because as much as sailors like company when they've been at sea for a while, no one is going to risk life and limb for a bit of barter."

"Then let's get the bloody hell there before the weather turns," Adam said, stalking from the cabin.

"He really is a great fellow," Peter observed as Gabriel finished the last of his coffee. "But she's his only daughter and. . . ."

"I understand how he feels," Gabriel said.

"With all due respect," Peter said, an edge to his voice that Gabriel hadn't heard before, "you do not."

Gabriel set his mug down. "I love her, Walters," he said. "I led her into danger, albeit unknowingly, and the last words that passed between us were not of love, but farewell. Of course Pearson loves her and is distraught. But I'm the man that put her in that position. From what you've told me, I know you understand that, since it happened with your Rose."

"Aye, I do. You're right. Sorry," and with that, Peter turned wearily away, back to the weather records of past voyages his captains had made before him.

* * *

The wind blew stronger and the sky remained gray, but the rain seemed no more imminent than it had that morning. Adam's patience was clearly on a short, fraying string, and even Peter began to treat him carefully.

"I'm going to make the run up to the ship now," Peter told them. "It's near dusk, they won't see us clearly, but in case any of these men are on deck, I suggest Gabriel stay out of sight until we start to go across."

"You're not going anywhere," Adam said. "We need you to captain the ship."

"Oh no, you don't," Peter replied. "I didn't come on this venture just to turn the wheel. My first mate Josephus is quite capable of handling the wheel and the ship while we're over there."

Adam turned to him. Gabriel smiled thinly. "Don't bother to try. I'll be the third one over, but after that, I will take charge."

Both of the older men looked a bit taken aback. "I know whose men have her, and I know more about how they operate than you do," Gabriel continued relentlessly. "You're welcome to pummel anyone you like who deserves it, but if we can get her out without a fight, that's preferable."

"Agreed?" He gave them hard looks all around, and despite muttering from Adam, they finally consented.

In the end, getting aboard the ship wasn't difficult. Asking questions without arousing suspicions was. Gabriel didn't see any faces he recognized, as he had expected.

When the visit had been extended to its maximum possible limit—three men on a rescue mission hadn't thought to bring goods for bartering—Gabriel decided they had nothing to lose.

He pushed to the front of the group, standing next to Peter. "You have a female passenger," he said without preamble.

"We have nothing of the kind," Captain Travis, a blustery Yorkshireman, said.

"You can drop the pretence. How much were you paid?" Gabriel asked. "I'll double it."

The captain's eyes widened. "I carry naught but tobacco," he said.

"Don't try my patience," Gabriel said. Adam and Peter stood close beside him, and under the menacing glare of three pairs of eyes, Travis gave up.

"Triple it," the captain said, "and I'll consider it."

"Triple it," Gabriel said, "and fetch her."

"Now that I can't do, your lordship," Travis said, his manner changing now that he'd won an exorbitant price. He also appeared to recognize Gabriel's accent and air of authority, even though he was younger than the other men present.

"Why not?" Gabriel asked in an even voice.

"The two men that brought her on board don't let her out."

"What?" This from Adam in an outraged voice.

"You must be her father," the captain said. "You've got the same looks. They aren't mistreating her. Where is there to go on a ship?"

"Where do they sleep?" Adam continued in the same tight, dangerous voice.

"Not with her, oh no, sir," he said, turning to the angry father. "They stay strictly away from her

My cook brings her dinner, and the cabin boy reg'larly empties the chamber pot."

He leaned toward them, almost confiding in his manner. "I let her up on deck at night, sirs. 'Tis cruel keeping her locked up all day. She's no trouble, not a little thing like her."

"Where are they now?" Gabriel asked.

"They're in their cabin. They'll be first in line at suppertime, leastways the big one will."

"Then fetch her now," Gabriel said.

"I can't do that, your lordship."

"What do you mean? You must have the key if you let her out at night," Gabriel said, beginning to feel as frustrated as Adam.

"There's a bar over the door but yes, there's a key also. They keep it with them during the day. I only get it at night."

This was like no shipboard procedure Peter had ever heard of, not that there were any rules regarding females, since they weren't allowed on naval vessels.

"And how do you manage that?" Peter asked.

"I make Harry and Nate—they are the men who brought her aboard—give up the key to the purser at night. For safety, I tell them. In case there's a ship's emergency. Then when they're asleep and they snore something fierce, both of them, I let her out to see the stars and the moon."

"That's all you do, I trust," Adam said, menace evident in the lowered range of his deep voice.

"Of course, sir, of course," Travis said hastily.

"Well, we're not going to wait until after dinner and brandies," Gabriel said.

"We don't have any time to stand about," Peter

put in. "Don't you feel the storm brewing?" he asked Travis.

"Oh aye, the wind has picked up again. It'll storm before morning."

"I think it'll storm considerably before that."

Just then the lookout in the crow's mast called "Lightning-ho." The storm was fast approaching. They had to get Violet and get back across in the rope and pulley contraption that had brought them over the bucking sea.

"This is your chance to bash heads, sir," Gabriel said as respectfully as he could to Adam, considering the topic.

"Oh no, I don't want no fighting on my ship," the captain cried, alarmed.

Peter snorted. "I've never been aboard a ship that didn't have fighting."

"Peter, where are the cabins likely to be?" Gabriel asked, ignoring Captain Travis.

Peter pointed, the rising wind beginning to whip his voice into odd syllables. "There, under the quarterdeck. The crew will be down in hammocks in the hold. We have to hurry."

"No," Travis said, looking around for his men.

"You made this deal, Travis, now you're going to keep it," Gabriel said. "Let's go," he said to the other two. Come after us and we won't be responsible for your safety or your life," he said to the Yorkshireman.

"I'm only a merchant shipper, I don't want trouble," Travis said, raising his hands in a warding gesture. "Just get it over with."

Glancing at the sky that had turned the sullen hue of imminent, heavy rain, he turned back to the men. "You don't have much time."

They moved silently down the companionway. Travis indicated with a jerk of his head which cabin was Nate and Harry's. The one beside it was Violet's.

Gabriel said they should take care of her captors and get the keys. If he or her father called out to Violet first, they might alert the scoundrels.

Travis backed away as the three men converged on the door. Adam produced a pistol from his waistband, hidden until now under the middy shirt they were all wearing. He nodded to Peter and Gabriel to proceed. Peter knew the bunks would be one on top of the other; Gabriel would take the top and he would take the bottom one.

Slowly Gabriel lifted the door handle, hoping it wasn't barred from the inside. If it was, they would lose all element of surprise. Fortunately, the men inside had no reason to fear an attack. Gabriel saw immediately that they had the wrong opponents. He was younger than Peter and Adam and should have taken on the huge man in the lower bunk.

But there was no time to suggest changing their plan, because the skinny man with the scarred face reached for a pistol from under his pillow, while the man below pulled an evil-looking dagger from beneath his.

Then the small cabin erupted in a melée and Gabriel knew Adam couldn't get a shot off in these close quarters without risking them all. He might not be too well-disposed toward Gabriel just now, but Gabriel didn't think his beloved's father would shoot him, at least not until they got the key to Violet's door from the two criminals.

But their plan turned out to work perfectly well,

because Gabriel didn't have much trouble subduing the thinner, wiry man. Like Adam, his pistol wasn't of much use in the confines of the cabin either. And once Adam had his pistol trained on thin Harry, the big one folded.

"Don't hurt Horrid," he cried.

"Brick, you're an idiot," Harry said. "You could have taken them. Cross me garters, but the only one under forty is the bloody Duke."

"Horrid, is it?" Gabriel said, feeling a tiny spurt of amusement for the first time in days. He had Horrid Harry's arms twisted behind his back. Adam held the pistol on Brick, while Peter ripped sheets apart for tying them up. "You must be the brains of this grand strategy. Give me the key."

"Horrid," Brick whispered, but the big man's voice came out as loud as a normal man's would, "how did they get here?"

"What difference does it make?" Harry said, his pockmarked expression sullen. "They're here. Probably flew or something."

Brick's eyes got wider. "Really?"

"No, you simpleton, the captain sold us out."

Gabriel had fished the key out of Harry's waistcoat pocket. He'd already taken the pistol away, so he pushed Horrid at Peter as soon as his hands were bound. Adam had his hands full with Brick, who seemed about to collapse in tears, but he was too big to ignore. He'd need stronger bonds than Harry. Gabriel estimated that would take a few more minutes.

He knew they had to get back to their own ship, but he was going to open Violet's door, even if it made her father more angry. How much angrier could he get anyway?

Peter divined his intention as soon as he saw the key appear, and gave Gabriel a quick wink. Adam realized it only when Gabriel opened the door, but now they were two on two and he couldn't follow Gabriel. He glowered under dark brows as Gabriel left, a look that promised retribution later.

There was only one thought on Gabriel's mind now: get to Violet. He left the cabin without a backward look, confident that the two older men were no strangers to a scuffle and could handle the ruffians.

TWENTY-FOUR

O Western wind, when wilt thou blow
That the small rain down can rain?
Christ, that my love were in my arms,
And I in my bed again!

—Anonymous, c. 1530

As he approached the door, Gabriel was surprised that Violet wasn't shouting and demanding to know what was going on next door. When he lifted the wooden bar, then unlocked the door, he found out why.

As he entered the room, she shoved a piece of wood into his stomach, the type used to bar the inside of the door. Only officers' quarters had inside and outside bars—crew quarters were barred from the outside.

Only Violet would attempt to ambush her captors.

Stumbling forward into the dim light, he saw the block of wood raised over his head from the corner of one eye. His midsection was still sore from the blow administered a few days ago by her father, so he had no strength to fling his arms up and protect his head.

Thank God, she recognized him just in time. Dropping the bar of wood, Violet flung herself into his arms with a glad cry. It would have been exceedingly gratifying if his stomach hadn't been bruised. As it was, her arms encircled him precisely where she had just jammed the bar.

Groaning, he went to his knees, bringing her down with him. "Gabriel! Are you all right?" she asked, still holding on to him.

He couldn't keep his balance. Twisting, Gabriel turned his body so that she fell against him instead of hitting the floor. He hit the wood floor instead, and once again had the breath knocked out of him.

"Bar the door," he got out between wheezes.

She looked at him. "Now," he insisted.

Picking up the bar she'd used before, she barred the door from the inside, just as a senior officer might have done to protect himself if the crew were about to mutiny.

"Why are we locking ourselves inside if you are here to rescue me?" she asked, dropping to her knees beside him. "Are you all right?"

"You mean other than what you did to me just now?" he said, still wheezing. Apologizing profusely, she helped him sit up.

They looked at each other. "This isn't how I pictured a reunion," she said at exactly the same time he did. Then they both laughed, until Gabriel started wheezing again.

"Surely I didn't hit you that hard," she said, still on her knees beside him, Margery's once-beautiful dress crumpled and stained beyond repair.

"On top of the blow your father dealt me, my

midsection hasn't quite recovered," Gabriel confessed.

She looked around. "My father? He's here? You're still alive?"

"Only long enough to rescue you, I think. Then he plans to take me apart. Why do you think I told you to bar the door?" He gave her a tired grin and she started to laugh.

He raised his hand to her soft cheek, looking at her closely. She seemed tired but he saw no bruises on her. And she certainly hadn't been cowering against a wall, so her remarkable spirit was in no way quelled. He dared to believe that perhaps 'twas as the captain had said, and that no one had harmed her.

Then what he'd said a moment ago registered with her. "My father hit you? That's why we're in here?" Her amazing aquamarine eyes had begun to sparkle again at the absurd idea that he was cowering in fear of her father.

"No, Violet. This is why we're in here with the door locked." He reached out and slid his hand under her mass of tumbled hair. With his other arm he pulled her onto his lap. Then he crushed her mouth to his and held her tight against him as if he would never let her go.

She melted beneath him, and he experienced the most profound sense of rightness. He had felt it only with her. For as long as he lived, he would find this sense of belonging only with her.

And then, damn if he didn't have to break the kiss first, because he still lacked air. He leaned his forehead against hers. "Violet Amanda Pearson, you will be the death of me yet."

"I thought that was going to be my father," she

said, pulling back to feather kisses along his temple. He captured her chin and put her busy mouth to better use kissing him again.

He heard a boom of thunder and broke the kiss quickly to their mutual dismay, silently cursing fate and fathers. "It may be the weather that kills us, if we don't cross back to our own ship at once." He rose to his feet, Violet scrambling up with far more grace than he.

Before she could ask any more questions, they both heard the pounding on the door and the unmistakable timbre of her father's deep voice.

"In case he doesn't let me see you again, my love," Gabriel said, "say that you'll marry me."

She leaned against him, as reluctant as he was to let go.

"Just like that?" she said. "No reserve, no conditions? What about your household?"

"No, love, none. I will help them start new lives, but my life belongs to you, now and forever."

"In that case," she said, smiling up at him, "let's tell my father so he doesn't think your intentions are dishonorable."

"I don't think that's going to matter much right now," he said, but she'd already unbarred the door. Violet threw herself into her father's arms with nearly as much abandon as she had with Gabriel, but she turned and smiled at him as her father gathered her close.

Then Peter appeared in the doorway, looking more worried that Gabriel had seen him at any time in their short acquaintance.

"We have to go now," he said urgently. "The storm is almost upon us and the seas are already high."

"Uncle Peter," Violet said happily.

He blew a kiss at her, but didn't smile. "Thank God you're safe. Let's get you off this ship, shall we?" he said.

Violet slipped from her father's embrace and went back to stand beside Gabriel. "I know you've met, but this is my betrothed, Gabriel Isling, Duke of Belmont."

"We've met," Adam said, his voice still carrying an edge.

"I know there is a lot to explain," Violet began, but Peter interrupted again.

"Later. We must go now," Peter said, grabbing Violet's hand to pull her out of the cabin.

She clung to Gabriel's hand, but he pushed her gently in the direction of her family. "Go, Violet. There will be time to talk later."

Violet wasted no more time, but neither did she drop Gabriel's hand.

As the two older men walked down the companionway behind Gabriel and Violet, Peter nudged his brother-in-law. "Give it up, Adam. She loves him."

"But does he love her?" Adam asked, still reluctant to be convinced.

"I'll wager every bit as much as you and I love Lily and Rose," Peter said. "Now get your mind back to the business at hand. This could be an extremely difficult crossing."

When they stepped out of the ship's interior, gray rain pelted them, and the sky was nearly indistinguishable from the sea. Their nearby ship bobbed precariously on the waves, sometimes disappearing from view by a swell or a gust of rain.

"Violet should go first," Gabriel said.

"Actually, one of us needs to go first," Peter said.

"Why?" Gabriel knew Violet's safety was their principal concern.

Peter moved close to Gabriel and lowered his voice. "To find out if it can be done at all. Otherwise, we'll have to wait here and hope we can stay within sight of our own ship."

"I'll go," Gabriel said immediately. Peter then beckoned to Adam, who reluctantly left his daughter's side.

"Violet, I'm not doing this to save myself," Gabriel said. "Peter wants one of us to go ahead of you, to make sure the crossing can be carried out safely."

"I would never have thought that," she said.

"No, but your father might." From the muffled sounds of argument he heard, he expected Adam was demanding to go first. Nevertheless, Peter was the captain and however reluctantly, Gabriel felt certain that Adam Pearson would concede authority over this aspect of the rescue to the most knowledgeable man.

"Gabriel, this isn't safe. You shouldn't go," Violet said, tugging at Gabriel's hand. He had just found her, how could he bear to part them again?

"And who would go then, Violet my love?" he asked quietly, leaning toward her in the shelter of the companionway's threshold. "Your father? Your uncle?"

There was nothing she could say to that. So she watched in silence while the rope and pulley were rigged up and Gabriel climbed into them. The ship's captain, Captain Travis, the one who'd let her out quietly at night a few times, was nearly frantic with his insistence on haste. He was afraid that the ropes linking the two ships would pull them into a collision if the wind changed.

"Quiet, man," Uncle Peter finally roared above the noise of the storm. "We don't want to be here any more than you want us here. Now shut up and help or get out of my way."

Gabriel swung out over the side and a swell immediately broke over him. Violet screamed, then tried to silence her terror, not wanting to distract her uncle and the sailors who were helping.

When the dark head reappeared, she released a breath, then kept her eyes on him as best she could during the long minutes that followed.

The only thing more frightening than seeing him go across the boiling expanse of water was seeing him come back.

"Why the hell did you do that?" Peter asked as soon as Gabriel swung aboard again. "You've already proved it can be done."

"I'm going to have Violet tied in with me," he said. "She won't have the strength to manipulate the pulley, and the sea is too treacherous to be passive for the whole trip. We must get her across as quickly as possible."

There was no time for talk or for anyone to argue about who should accompany Violet. Gabriel pulled her close and Uncle Peter tied her up snugly with him. She was already wet when they went into the water, because Gabriel was drenched. Then there was the sickening feeling of swinging out into space with nothing solid beneath her. Immediately sea spray broke over them, and Violet began to shiver.

"Hold on," Gabriel said. "Just hold on. I won't

let you go." Violet ducked her head into his chest, closed her eyes, and prayed.

"Open your eyes," he shouted. As her eyes flew open, she saw the crest of the wave descending. "Take a breath just before it breaks. Close your eyes again and hold on!"

She did as he said, but was still unprepared for the sheer terror of the weight of water crashing in on them. Instinctively she clung more tightly to Gabriel, whom she could not see but could feel. Nearly out of breath, she felt her lungs burning with the effort to keep the water out.

The end of her endurance—seconds, minutes, she would never know—came far too soon. The sensation of water pressing in on her was just as powerful as before, but she could no longer hold her breath.

Just as she was nearly forced to open her mouth, she felt a sharp pull upward, then she and Gabriel smacked into something hard and un-yielding.

It was the side of the ship. She and Gabriel were being pulled up when she became aware that Gabriel was silent and limp beside her, his head lolling back.

She screamed at Uncle Peter's crew as they pulled her and Gabriel aboard. "Something's happened to him. Master Josephus," she called to Uncle Peter's first mate, whom she had known since she was little. "Help me."

"Miss Violet, I have to get your father and your uncle over. Jeremy will help you with the Duke."

There were few hands to spare with the effort to get the other men across, but Jeremy helped

her move an inert Gabriel off the deck and into
the passageway, out of the rain.

There, she cradled his head in her lap, after
making sure that he was breathing. It was the blow
he'd taken as they had struck the side of the ship
that had knocked him unconscious. He hadn't
drowned.

Her father found her that way, her tears wetting
Gabriel's face even as she tried to dry him off
with toweling and warm him with a blanket someone had draped around her shoulders.

"Are you all right?" she asked.

"I'm fine," Adam replied. He turned his head
to look at the rope that still swung between the
ships. As they watched, a figure took the same
plunge into nothingness that they had both just
experienced.

Someone brought her father a blanket. He
stood looking down at her as tears she didn't
know were falling continued to track down her
face. He bent down to her, touching her cheek
with his fingertips.

"He'll be all right, my darling," he said in the
warm voice she had always associated with her father, not the angry man who'd been on board
the other ship.

"He has to be, Papa," she said simply. "He has
my heart."

"I can see that," he said, his gaze following her
hand that stroked Gabriel's dark hair back from
his brow. "I'll get someone to help take him to
his cabin," he said, turning away. "Uncle Peter
will be across at any moment, then we can sail
out of this storm and on to home."

Although Violet said nothing further to her father, the word "home" crystallized everything for her in one blinding moment of clarity. She followed the sailors carrying Gabriel, waiting outside demurely while they stripped him and bundled him in blankets. Then she went in and sat on the edge of the bunk where he still lay pale and lifeless, his pallor alarming under his tanned skin. She left him only long enough to take off her own drenched clothes and to wrap herself in another blanket.

Gabriel was her home, her world, her life. She didn't care where they would go, or even if she ever saw London, as long as she didn't have to be apart from him. She leaned her head against his chest just to reassure herself that she could still hear his heartbeat.

Exhaustion quickly claimed her, and she fell asleep in that position, one arm draped across Gabriel's chest, her ear pressed to his chest where his heart beat strong and steady.

Peter and Adam found them like that some time later. The men had both dried off and changed clothes. Peter's helmsman had maneuvered them out to the storm's edge, and then away. Once they had reoriented themselves, Peter was able to make course corrections by sighting from the stars overhead.

A sailor followed the two men with plates of hot food. Adam took the tray while Peter opened the door quietly. Violet slept with her head on Gabriel's chest. As they watched, Gabriel stirred, lifting a hand to thread it through Violet's hair, as if to assure himself she was really there.

Gabriel heard a sound at the doorway with his

acute perception, because he turned his head just at that moment. The look he gave Violet's closest male relatives was both grave and intense. It said that he had no need to stake a claim, no need to prove anything to her father or uncle.

Both men saw the tenderness in his touch, saw Violet turn her face toward him in sleep, a faint smile touching her lips as if she knew where she was and who she was with.

Peter entered the room silently while Gabriel turned his storm gray gaze back to the woman who rested so trustingly against him. Putting the tray down on a nearby table that was bolted to the floor, Peter turned and went back as silently as he had come.

Adam stood looking a moment longer at the tableau, then nodded at Gabriel. They closed the door quietly behind them.

"Peter, when was the last time you performed a shipboard wedding as the captain of this vessel?" Adam asked, throwing an arm around his brother-in-law's shoulders.

"Never, to be precise," Peter answered with an amused glance at Adam.

"Find your Bible," Adam said. "There'll be one tomorrow, or as soon as he recovers."

"I think he's recovered now," Peter said.

"I don't want to hear it," Adam said. "Right now, they are too exhausted to be moved." The two men smiled at each other.

"Now, tell me how many days it will take to get us back home in this leaky bucket of yours," Adam said.

* * *

Gabriel wanted to give Violet all the time she needed to sleep, but his headache and thirst forced him to change position. He had managed to pull her legs up onto the bed so that she rested fully against him now, and she grumbled sleepily as he tried to sit up.

His vision swam alarmingly, and he put out a hand to keep the world from spinning. He touched her head. She sat up.

"Gabriel, be careful. Lie down. You've been unconscious."

"Then this isn't a dream?" he asked, leaning against the bulkhead and reaching out to draw her back into his arms.

"Is what a dream?" she asked.

"That you are here, that we are together, that you will be my wife, and that your father and uncle haven't killed me yet."

"They're probably waiting until you recover," she said with a teasing grin.

"Kiss me, Violet," Gabriel said. "I don't want to talk about your family right now."

"I love my family, but you are my world now."

"And you mine," he said, his gray eyes as luminous as she had ever seen them. Cradling the back of her head with his palm, he inclined his head toward her. They indulged in a long, heartfelt kiss before he broke it off.

He titled his head back again. "I'm sorry, Violet, I don't know whether it's the salt water I drank or hunger, but my head is spinning, and I don't mean from you."

"I'm not offended," she said, climbing out of the bunk wrapped in a blanket to fetch the food her father and Uncle Peter had brought.

"I wanted to spend this time making love to you, before your father or uncle decide to avenge your honor," he said, realizing that a sitting position was the best he was going to be able to manage for right now.

Violet brought over the cooked chicken and biscuits, and they both went at the food with hearty appetites. There was grog that neither of them wanted, and lemonade from fresh lemons that had been brought on board when the ship left Williamsburg, and this they did drink.

Finally, she wiped her mouth with a napkin, and leaned toward Gabriel once more from her cross-legged position on the bed.

"I don't think we have to worry about that," she said with a smile.

"Your father and uncle surely aren't going to let us stay in this cabin together," he said, remembering Adam Pearson's touchiness. He thought he had a way to go to win the older man over.

"Oh no, I think they will," she said, her smile turning into a full-fledged grin.

"What do you mean?" he asked, wondering if she'd taken a blow to the head as well.

"I believe we're going to be married tomorrow to keep us honest. You do know that's the prerogative of a ship's captain, don't you?"

"Is it real?" he asked.

"Yes, 'tis a true marriage. Mama will insist on a wedding at home anyway, but this will be to satisfy my father and uncle."

"Then perhaps we should give them something to worry about, hmm?" he said, starting to nuzzle her neck.

"Does this door lock from the inside?" Violet asked.

Gabriel looked away from her long enough to see the bar, similar to the one on the other ship. "Yes."

"This time, I'm locking us in," Violet declared. And she did.

"How's your head?" she asked as she returned to the bed.

"It's been better," he admitted.

"Then lie down," she said. "Let me take care of you." Gabriel slid down until his head rested on the mattress.

"This is better, but don't let me fall asleep, Violet," he said.

"You can fall asleep afterwards," she promised. She dropped her blanket and crawled in beside him. He turned to her, gathering her against him.

"You're not dressed either," he said as he felt their flesh come into contact. "I like that."

"So do I," Violet said, starting to explore him with her hands, running them down his strong chest, his muscular arms and legs.

"But I don't think I'm going to be able to do anything about it with this vertigo," he said into her ear.

Violet slid lower and began kissing his chest. "You don't have to," she said. Eventually she rose above him, guiding him to her with ancient feminine intuition. Her hair spread around them, brushing his shoulders, enclosing them in a private world where nothing existed except the two of them.

He held her hips with his hands, and called out er name as he climaxed deep inside her. His triggered hers in a rush. She arched in ecstasy, then slid down to rest on his chest, exhausted but never happier.

"I'm sorry for the pain I caused you, my love," Gabriel said a short time later. "Even sorrier that I led you into danger."

"As long as it led you back to me and not away," she said.

"Never again," he pledged. "I'll never leave you, no matter where we go."

"Where are we going?" she asked, tasting the salt on his skin with her tongue.

"Didn't you want to travel, love?" As he spoke, he spread her hair out, caressing her back with the long tresses.

"Only if 'tis with you."

"It will be. I would like to move the ladies to Charleston, but we don't have to live there if you don't want to."

"Is Lord Albie still a threat?"

"We left strong messages with those men of his. And if we go to London for our wedding trip, I will make certain to deliver that message again in person."

"Mmm," she said against his neck. Her limbs were relaxed and limp.

"Sleep, my love, I'm right here."

"You sleep too," she murmured. "Unless I'm too heavy for you?"

The laugh rumbled in his chest. "Never."

Locked in each other's arms, and needing nothing else in the world, they fell asleep together, as they would every night for the rest of their lives.

COMING IN MARCH 2002 FROM
ZEBRA BALLAD ROMANCES

__LIGHT A SINGLE CANDLE: The MacInnes Legacy

by Julie Moffett   0-8217-7270-8 $5.99US/$7.99CAN

Bridget Goodwell is determined that nothing will prevent her coming wedding. But three weeks before the ceremony, her first love drops anchor in Salem's harbor, threatening everything she has planned. Bridget is horrified to discover that her love for him will lead her to an ancient curse—unless the passion between them breaks a powerful spell. . . .

__LUCK OF THE DRAW: The Gamblers

by Pat Pritchard   0-8217-7254-6 $5.99US/$7.99CAN

Cal Preston wins a half interest in an eastern Colorado ranch from a reckless youth. Cal finds his way to the property, where he is met by widowed owner Lily McCord. Without his help, she will lose the ranch—and he can't stand by and watch that happen. Now Cal is prepared to do whatever it takes to keep Lily in his life, even if it means risking everything to win her heart. . . .

__THE SEDUCTION: Men of Honor

by Kathryn Fox   0-8217-7243-0 $5.99US/$7.99CAN

Journalist Samantha Wilder was certain that at least one of the North West Mounted Police had to be on the take. But even cynical Sam was shocked when clues led to well-respected Inspector Duncan McLeod. Still, the truth had to be told, and she would be the one to tell it. Until Duncan's passionate kisses had her falling in love with the subject of her investigation.

__TWICE BLESSED: Haven

by Jo Ann Ferguson   0-8217-7309-7 $5.99US/$7.99CAN

Emma Delancy ran from her past to Haven, Ohio, seven years before. Then handsome newcomer Noah Sawyer accused an orphan boy of stealing, and Emma found herself fostering the youngster. Destiny seemed to throw them together at every turn. Emma knows her secret will only make matters worse—unless the love they have found can shelter the family they long to make . . . together.

Use this coupon to order by mail.
ALL BOOKS AVAILABLE MARCH 01, 2002.

Name_____

Address_____

City_____ State _____ Zip _____

Please send me the books that I have checked above.

I am enclosing $_____
Plus postage and handling* $_____
Sales tax (in NY and TN) $_____
Total amount enclosed $_____

*Add $2.50 for the first book and $.50 for each additional book.
Send check or money order (no cash or CODs) to: **Kensington Publishing Corp., Dept. C.O., 850 Third Avenue, New York, NY 10022.**
Prices and numbers subject to change without notice. Valid only in the U.S.
All orders subject to availability. **NO ADVANCE ORDERS.**
Visit our website at **www.kensingtonbooks.com.**

BOOK YOUR PLACE ON OUR WEBSITE
AND MAKE THE
READING CONNECTION!

We've created a customized website just for our very special readers, where you can get the inside scoop on everything that's going on with Zebra, Pinnacle and Kensington books.

When you come online, you'll have the exciting opportunity to:

- View covers of upcoming books
- Read sample chapters
- Learn about our future publishing schedule (listed by publication month *and author*)
- Find out when your favorite authors will be visiting a city near you
- Search for and order backlist books from our online catalog
- Check out author bios and background information
- Send e-mail to your favorite authors
- Meet the Kensington staff online
- Join us in weekly chats with authors, readers and other guests
- Get writing guidelines
- AND MUCH MORE!

Visit our website at
http://www.kensingtonbooks.com